PRAISE F'S
INTERGA. ...IOW

"...a femme fatale noir story with a feel-good gloss. The characters are endearing, even the baddies...Space opera fans who enjoy a generous helping of antics and drama will revel in this adventure."

—Publishers Weekly

"An epic space adventure full of fascinating characters, pulse-pounding action, and wicked twists. I'm ready to run away with this circus!"

—Mary Fan, author of *Starswept*

"Filled with themes of acceptance, hope, activism, and friendship, *Jack Jetstark's Intergalactic Freakshow* is a jaunty debut...readers will root for Jack and company and will look for more from Rossman."

—Booklist

Jack Jetstark's Intergalactic Freakshow

JENNIFER LEE ROSSMAN

World Weaver Press

JACK JETSTARK'S INTERGALACTIC FREAKSHOW
Copyright © 2018 Jennifer Lee Rossman.

This is a work of fiction; characters and events are either fictitious or used fictitiously.

Published by World Weaver Press, LLC.
Albuquerque, New Mexico
www.WorldWeaverPress.com

Edited by Sarena Ulibarri
Cover designed by Sarena Ulibarri.
Cover images used under license from DepositPhotos.com.
Interior illustration by Jennifer Lee Rossman, © 2018.

*

First Edition, December 2018
ISBN-10: 1-7322546-3-X
ISBN-13: 978-1732254633

Also available as an ebook.

JACK JETSTARK'S INTERGALACTIC FREAKSHOW

To all the freaks I've been lucky enough to call my crew

CHAPTER ONE

The crowd grew restless in the renovated cargo bay of my carnival ship, muttering amongst themselves and drifting toward the exit. But they wouldn't leave; they never left, not before the show started. The draw was too strong, their thirst for the bizarre and grotesque too unquenchable. They would stand in that dim alcove of the *Rubeno Mardo*'s cargo bay for hours if I let them, just for the briefest glimpse of the exotic performers promised by the advertisements posted throughout town.

Across the tapestry of the universe and all its vast and varied cultures, there ran a single, unifying thread: no one could resist the allure of the words "not for the faint of heart" written in a scandalous, jagged font and followed by four exclamation points. Good marketing knew no bounds.

From my post in the shadows, I looked out over the audience with satisfaction. Used to be I couldn't see the floor between the people, the way they crowded in. Now it seemed I saw more of it every show, but I couldn't complain about the turnout on this night, nor about the revenue they brought in.

There was something to be said for docking on the less affluent moons and planets. Sure, the rich people floating around on their space stations and on the hoity toity worlds that governed their solar systems had coin enough to melt down into disposable flatware, but they spent it on electronic gadgets that numbed their brains, not on the kind of quality entertainment we offered.

On the farming and mining colonies, where the only forms of entertainment were swatting mosquitoes and throwing rocks at neighbors, the arrival of a carnival ship made for a major event. They saved up all year for a night's diversion from their hard lives.

And I was all too glad to provide it for them.

"We made a killing tonight," my pilot Lily whispered in my ear, her bright smile evident in her voice. "Might even be able to afford the fuel to get us to the next gig."

"We'll be fine," I said, not really listening as a person in the crowd drew my attention. "I think we found another one."

"Who?"

I pointed to the girl, dressed in her best flannel shirt and black slacks, with most of the hay brushed out of her coppery hair. She was a teenager, but the electric fascination in her eyes as she waited for the show to begin wasn't the excitement of a mere child. Something about our world spoke to her. Maybe the opportunity to travel the galaxies, maybe the camaraderie of a carnival family, or maybe just the chance for something more than the lot life had given her.

Whatever the case, she'd be part of the crew before we departed the next day. I was sure of it.

"She could just be excited for the show," Lily argued, crossing her arms. "It doesn't mean she's one of us."

I nudged her with my elbow, grinning. "Why do you doubt me?"

"Because you refuse to." She pointed a long, manicured nail at the crowd. "They're waiting," she said, disappearing into the darkness as she went back to her mark.

"Can't rush the music," I said, yet even as the words left my mouth, the old receiver crackled to life beside me, playing the first notes of my intro.

Adrenaline surged to my heart at the sound of the slowly rising tones of the eerie, wordless song, and I hurried to my post on the catwalk. Her voice sounded more like a warbling violin than it did a singing woman, which only added to the ethereal ambiance. A murmur went through the crowd as I emerged from the shadows high above the stage. I felt alive, fire burning through my veins.

"Ladies and gentlemen and nonbinary gentlefolk," I boomed, the music growing high and tense, "consider this your last warning. You are about to bear witness to creatures and abominations from the farthest reaches of the known universe, horrors the human eye was never meant to see. I cannot be held responsible for the effects these sights have on your psyche. Some people never recover from the shock, so I encourage those with sensitive dispositions or weak hearts to leave now."

No one left; no one ever left.

"Then be prepared to gaze upon the unnatural freaks of the stars!" I triggered the curtain drop at the musical cue, and the audience gasped at the mere sight of their silhouetted forms. "Notice there is no glass, no barrier between them and you. Jack Jetstark's Intergalactic Freakshow uses no such safety measures, but it wouldn't matter anyway, as they've broken through everything we've tried. Keep your fingers to yourself folks; they most certainly do bite."

The audience inched back with a collective squeal of excitement from the children, eyes wide and hands clenched in anticipation.

"Our first specimen, or should I say specimens, were born on a distant planet in the Ilex system. Or maybe they were hatched, or created… no one quite knows for sure."

The first spotlight clicked on, illuminating the three-headed form that elicited shrieks of terror from the crowd.

"Behold! The fused bodies of the Fago triplets! Three brothers found in a distant monastery, two joined at the skull, two joined at the liver, all three sharing a single mind."

The triplets swayed to the beat, their skin stretching between their shared abdomen and their bifurcated skulls moving as one. They stared at the crowd with dead eyes, mouths gaping in slow synchronization as they moved forward in a shambling lockstep, lost in a deep trance.

"The greatest scientific minds are unable to tell if they are three individuals or a single, nightmarish organism. They feel the others' pain, hear the others' thoughts." I paused, letting the notion run wild in the minds of the audience, the room silent save for the quiet singing. "Is anyone among you brave enough to come forward and help them demonstrate their abilities?"

No one volunteered, no one dared move or even breathe lest they be noticed and called upon. And then a girl stepped forward as the crowd shrank away, glad to let her be the sacrificial lamb. And wouldn't you know, it was the girl I'd pointed out before the show. I hoped Lily was paying attention.

"Whisper something to Theon," I instructed. "He's the one on your left, their right, attached to his brother at the torso. Don't make any sudden movements."

The girl approached with shaking hands and wide eyes that darted between the triplets' dark-skinned, ashen faces, only giving the occasional glance to the points where their bodies connected. She recoiled as Theon reached an arm toward her, but still put her lips to his ears and said something inaudible to the rest of us.

Theon cocked his head to the side and Parthen's face, in the middle, contorted into a silent, pained scream. Finally, the thought passed to Pneuman, who shared a lobed skull with Parthen, and he cried out, "Hello, world!" much to the delight of the crowd, the girl in particular.

The triplets began writhing without warning, though anyone listening to the rising tension in the song might notice it was scripted, their limbs flailing and jaws snapping as they grabbed for the girl.

"Get back!" I shouted as I fumbled for the control panel. I flicked

JACK JETSTARK'S INTERGALACTIC FREAKSHOW

off the triplets' spotlight, and they receded into the shadows just in time to prevent the frightened crowd from fleeing.

It was a delicate balancing act, scaring them just enough to get their adrenaline pumping, but not so much that they demanded their money back.

I let them settle down and calm their heart rates while the song shifted to what I liked to call its tribal stage, filled with low, short notes and the drumbeats of palm against palm. That part always got to me, hearing the musician's hands that had once touched mine, and I noticed an unintended warmth come into my voice as I went on with my patter.

"We've all heard tales of Earth, of how its people destroyed themselves in nuclear warfare, leaving the planet a lifeless, radioactive lump of rock. For the most part, those stories are true, but the Earth isn't devoid of all life."

The next light turned on, introducing a hunched, hairy form resembling a gorilla but just human enough to be disturbing. Glowing blue eyes glared out from beneath a brutish brow.

"A colony of humans survived the war. At least, they used to be human. In the ensuing centuries, living in the fallout of bad decisions and eating toxic, mutated beasts, the survivors changed into… well, into something awful. I personally captured this one in the wasteland once known as Japan. I call him Merulo. He doesn't speak, and eats only what he can catch." I grinned as I delivered the line that never failed to horrify. "Did I mention that he loves children?"

Merulo sprang forth amid a wave of shrieks and nervous laughter, walking on his knuckles and bare feet, his hulking chest expanding and contracting with his deep, rasping breaths. His dark brown hair hung in matted cords along his body, his upper lip curled to display sharp, crooked fangs.

He prowled the stage, grunting at the men in the audience to assert dominance. One man in particular attracted his attention and he stood on his hind legs, stretching to his full, imposing height of seven feet, and let out a roar that shook the walls and sent the crowd retreating to a safe distance.

I cut the lights, making everyone in the crowd strain their ears to locate the mutated man-beast before he attacked. They had to know it was all an act, but part of their brains could never be convinced. That excitement brought in the revenue.

The music slid into a softer, almost seductive passage, with notes that curled upward and whispered promises of eternal devotion. My cue to turn on the center light.

Lily stood with her back to the audience, her short blonde hair just brushing her tawny wing feathers.

"Folks," I said, my face growing warmer as the song echoed in my heart, my finale fast approaching, "we leave you with a creature from the softer side of the universe, to soothe your minds before you go out into that darkest of nights."

Lily ruffled her feathers and unfurled her long wings to a round of soft, awed applause.

"An angel, ripped from the mythologies of old, a being of unknown origin who fell from the stars. Or was she cast out of the heavens? She'll never tell."

She wrapped her wings around herself and spun to face the audience. One wing covered her body, the other hid the lower half of her face, leaving only her long legs and piercing gold eyes exposed. She took cautious, deliberate steps forward, teasing glimpses of her body as she swapped wing positions but never showed anything she didn't want them to see.

"A more beautiful abomination you'll never find, but you will do well to remember that she is not one of us. She is a monster, no matter her outward appearance."

People—men mostly—crowded unafraid at the edge of the stage. Lily knelt before them, inching forward as the music swelled, drawing in a willing participant with her seductive eyes.

"The other freaks, those you feared and recoiled from, will do you no harm." I began my descent to the stage for the finale. "You, sir!" I addressed the man with his face mere inches from Lily's. "Beware, for she is the only danger on this stage. That is no angel; that is the man-eating harpy!"

Before he had the chance to react, Lily flung her wings out, baring the razor-sharp beak where her nose and mouth should have been. She let out a screech and flapped her wings, launching herself up to hover above the stage where Merulo and the triplets stood in dim lighting.

I stepped in front of them and breathed a plume of fire toward the high ceiling, the song reaching its rapid, sonorous climax. It hit its crescendo and broke into an abrupt silence, the lights and my fire going out at the same time and plummeting the crowd into a darkness broken only by the light pouring through the door that led outside.

A cool, peaceful exhaustion washed over me, and I left them with a final declaration in a calm drawl: "The freaks I've brought to you tonight are just a small sampling of the horrors I've encountered in my travels. You think the universe is a blank slate where you can write your own stories. We don't realize other races exist, but I've shown you they do. Their stories are written in the stars. And some day, they'll come back for what's theirs."

***

I leaned against the steel wall of the control room that doubled as our living room, decompressing from the show with my crew, who doubled as my performers. A lot of the *Rubeno Mardo* took on double duty; designed as a small transport ship intended for a crew of one or two people for short hauls, she lacked much in the way of amenities, and we'd redone most of her insides to make sleeping cabins and recreation rooms. A good portion of it was makeshift, with people sleeping in the renovated armory and engine room, and a small kitchenette made of salvaged appliances wedged in the corner.

Not a lot of money in the traveling carnival business anymore.

Enough to make a living, but not like it used to be, back when fleets of enormous ships traveled the skies, bringing roller coasters and virtual reality machines to the residents of the universe. Sometimes it felt like we were the only ones out there, with our meager rides and food stalls offering unhealthy fried things on sticks; nothing special that couldn't be found at any summer funfair on any planet, moon, or decently sized asteroid.

But people wanted to see the unusual, to be scared out of their wits by the alien creatures from the far-off places they could only dream of visiting. Therein lay the appeal of the sideshow, without which our profit margins would wither to nothing and the *Rubeno* and I would be stuck delivering cargo again. She was built for that kind of work. Me, not so much.

I much preferred life as a space carny. If nothing else, it was a more enjoyable way to make a buck, and far less lonely. In a world that shunned and ridiculed, our little piece of space was a welcoming reprieve. It was a home, it was a family.

Merulo warmed up dinner in an old food heater, setting chipped plates on the table while he attempted the impossible task of wrangling his unruly mop of black hair. The triplets eased their pained minds by chatting among themselves and watching game shows on a screen made mostly of static. And Lily sat in front of a lighted mirror, removing the heavy mascara that made her eyes pop while undoubtedly planning our route to the next planet in her brain that never slowed down.

She noticed me watching and arched a thin eyebrow. "What?"

"It's just nice," I said. "All of this. It isn't like the world out there. It's real."

A small voice spoke from behind me. "It's fake."

I turned to see the girl, the one with the bits of hay in her red braid, standing in the doorway. Shock and disillusionment cast shadows over her freckled face, the horrors of the show paling in comparison to this glimpse backstage.

"How did you get in here?" I demanded, not expecting any trouble but sure that I had locked up the carnival entrance as well as the stairwell leading to our living quarters.

"Is any of it real?"

I looked back at my crew, this time through her eyes; disturbing sights to say the least. A wildman in a robe and eyeglasses, a jovial grin on his chubby face. Conjoined triplets separated and sitting on opposite sides of the room, the sickly pallor having been wiped from their dark skin. An angel in jeans and a crocheted shawl, her beak transformed into a nose and her bare shoulders showing no sign of ever bearing wings.

Even I'd changed since the show, from the fire-breathing barker who spouted words with ease to a broody slacker in a vest who'd couldn't turn a phrase to save his life.

Not hard to understand her surprise. The only thing worse than seeing terrible, man-eating monsters was seeing them without their disguises, seeing that; deep down, they were only human, same as anyone else. I liked to keep that particular fact a secret, as people tended to pay much more to see anatomical anomalies than they did to see ordinary people, but I didn't see a way out of this. She looked too smart to fall for anything I could pull out of thin air.

"Is it all fake?" she asked, stepping into the room.

I put my arm out to stop her. "I asked you first; how did you get in here?" I tried not to sound too upset, but the thought of someone trespassing on my ship, my *secure* ship where my people expected to be safe, infuriated me. If a mere girl could get on board without triggering the alarms, why not a crew of galactic pirates?

The girl retreated, her gaze flicking from one person to the next before landing on me. "I'm sorry. It's just... it's what I do." She fiddled with her hands and tugged down the sleeves of her red and black jacket.

"What does that mean?" Lily asked, coming to my side and taking over the interrogation while the others watched with caution.

"It'll be easier if I just show you." The girl closed and locked the door behind her, then knelt to peer at the electronic lock. She placed her palm over the device and the lock clicked open a moment later. She pushed open the door and turned to us, the faintest hint of a smile on her lips.

"That's impossible," Theon said as he came to inspect the lock, sounding almost insulted at the breach in security. "I installed it myself. It only opens with our keycards." He gave the girl a sideways glance, his dark, deep-set eyes narrowed. "They're electronic."

She shrugged, offering a wide grin that showed too many teeth. "So am I."

No one quite knew how to respond to that, and silence fell on the room, broken only by the steady whirring of the food warmer and the cooling fan on the control panel for the ship's various electrical systems. As a precaution, I went over and locked the door with my handprint as well. No need to take unnecessary risks.

"I can bypass that, too."

"Who are you and what do you want?" I asked.

"I'm Cara. I just wanted to meet them, learn more about them. They're fascinating." She paused before adding, "Now, even more so." Her voice wavered, so quiet as to border on a whisper, but she held her chin high and maintained eye contact. I sensed a bravery inside her, maybe so deep she didn't see it for herself. But it was there. Had to be, or else she never would have snuck onto the ship, never would have stayed after discovering our secret. "So it's all just an act?"

"Most things in life are," I said. "Best acts just come from places of truth."

She motioned to the triplets. "But I mean... They aren't really conjoined."

Pneuman laughed, relieving some of the tension that had built up in the room. "We aren't that interesting. Parthen isn't even related to us."

Theon reached across the tattered sofa and gently peeled away the bald cap from Parthen, the middle triplet, to reveal a head of long, black braids with purple highlights that set her starkly apart from the boys and their crew cuts. "Parthen's not even really a *guy*."

"It's complicated," Merulo assured her, smiling to show a mouth of ordinary human teeth. He looked to me for confirmation. "Am I setting an extra plate, Jack?"

I scrutinized Cara through narrowed eyes, sure she was one of us but needing confirmation. "What happened when the music started?"

She furrowed her eyebrows, rolling her palm absently across the doorknob as the cogs spun in her skull. If I was right, she had two answers in mind and had to decide which one I wanted. "Well, the curtain went up—"

"No. Not on stage. Inside you."

After a long moment of hesitating and tugging at her sleeves, Cara gave me the answer I was looking for, inelegant and unscientific as it may have been. "I felt like I was made of magic."

I nodded my approval and tossed her a keycard. Not that she needed one, but it felt like a nice gesture to welcome her in. "Set another plate, Merulo."

CHAPTER TWO

We gathered the following evening in the shadow of the *Rubeno Mardo*, her angular zeppelin shape silhouetted against the setting suns of Hodge and the dome of her bridge glistening in the last light of day. Her mirrored tail fins, one of her few parts not yet overtaken by the rust growing up her hull like moss, reflected the lights of the town in the valley below.

People wouldn't bother us here in the desolate airfield far from farms or cities, as nobody had reason to go there except when a ship came, and we'd been the only ship to take off or land in weeks. Not exactly a hub of tourism or trade; probably a different story around harvest time, but I wasn't looking to stick around and find out.

Ideally, I had wanted to leave that morning, but explaining how the show worked ended up being too complicated and, to paraphrase Cara, it would be easier just to show her.

"They don't look as... scary tonight."

Couldn't agree with her more. Within a few seconds of arriving at the airfield, Cara had pinpointed the one aspect of costumes that led to the demise of countless other shows: people could spot the seams on fake conjoined siblings even in the dimmest of lighting.

It was almost laughable to suggest these were the same freaks from the show, and I understood the skepticism Cara regarded them with.

Merulo was tall and full-figured, but cheerful and downright cuddly compared to the beast he would become. His dark hair falling across his shoulders and his neat goatee were the only hint of the fur that would sprout on the rest of him, and he wore a loose caftan— we'd learned long ago that his shifting muscles and fat would tear the seams of any tighter clothing.

The conjoined triplets weren't conjoined, though under Parthen's camouflage jacket she wore a shirt that bared her midriff in preparation of melding her skin with Theon's, and the left side of her hair was shaved to better connect to Pneuman. And though Theon and Pneuman were identical twins, they couldn't have looked more different—Pneuman a sweet, goofy kid wearing an old souvenir freakshow shirt we used to sell, and Theon serious and somehow more attractive, to me at least, in a tight shirt and jeans.

And other than a few feathers in her hair for dramatic effect, Lily looked as much like an angel as I did. Still unbelievably gorgeous and not shy to flaunt it, but entirely human.

"First thing you've got to know," I said, brushing my hair from my face as the wind began to pick up, "is that we're all freaks. Everyone in the whole universe, for one reason or another. Most try to hide this fact. A few of us embrace it, not so much because we want to but because there's nothing else for us. So we show people the terrifying and unseemly parts of us no one wants to see, and we charge 'em good money to see it."

Lily stepped forward and knelt to display her shoulders and back, all bare, featherless skin down to the dangerously low neckline of her sequined dress. "See? No wings."

"But you flew," Cara insisted. "If it isn't costumes and harnesses, then what?"

I held up the receiver, a small wooden box the size of my hand with a speaker on one side and images of galaxies and solar systems carved into the others. Not the most advanced technology, but I wouldn't have anything else.

I checked the time. Soon.

I debated how much to tell her. No matter how many times I tried to explain it, it never sounded remotely plausible, but I had to warn her. Seeing the end result was one thing; seeing it happen before your eyes was another matter entirely, though the complete truth was an ancient burden none of them deserved to be saddled with.

"The music plays," I said. "Same song, same time every night, and it triggers something inside us. That feeling you had, like you were made of magic? That's what it feels like when your DNA recognizes a song, even if you've never heard it before."

She stared at me in eager anticipation, nodding slowly. Whether she actually believed me or was just humoring me, I couldn't say, but it was a nice change from the usual interruptions of "that's impossible" and "science doesn't work that way."

I cast a sideways glance at Theon, who had given me more trouble than the others, and continued. "Makes you feel alive, like there's a purpose to your existence and you can do the impossible, and that ain't just in your mind. We're all freaks, but we—" I motioned to my crew. "Well, we're different. Our bodies hear that song, and it triggers our genes to change, to grow into... I don't know, the true selves that live in our heart or some sentimental crap like that."

"How poetic," Lily said with a laugh. She looked up at Cara. "I know it's hard to understand. It happens to me every night, and I still have no idea how it works, but I can fly, Merulo becomes the feral wildman, Parthen and the boys really can read each others' minds and feel each others' pain... Jack breathes fire and gains the ability to give impassioned speeches without sounding like an uninterested jerk."

I checked the time again.

"So what changed in you?" Pneuman asked with earnest interest. "During the music, I mean?"

Cara hesitated, almost like she was afraid of hearing the absurdity out loud.

"I turn into a wild beast," Merulo pointed out quietly. "And these three grow into one, psychic organism. Whatever you're about to say will probably be the most normal thing we've heard in months."

After another moment's thought, Cara rolled up her sleeves. Her arms, though pale peach and freckled like her face, gleamed in the diminishing sun.

I reached out to touch her. Cold, almost metallic. That explained how she opened the lock.

"You're a cyborg," I said, tapping my nail on her forearm to hear the clinking sound. They just couldn't get the texture right, no matter how hard they tried.

Her moon didn't seem like the type of place to have a neurologist trained in bio implants, and I doubted anyone there could afford to travel to see one.

"Fancy. Who wired it into your brain?"

"I did it all myself." She held up a hand and demonstrated the various functions and attachments installed in her fingers, glossing right over the fact that she had just admitted to performing brain surgery on herself. She yanked her sleeves down. "And I'm not a cyborg," she clarified. "I'm just good with electronics and I like gadgets. My dad says it's bad to be a cyborg."

"Well, I tell you what. kid. You can't make a person change by pointing out their flaws, but you can be the one person who doesn't try to."

"I've always had a connection to electronics," she said, shyly extending a hexagonal wrench from her forefinger, "like I could talk to them. But when I heard the music… something happened."

I checked my watch. Not long now. "Yeah, something always happens. What matters is what happened to you, kid."

"They… talked back." Her words came slow at first, her reluctance to being different still holding her back, but as she talked, she grew more excited, more animated. "I could hear the messages stored on the phones of everyone around me, could see the last videos that played on their contact lenses. I could see the blueprints of your ship in my head. She's an Aldebaran cargo ship, Highwire model. Superluminal capability, more weapons than she came out of the factory with, and she has a capacitor that should be repaired soon. And I felt like, if I wanted to, I could touch any source of power on the ship and control everything remotely."

"Ready to feel that way again?" I asked, holding out the transmitter as showtime approached.

And passed.

It was time, but the music didn't play. *The music didn't play.*

Why didn't the music play?

I tapped the transmitter, shook it, slammed it against the palm of my hand. Nothing. I checked the time again, made sure my watch was in working order and compared its time to that on the broadcast billboard in the valley, one of the main ways information was shared in rural areas without affordable access to wireless. My watch was set to what we called *Rubeno Mardo* standard time, a way to keep our internal clocks in sync when visiting planets with days of vastly different lengths, but it was easy enough to do the conversion. She was definitely late.

A cold blood pumped through my veins, my heartbeat echoing in my ears as my world threatened to come down around me. Why wouldn't it play?

"Jack?"

I pulled away from Lily's touch. "Showtime," I said, pacing the hillside and holding the transmitter up to get a better signal. But that couldn't be the problem; it played even when we performed in the underground cities of Rosmarus. "It's played every night for ten years. Why not now? What happened to her?"

"I don't know." She looked scared, they all did, but not because of the music. That didn't matter to them, not like it mattered to me.

"Are you okay?"

The song started. Sixty-five seconds late, but it finally started, and the first notes calmed every one of my nerves and set fire to my icy veins.

Something was wrong. Horribly, world-changingly wrong, but for the next eight minutes and thirty-three seconds, I didn't let it bother me. Couldn't even if I tried, because she *sang*.

Pneuman, Parthen, and Theon's heads and bodies merged with each other, and they briefly played the part of the zombie-like psychics before returning to their usual, alert appearance. Merulo's eyes began to glow, his hair growing thicker and his face contorting into a primitive muzzle. Lily's wings rose up from her shoulder blades and unfurled to their full, impressive plumage.

And Cara, well she looked like she didn't know whether to laugh or cry as she saw the transformation that took place behind the curtains and finally felt like she belonged.

I knew that feeling; felt it every night without fail, and it never faded. Each time felt like the first, like finding yourself in a group of strangers.

I probably should have kept my mouth shut, let her experience it without my commentary, but the urge burned inside me, fueled by the song and giving off smoke that curled upwards from my mouth when I smiled. I buttoned my vest, brushed back my hair, and stepped forward.

"Gaze upon the medical oddity, their fusion now so real that their shared organs are visible in X-rays! See the wildman, his grunts and chest-beating a conscious act but his instincts and rage a dangerous and untamed force! Watch the angel fly, no wires or apparatuses, as beautiful as she is deadly!"

I turned now to Cara and gestured emphatically toward her, my voice growing louder in anticipation of seeing her new, exciting power.

"Welcome to our family the cyborg! Half human, half machine, able to communicate with both and bend them to her will with only a single touch!"

We stepped back to give her room to work her magic.

Cara approached the *Rubeno Mardo* with a bold confidence, the ship dwarfing her already small stature. She put a hand to the great iron hull, and the *Rubeno* sprang to life, her warning lights blinking and flashing and the gangplank opening and closing. Her wings pitched, her landing gears retracted and extended, and her tail turned to reflect a different part of the city behind us.

And a woman's face appeared on the mirrored fin, that same radiant face I saw every time I closed my eyes.

I whirled around and looked down into the valley. Diantha's image glowed from the news billboard, complete with flashing graphics and words scrolling underneath. It had to be important but I couldn't read it from where I stood.

Without a second thought, I flew down the hill, my feet barely touching the ground and the fire burning hotter in my lungs with every step, the music growing to its climax just as I reached the center of town.

Her face loomed over me, half hidden by a dark veil like she'd been caught unaware by a paparazzi drone. She looked scared, her face streaked with tears, but strength and resolve glinted in those big, brown eyes and I couldn't remember her ever looking more beautiful.

The text below her told the developing story of an assassination plot, and my heart stopped. No. Not her, she couldn't be...

But she wasn't the victim. Earlier in the day, Garon, leader of the planet Vespi as well as the intergalactic corporation VesCorp, had fallen ill and succumbed to a poison which investigators declined to disclose. His family—a daughter and my ravishing queen Diantha—had been secreted away when their food was also found to contain traces of the poison. Both were in good health and had returned to the capitol later in the day, at Diantha's insistence. The assassin had yet to be apprehended, and security had been increased tenfold.

I stared at her picture as the story repeated, until they finally replaced it with another one. Seemed there was a reported uptick in mosquito populations and unexplained disappearances on some moons. No connection had been found, but that didn't stop people from speculating.

The music faded, ending sixty-five seconds later than normal and leaving me exhausted and overwhelmed. Was I supposed to do something to help her? Travel across the universe to protect a girl who had more armed guards than the sky had stars? Yes, I think I was.

Someone called my name. I turned to see Lily standing wingless atop the hill. The others joined her, disheveled and broken.

I looked at my hand. I still had the receiver. What must have happened to them once they were out of range, when the music suddenly stopped affecting them... how it must have felt for the music to end in the middle with no warning.

I didn't say anything as I went up the hill and back to the ship, but I don't think they expected me to. Most of them knew about Diantha, anyway, and I didn't feel like explaining it to Cara just then.

This was our signal.

***

I was young and foolish, more stars in my eyes than in all the known galaxies. Looking back, it should have been obvious that something was up. After years of begging him to take me on one of his runs, why would my father finally relent now?

As it turned out, an extra pair of hands just made the work go faster, and when your work was smuggling stolen goods through a warzone, speed was key. If he was caught bringing supplies to a moon threatening to rebel against its planet, there could have been major prison time. And dear old Dad graciously chose his eighteen-year-old son to be his accomplice.

Not like I really cared. I got to leave our muggy little rock, see the night sky unfold into infinite nebulas and galaxies, and set foot on the moon of another world. Everything I had ever dreamed of.

Not much to write home about, Vespi 3-14, with a single city and rolling fields of lavender its only defining feature for miles in every direction, but I loved it. Loved every minute I spent hauling unmarked boxes from the *Rubeno Mardo*'s cargo hold and sweating under the infernal sun. I never wanted to go back.

I got the impression most of my father's work involved leaving stolen goods in a shack somewhere in exchange for a bag of money left by an anonymous buyer. Lucky I didn't have an opinion of him that could be tarnished.

One box, a big one half my height, was actually labeled, with an address in the city.

"Some of my business is legit," Dad said indignantly. "But you better go, in case it's a sting. They don't have warrants out for you yet."

I left him with the rest of the cargo and dragged the dolly over the uneven terrain toward the city of gleaming pink marble, glad for an opportunity to see more of the moon.

Except for the primitive stone villages and the VesCorp mining camps, the city was the only thing resembling civilization on Vespi 3-14. Couldn't tell you why they didn't build more like it, only that it was gorgeous. Everything my home wasn't.

Towers a dozen stories high, cobblestone streets, and not a single drunken oaf yelling at his wife to make him supper. That settled it. If the rest of space was anything like Vespi 3-14, I wanted it to see it. All of it.

I found the address easily enough, a music store carved from what looked like a single block of marble. Behind its glazed windows sat all manner of instruments I'd only seen in books, and standing on its steps… I'm not one prone to hyperbole, but she may have been the most beautiful sight in all of space.

She wore a simple dress, two-toned blue and ruffling around her feet in the breeze, and had her curly brown hair teased up in a braided bun. Light beamed from her face, and I'd wager her radiance could have outshone any supernova. She turned at the sound of the dolly rattling down the street, and my legs threatened to give out when she smiled.

"Is that for me?" she asked, peering at the crate. Maybe it was just the local accent, but her voice sounded like music.

I tore my eyes from her to glance at the name written on the label. "Diantha Perlo?"

"That's me," she said, smiling again, this time at me.

After that, it was hopeless. I'd have done anything to make her smile like that. I had just opened my mouth to introduce myself when something behind me drew her attention. I followed her line of sight to see large Vespi ships pursuing something in the cloudless sky.

My father's ship.

"Bastard," I swore under my breath, then looked at Diantha and muttered an apology. Someone as fine as her shouldn't have had to listen to my foul mouth. "I think my dad just left me stranded."

"Bastard," she agreed, and set off for the field where we had set down.

"Your crate," I said, running to catch up.

"People are good here," she said simply, and that explained everything. Back home, you didn't let anything—spouse and home included—out of your sight unless you didn't mind someone stealing it.

When we reached the field, any hope that someone else had simply stolen his ship drained from my body. I don't know why I even considered any scenario other than him leaving me. Never should have expected anything better from him.

More big ships hung in the sky. Military crafts from up on the planet. A few crates were scattered about, with his vest slung over one. A note scrawled beside it read, "War gettin' worse and they ain't playing around with smugglers. Have to fly her through a minefield. Take care of the vest for me, kid."

"He isn't coming back," I said, picking up his vest. Tattered old thing, but as close to a signature as he had. I couldn't remember ever seeing him without it, so he must have expected the worst.

Diantha lay a hand on my arm. "On the bright side," she said, "you would look good in a vest."

CHAPTER THREE

I lay awake for hours, staring up at the stars painted on the dull sheet metal ceiling and turning the receiver over in my hand as the *Rubeno Mardo* rocked back and forth. Only my rusted heap could find turbulence in the glassy calm vacuum of space.

Something clanged against her hull. She took a lot of abuse, my old ship, but she kept going, kept persevering through whatever space threw at her. I knew she couldn't go on forever; bolts fell off whenever we set down and her props wore out as fast as we replaced them. And Cara was right—there was a capacitor that needed replacing.

She was a good ship but not built for this kind of stress. One of these days, she'd give up pretending that she was.

As for me, I gave up pretending to sleep, sat on the edge of my bed with a pen and a pad of paper, and set to work trying to find a place in the show for Cara, making diagrams and timelines and reworking the script. There just wasn't time to fit in another performer, not without cutting someone off and depriving the audience of properly built suspense or seeing an angel take flight. I think that might have been why I'd stopped actively looking for more freaks.

Couldn't say for sure there'd ever be a show again, if I couldn't rely on the music playing on schedule, but it gave me something to do besides worrying about Diantha. There was nothing I could do about it until we got to Vespi, at least a three-day flight, except go to the bridge and yell at Lily to fly faster. Not like she'd listen anyway, so I worked on the show.

I heard footsteps enter the room some time later but didn't look up. The mattress shifted and a red braid dangled into my field of vision. "Can't you just make the music play longer?" Cara asked, reading over my shoulder as I arranged and rearranged our performance time without success. "Or just play the song twice in a row?"

I crossed off another attempt at fitting her in, and tapped my pen on the pad of paper. If I didn't talk so much at the beginning, or if we got rid of the audience participation and just had the triplets demonstrate their psychic ability on their own...

Did she ask me something? I looked up. "What?"

"If the music played longer, you would have time for everyone. Right?"

I went back to my planning. "I'm not in charge of the music, kid."

"But maybe if you talk to whoever is—"

"She's a little busy right now."

"Right, but—"

"It just doesn't work that way."

With an exaggerated sigh, Cara left my bed and wandered around my room, poking around in my belongings and running her hand over the communication panel on the wall.

"That stopped working ages ago," I told her.

She put her face up to the device and peered into the speaker holes, then went at it with a screwdriver that extended from her forefinger. The dark screen flickered to life and its buttons glowed a bright blue in the dim light.

I raised an eyebrow and wondered if she hadn't just found a place on the crew as our engineer. "I… would've gotten around to fixing that eventually."

"I might as well do it," she said, coming to my side and reading my notes again. Did this kid ever sit still? "Don't you have tablets?" she asked, crinkling the edge of my paper. "They make ones that can draw the thoughts right from your head."

"I've got an old-fashioned mind. And paper can't be hacked."

"It isn't that important," she insisted, watching as I crossed out yet another composition that would have left no time for Merulo. "Me being in the show, I mean. I like just being with people like me, getting to see the places I've only read about."

"That's the idea," I muttered, paying as little attention as I could. Not that I didn't like her. She seemed like a good kid, if a little excitable and flighty; I just had other things on my mind. So many things, all pushing for my time and energy.

"Is it?" Cara asked, her interest piqued. "Is that why you do this?"

"One of the reasons." I flipped over my paper and started a rough sketch of a robot costume. Maybe Parthen could make the covers for the legs out of spare heating ducts… Or was it scarier, more interesting, if the robot looked just like a human? They could take over your job, maybe even replace you in your life, and no one would ever know.

"But why a freakshow?"

"Did you see us?" I asked. "We're freaks."

"For a few minutes once a night," Cara argued. "There are other ways to make a living. Why *this* way?"

I sighed and put down my pen; I wasn't going to get any work done anyway. "We're freaks all day, kid. Just can't always see it."

Another collision rocked the *Rubeno*, this one larger than the last. Must have been going through a debris field.

"The show fills a need," I explained to Cara. "See, we used to be a scared little species confined to one planet orbiting one star. There used to be mysteries lurking in the woods, under the oceans, even in our own bodies, but we found all the answers. So we'd look up at the night sky and imagine all the amazing things we could see, if only we could travel through space."

Cara sat on the edge of my bed, hanging on my every disillusioned word like it was a bedtime story.

"We made up stories about the alien races that lived on all the worlds just beyond our reach, sent out probes just to find life out there and make us feel like we weren't alone in this great big universe. When we didn't find anything, we invented ships that could travel farther and faster than any before. Now we could see with our own eyes all there is to see, and we saw that there ain't much to see. Just empty space and dead planets, not even a hint of a long-lost civilization to be found."

The ship thundered and shuddered. Another piece of space junk. And here I thought someone who had wings might make for a good pilot.

"All the mysteries of the universe lay dead at our feet," I continued, trying to keep Cara's attention away from the crashing sounds that made her jump. "We'd gone all the way to the stars only to discover what we already knew: that we were alone in an infinite, empty blackness and that nothing could amaze or excite us anymore."

"So you put on a freakshow?" She sounded unconvinced. "And you lie to them?

I shrugged. "People want to believe there's something more to life, that they haven't read all the books the universe has to offer. They need to believe, not just in angels and telepaths and nuclear holocaust survivors, but in the *possibility* of those things existing. Doesn't matter if it's a lie. It gives them hope. Sometimes that's all you need."

"Wouldn't it be just as effective to show people who undergo metamorphosis when they hear a certain song? Isn't that just as exciting?"

Before I could answer, the ship lurched to the side with an awful scraping sound. I teased her, but Lily was actually an excellent pilot;

this was no debris field.

I got up without another word and stalked through the corridors of the *Rubeno*, her lights dimmed to simulate the twenty-four hour cycle we humans needed to function but couldn't find on most planets. Her cycle was synced up to a moon that never saw night, but the people there still kept a schedule and darkened the lights in the evening. To the same end, our crew quarters lacked windows to eliminate the light of passing stars. Never minded it much before, but now it pissed me off. What was going on out there?

Parthen and Theon stood in their doorway, disheveled from sleep but on high alert.

"What's going on?" Theon asked, arms crossed over his bare chest.

I threw my hands up helplessly as I passed. "I'll let you know as soon as I figure it out."

I reached the stairs leading to the domed bridge on the top of the ship, and met Merulo on his way down. He brought me up to date with a single word, his voice bordering on excitement and his grin visible even in the dark.

"Pirates."

Great.

We both headed up to the bridge, where the expanse of space surrounded us in all directions and the round command room sparkled with the thousand tiny lights of every button and dial. Field of stars wherever you looked.

It wouldn't be the first time we'd been targeted by a ship that flew under the radar and around every law. The *Rubeno Mardo*, though long since converted on the inside, still bore the markings from her past life as a cargo ship, and this drew in pirates and marauders like unscrupulous moths to a flaming pile of money. Usually only took an explanation of the situation, and sometimes a small payoff, to avoid being boarded.

Lily sat in the big chair at the head of the control panels, hands flying across switches and levers as she grumbled to herself.

"What's the situation?" I asked, coming up beside her.

She gestured at the blackness of space all around us, empty save for the rocks and metal scraps that struck us periodically. "I don't see anyone," she said. "They must be cloaked or something. I'm trying to communicate, but they're not responding, and we keep getting hit."

Even as the words left her mouth, a rock appeared in front of us and hurtled toward our ship. Lily swung the *Rubeno* around, but it struck with a reverberating thunder and we all had to hold onto something to remain upright. Never even had time to perform evasive action.

"I don't know what kind of pirate can afford a cloaking device," Lily said, a shrill edge in her voice.

"Probably stole it, " I said, and nudged her shoulder. "You've been up all night."

"So have you." She stayed put and gave me a look. "And I'm kind of an owl."

"Kind of," I agreed, and nudged her again. For all her confidence when it came to dealing with people, I knew how she could get when the other party wouldn't participate, when she wasn't in a position of power. "Take a break, Lily."

"I'm fine—"

"Captain's orders."

She stood, giving the invisible ship one last glare, and sat with a huff in one of the other chairs.

I took my seat, Merulo at my side, and we got to work. Radar showed nothing, gravitational field detector didn't find so much as a blip. I gripped the throttle, my heart pounding in my ears, and searched the skies for a gap or disturbance in the endless sea of stars that could indicate bent light around a cloaked ship.

Something had to be out there. Rocks and scrap metal didn't hurl themselves, not with this precision.

I gritted my teeth, wincing as something scraped against the hull, and absently tapped at the keyboard to transmit a message of goodwill that I doubted they'd bother reading.

Pirates, at least the kind I'd encountered, liked to force their way aboard ships, keeping them intact to add to their fleet or sell off once they'd dealt with the crew. These invisible buccaneers seemed intent on breaching our seal, drowning us in a vacuum and rendering the *Rubeno* useless.

"She's strong," Merulo assured me, always the peaceful optimist in times of crisis. You wouldn't think that would be so irritating, but he found a way.

"Not what I'm worried about," I said. "They've got some high tech here, probably filched from some military somewhere; why use it to fling rocks? Don't they have lasers on board?"

"That would give away their position," he mused, leaning back in his seat and tracing his fingers around the big, red button on his console, no doubt itching to press it.

The hatch opened in the floor behind us, and Pneuman, Parthen, and Theon took to their stations—Parthen monitoring our various systems, and Pneuman and Theon on the comms.

"Do you want to talk about her?" Pneuman asked when I didn't greet them, correctly interpreting my distraction.

I banked the ship as a rock came our way, and managed to have it only ding the starboard wing. "Sure, this is the perfect time to discuss my love life," I growled. "Where's the kid?"

"In your room," Parthen said. "She's scared but says she wants a seat on the bridge for the next siege."

"I'll go sit with her," Lily said, and disappeared down the stairs.

I flicked from one optical lens to another to try to see *anything*. The sky blinked from vivid splashes of colored heat signatures to a grayscale starscape intensifying any point of light as the dome around us filtered out various parts of the visible spectrum.

Still nothing.

I started wondering if maybe there wasn't a ship at all. We could have wandered into an anomalous gravitational field that accelerated the natural orbit of an asteroid belt and...

Who was I kidding? I had no idea what was going on.

"Any theories?"

"You aren't over her yet," Theon suggested.

I narrowed my eyes. *Frigging smartass.* "About the ship."

Merulo thought for a long moment, his eyes unfocused on a point far off in space. He swiveled his chair until he made a full, slow revolution, then craned his neck to stare straight up. "Theon's wrong," he said at last. "I think you are over her."

Something struck us from behind, and I couldn't contain my frustration any longer. "We're being attacked, Merulo! My feelings for Diantha—"

"He means the other ship," Parthen interrupted, chewing one of her braids anxiously. "I think you're over her. Or she's under us. However you want to phrase it, she's not throwing things at us— she's sucking them in with her tractor beams."

Well, now. That changed the situation considerably. The pirate ship could have cloaked itself from radar and the like, but it would have been visible in some capacity, in some wavelength of light. Unless it had found shelter below our very hull, the one place we couldn't see from the bridge.

I looked at Merulo and raised my eyebrows as we secured our five-point harnesses. "Ready?"

A ferocious grin overtook his serene face, and he grabbed the controls of our weapons system with a grip that turned his knuckles white. "Always."

I tapped the *Rubeno*'s intercom panel and used a few choice words to keep Lily and Cara up to date on the latest developments. "Hold on," I said with a smirk, "we're gonna do something ill-advised and reckless."

With that, I rotated and engaged our thrusters with full power, inertia pressing down on us as we shot upward.

Now, someone smarter and more pedantic than me (Theon, for

instance) might find fault in the way I phrased that, what with space being a directionless void and all. But the way I see it, if you have artificial gravity, you have directions; up is the way you look when you roll your eyes, and down is the way you fall when you're drunk.

We had artificial gravity, and so we went up, then spun forward to face the other ship amid the distant crashing of unsecured objects falling into walls. Hopefully they took my warning to hold on literally.

We must have taken the pirates by surprise. A small patch of space wavered, its stars shimmering more than usual as the light bent and warped around the invisible ship. The affected area shrank from view and the barrage against our hull ceased, leaving us floating in the still and silent infinite.

"Since when do pirates just retreat like that?" Merulo wondered, echoing my own thoughts but without all the cursing.

"They don't." I gunned the engines and gave chase without a second thought.

"Are you sure about this?" Pneuman asked. "They aren't bothering us anymore. We could let them go."

I probably should have let 'em go, should have thanked the universe for our good fortune and set to work fixing the damage.

Probably should have done a lot of things differently, but maybe I wasn't quite at my best that night. Couldn't be sure; I only knew that someone had attacked my ship, and I intended to find out who.

I pushed our engines to their limits, ducking and weaving around asteroids and pleasure vessels but never gaining ground.

Even with my eyes locked, unblinking, on the blurred space in the distance, I could see Merulo staring at me, waiting for the command he lived to hear. When I saw nothing but clear space between us and them, I nodded to him.

"Fire."

My quiet and meditative first mate erupted in a blaze of primitive war screams, pressing the big red button as hard as he could and guiding our missiles toward the target.

I had to laugh. He touted the virtues of peace, rallied against wars, and even suggested we reduce our weapons store, but get that man at the control of a rocket launcher and he became this bloodthirsty warrior, stopping at nothing until he destroyed his target. A tangle of contradictions, and I wouldn't have wanted anyone else at my side.

The pirates dodged every missile, gliding out of their path with little effort as the ship slipped out of range.

The last one found its mark, setting its payload of oxygen and hydrogen aflame with a spectacular flash, and we let out a cheer, Merulo's tenfold louder and more enthusiastic than anyone else's.

As the glow of the impact faded, the pirates' cloaking slipped for the briefest of nanoseconds. I couldn't hope to make out any detail at that distance, the ship just a speck in my vision, but our radar picked up an image and flashed on our screens the distinctive, triangular silhouette of a Vespi warship. Not a typical pirate vessel, as Vespi ships rarely let themselves get attacked, much less skyjacked.

Our engines whined as the throttle met the console and refused to go any farther. The other ship vanished from view and from the reach of our equipment, but I refused to give up the chase.

"We'll never catch them," Merulo warned.

That warship could have destroyed us. Even without its weaponry, it could have crushed the *Rubeno* on its windshield and never even noticed. So why didn't they? Why antagonize us, damage us, only to flee when we fought back?

"Have you checked our fuel levels lately?" Parthen asked with concern.

Space blurred, pieces of rock and other floating debris flying past at speeds I'd never seen. Didn't even know the old girl could go that fast.

"Jack!" Parthen's voice hit a sharp note that drew my attention.

"What?"

She jabbed a finger at the fuel gauge. Running on the low end, but it looked fine to me.

"We've got enough."

"Enough for what?" Theon challenged. "Not enough to get us to tomorrow's gig, much less get us all the way to Vespi. Not enough to reach the other ship, even if we could come close to matching their speed."

When I didn't respond, Merulo reached over and took the throttle.

"I got it," I snapped, pushing his hand away. I glanced at him from the corner of my eye. He stared at me with deep concern bordering on fear.

What was I doing? What did I seriously think would happen if by some miracle we did catch up to the pirates? I let up on the engines, grinding my teeth and calling myself every awful word I could think of, then released my safety harness and handed over the controls without another word.

I crossed paths with Lily and Cara in the corridor.

"Want to tell me what that was?" Lily asked in a fury as Cara, smiling with inexplicable satisfaction, went up to the bridge.

I kept walking. Trying to explain why I did something I couldn't explain didn't rank high on my list of ways to spend the night. "Ask Merulo."

"I'm asking *you*." She pursued me all the way to my quarters and stood in the doorway, glaring at me. "It's because of Diantha."

"If you already knew the answer, then why bother asking?" I heard a growl creep into my voice, and tried to keep it out. Lily didn't deserve that.

"Because I don't know if *you* know it." She stepped into my room and leaned against the metal beam that secured my bed to the walls. "Someone tried to hurt someone you love—"

"I don't—"

She cackled. "Trust me, you do. It made you angry, and now you're lashing out at anyone in your reach."

Couldn't really argue with her there. I fell into bed, exhausted but too wired to find sleep or even close my eyes.

"And if you were on your own, I'd say have at those pirates," Lily said, looking down at me. "Chase 'em, provoke 'em, run out of fuel and get stranded in space by 'em for all I care. But you're not on your own. These people need you here, making level decisions that keep them safe. You're all they have."

Had to love her choice of pronouns. *They* needed me, implying that she didn't, that she could go back to being the bed-hopping, pickpocketing scam artist she used to be.

On second thought, I had no doubt she could slip right back into that life without missing a beat. They all could, but they never would. They needed this, the ship and the show. They needed a place to belong.

I let out a weary sigh. Had to love my choice of pronouns.

CHAPTER FOUR

We had just enough fuel—no thanks to me—to reach a trading outpost on an unnamed asteroid in the Zenda belt. Dead, dusty rock in the middle of nowhere, with no signs of anyone even trying to grow anything worth eating. They probably only bothered giving it a breathable atmosphere because the miners could work longer without lugging around heavy oxygen tanks.

I noticed the VesCorp mines as we set down on the surface: major excavating projects employing upward of a thousand men, judging by the size of the camps, using giant machines to dig deep into the core of the asteroid.

"Good thing there aren't any permanent settlements," Merulo said bitterly as we gathered any goods we had to trade. "If it isn't already uninhabitable, it will be when they're through seeping their toxic chemicals."

I nodded my agreement. There was a little town set up to service the mining camps, but they'd pack up and leave when the diggers left.

Happened all the time. Expedition discovers some valuable element, town springs up overnight and lasts only as long as the land keeps giving. Sometimes it'd be a week, sometimes years or even decades. Cultures developed in places like these, only to be broken apart and scattered across space when the next dead rock didn't have the resources to house the entire town.

All at the whim of the minerals and the people who went to any lengths to pull them out of the ground where they belonged.

My father grew up in a place like this. Never was the same after it disassembled, never could settle down or let himself feel too comfortable in any one place or with any one person. Probably where I learned it.

We disembarked in the late afternoon, *Rubeno Mardo* standard time. Supposedly also late afternoon on the asteroid, but its sky was a dark, evening blue and its low sun only a vaguely bright spot over the rocky horizon.

My feet skimmed down the *Rubeno*'s gangplank, feeling like they barely touched the ground. Most of the crew, experienced in the variable gravity of other worlds, handled the transition with a practiced ease, gliding across the craggy gray landscape. Cara fell flat on her face, to the great amusement of Theon.

Pneuman gave him a dirty look and helped Cara to her feet. "Just be glad you fell on a planet with reduced gravity. Hurts less."

Cara rubbed her nose. "Still hurts," she muttered, looking down at the traitorous ground.

"That's nothing," Pneuman said. He linked arms with Cara and helped her stumble over the terrain. Though technically the same height and build as his twin, Pneuman carried himself smaller and seemed to take up less space. "You should have seen my first time. The gravity was so low that I fell, bounced like five feet in the air, and fell again!"

"It wasn't that funny," Parthen said, hiding a faint smile. "He broke his ankle the second time down."

"But you fixed it," he said with an earnest grin. "She's very good at setting broken ankles. If you ever break an ankle, go see Parthen."

We came to the open air marketplace that dominated the town, a bright and colorful bazaar that stood out in contrast with its dark and dreary surroundings. Stalls and stands, each adorned by candles or oil lamps to ward off the asteroid's eternal twilight, offered a variety of food, clothing, and trinkets available for barter. Not a very technologically advanced society, but that came with the territory.

"Meet back at the ship in thirty," I said, slapping away a mosquito.

"I have some things in my room," Lily reminded me, referring to the jewelry and other gifts given to her by all the men who had fallen in love with her over the years.

"It's my fault we're here," I said. "I'm not letting anyone else pay for my bad choices." We had a few gigs lined up, but I wanted enough fuel to go straight to Vespi.

Lily and the boys disappeared into the crowd, dragging off boxloads of the scrap metal we collected for just such a purpose, leaving me with Parthen and Cara to hock the random assemblage of junk we didn't need. Like anyone ever really needed lace doilies and little statues of extinct ocean elephants.

"What do you call this thing again?" I asked Parthen, turning the gaudy figurine over in my hand.

"A whale."

As we made our way down the main stretch, I glanced at the wares peddled but never stopped long to look. Seemed no one had any fuel, at least not any amount worth buying, nor any idea where to find some.

"Based on its size," Cara said as she tripped yet again, "this asteroid should have somewhere around a hundredth of the gravity of my moon. But we aren't floating. It feels more like..." She paused to calculate. "Half the gravity of Hodge."

"Smart girl," cackled an older vendor. They beckoned us to their stall, where they displayed their silken scarves and leather goods with pride. "They can alter our gravitational field on the smaller planets, like your ship probably does. As much fun as weightlessness is, our bodies thrive in the conditions we had on our ancestral home."

I picked up a scarf and tossed it up. It floated down like a leaf in a lazy breeze, twisting and turning and taking its sweet time to reach my outstretched hand.

"But it isn't Earth gravity," I said, handing it back to the vendor. "If you're going to the trouble of altering—"

"The miners," they said with a dismissive wave of their wrinkled hand. "Less gravity, less friction, less energy needed to move the giant machines. VesCorp manipulates worlds in ways you can't imagine. You notice how warm it is, even without a sun? To keep the miners happy, keep them working day after day."

The person spoke with an easy, conversational tone, but sadness tinged their crinkled brown eyes. VesCorp owned this town, owned the people in it and controlled every aspect of their lives. Could be said they did the same for most of the universe, but it was worse on moons and asteroids, which were owned by the nearest planet— usually a planet in the pocket of VesCorp. Couldn't grow anything unless VesCorp said so, couldn't have the right gravity, couldn't complain because they didn't always own their houses or even rent the land. I doubted anyone could ever be truly happy working under VesCorp.

I gave the vendor the whale statue and a thin silver chain in exchange for a pair of gloves, far more than they were worth and we both knew it, but neither of us said anything. Maybe they could trade it for a good, decent meal; lower gravity over extended periods tended to waste muscle mass faster.

Their face beamed as they tucked the items into the pocket of their voluminous dress. They set the earthy brown gloves in Parthen's hand and patted her on the cheek. "Maybe don't flinch so much when people touch you," they advised, sounding like a wise old grandparent. "The right man might be afraid to hurt you."

Parthen accepted the gloves with a mumbled thanks and a deep scarlet came to her cheeks.

"Know where we can get a few cans of fuel?" I asked the vendor.

They pointed to a large tent that loomed over the crowd and other stalls. "You'd want to talk to Orion about that."

I nodded my thanks and we made our way to the tent, a massive plastic and canvas affair the size of a small house, complete with air conditioning and, I noticed as soon as I stepped inside, a gravitational field independent from the rest of the asteroid.

"Finally," Cara said with a laugh, letting go of Parthen's arm and walking confidently on her own in the familiar gravity.

Tourists and traders milled around the tent, examining its fine wares. No residents of the town could hope to afford the rarities offered here, obviously intended for more wealthy traders looking to take advantage of the asteroid's nonexistent laws against the selling of illicit goods. Narcotics, bars of pure uranium, and barrels of blood diamonds made up just a small portion of the inventory that would get you arrested on a more reputable rock. Birds and monkeys shrieked somewhere in the distance, and I saw an exotic lizard of some sort clawing at the bars of its cage.

"Merulo would kill this guy if he knew what was going on here," I said under my breath.

"Must make a fortune, though," Parthen mused with a hint of resentment, running her gloved hand over a display of jewel-encrusted dresses that each cost more than the *Rubeno* was worth, "being the only luxury goods emporium at the only outpost for parsecs around."

And instead of giving to the community, he spent it on himself. I'd never even heard of someone increasing the gravity of one isolated area. How much had that cost?

We wandered around the store, my field of vision crowded with too many displays of too much shiny crap no one needed. A gaggle of kids ran rampant through the store, touching everything and poking the animals.

"Hey!" The word shot through the noisy tent like a bullet, stopping the kids in their tracks. "What did I say about touching my merchandise!"

The kids scurried out of view. I looked for the source of the shouts and found an irritated man in a tight jacket and ostentatious pants with flashing lights down the seams, leaning back in a gilded chair and sipping a fizzing drink.

Orion, I could only assume.

The level of opulence, especially in the shadow of people who sold stale bits of bread to survive, disgusted me. I had half a mind to try to beg some fuel from the miners rather than deal with this shiny bastard, but I doubted they'd give me the time of day.

I walked up to the man, box of tradables in hand, and squinted at him. "How much fuel will this get me?"

He tipped the box toward himself and rummaged through its contents. "Not a drop, my friend. I'm not in the business of buying junk. If you can trade up to something good, we'll talk. If not, and I suspect not, you can go around buying up the few shot glasses of fuel they've got to trade out there." He waved out the door. "Might take you a few days, but you'll collect enough eventually."

"You'd lose our business."

He cackled. "I look like I'm gonna go bankrupt anytime soon?"

Something crashed to the ground somewhere in the tent, and the gaggle of children ran past. Orion grabbed the last one by the collar of his shirt and pulled him close.

"What did I tell you about touching Daddy's merchandise?" he growled in the child's face.

"Not to," the boy whispered, eyes wide in terror.

"And what happens if you break the rules?"

"You'll throw us in a crater."

"Damn right, so don't let it happen again." Orion released the boy and shoved him in the direction the others had gone. "One night leads to eighteen years of hell," he muttered. "Makes me regret ever setting eyes on their mothers."

"What a gentleman," Parthen said nervously under her breath as Cara positioned herself behind us.

"Would you give me some fuel if I got them out of your hair for a few hours?" I asked. "I run a carnival ship—"

"I honestly don't care if you run a slaughterhouse," Orion interrupted with a hearty chuckle at his own attempt at humor. "Time away from those cretins is well worth the price. Tell you what, I'll even let you keep one of them! Your choice. I'd suggest the grubby little blonde one."

I declined the offer. "Give us a bit to set things up, then send 'em to the airfield. *Rubeno Mardo*, tail number NGC 3370. It's the one that looks like a whale wearing a glass beanie."

"Look at him, confidently saying 'whale' like he's known the word all his life," Parthen whispered, making Cara giggle. With that, the girls and I left the climate- and gravity-controlled tent in favor of the heat and uncomfortable weightlessness of the outside.

"Awful man," Parthen said with a shudder. "Strike that—he doesn't deserve to be called a man."

Couldn't agree more.

Cara stared straight ahead as we walked, her eyes unfocused and her face about to shatter into despair. She'd probably never seen anyone like Orion, anything like this town. People didn't have the most exciting or luxurious lives on her moon, but I was willing to bet they went to sleep at night knowing that they'd have a place to live in the morning, and that some sleazy guy in a suit wasn't gonna come and monopolize the commerce.

Probably shouldn't have let her come with us, not with her being so young. Should have waited, swung around a few years later to pick her up. But I knew how hard it was, living in a world that didn't understand. She hadn't said anything about her old life, but with us freaks it was always the same old story, just with different characters. None of us would go back to that; once we heard the song, we belonged to the stars.

"Space ain't all farms and carnivals, kid," I said, squeezing her hard, metallic shoulder.

"I never thought it was," she said, her voice wavering. "I just thought... I don't know what I thought. That finally fitting in somewhere would make everything okay. And it has. And it hasn't."

"That's because the worlds suck, kid. Every one of them in their own way, but all of them suck." What more could I say without lying to her?

Parthen answered that for me. "We're born into a universe that doesn't care whether we live or die. Most of the people around us are just along for the ride and some of them actively sabotage your ride so theirs can be smoother. And when you're different..." She hesitated before choosing her words with a careful precision, "When you're seen as an unclean pariah just for trying to help people survive, it seems like no one wants to ride with you."

Cara stopped as we passed a table of machine parts, steadying herself as inertia tried to pull her along. The young proprietor of the rusted table pointed to a sign declaring the prices of the items. A pittance. If he sold everything, he might have been able to feed his family for a day. Maybe two, if they rationed.

"I've never really had friends." Cara pulled her sleeve down over her metallic hand, staring at an ancient analog clock. "There weren't many kids around and none of them liked me. Machines liked me, and we had a lot of those."

"What about your family?"

"Mom was always busy. And Daddy told me not to... not to talk to machines."

I could see the gears turning in her head, the smoke coming from her ears. Clocks like that, real old ones with the bird that popped out every hour, they could fetch a lot of money in working condition, enough to feed a family for months. And she could fix it, but years of being told not to do things that made her different weighed on her mind. Same old story, different details.

"May I?" she asked, picking it up.

"Five coins," the boy said, hope leaping to his face.

"It doesn't matter if the people who are supposed to love you don't like the person you are," Parthen prodded. "All we can hope for is to find the ones who do—the ones who make you smile when you don't think you have it in you—and keep them close."

Cara peered into the door at the top of the clock. "Like you and Pneuman."

"Theon," I corrected. "She's dating Theon. He's the one she shares the torso with."

"Maybe," Cara said, using her fingers to pry open the back of the clock and adjust the mechanism, "but she loves Pneuman."

She sounded so confident that I almost found myself agreeing with her, but there was no way I'd have missed a love triangle forming on my own ship. And definitely no way Theon the psychic would have missed it.

I turned to see how Parthen would react to this claim, and saw her walking off toward the airfield, arms crossed and head low.

Huh. Maybe Cara wasn't so far off. Not any of my business, though. I'd deal with it only if it started affecting the performance of the crew.

Cara made a final adjustment to the clock and set it to five. The little bird popped out of its door for the first time in probably a hundred years, and sang the time at the top of its screeching, mechanical voice. Why anyone would want something like that in their house is beyond me.

The boy accepted the repaired clock with tears in his eyes and tried to express his inexpressible gratitude by kissing Cara's hand.

She pulled away, yanking her sleeve down, and gave him an awkward smile. "Five *thousand* coins."

I smiled. Something to be said for finding a place to belong, for finding people who accept your true self, the person you are when you're not trying impress anyone. It changed lives; probably saved a few, too.

***

Colored lights and music filled the midway in the repurposed cargo bay, laughter and the sound of children's footsteps echoing down the two lanes of booths and rides under the dark ceiling painted to look like the sky over Vespi 3-14. The warm smell of fried dough mingled with the exhaust of the generators that powered the rides, producing an intoxicating aroma that could only be found in the dying breed of carnival ships.

Of all the reasons to travel the skies in a decrepit old ship with a crew full of lovable freaks, the laughter of children was one of the better ones. Smallest crowd we'd had in a while and hardly worth running the rides and manning the booths, but if it would get us fuel, I didn't care.

To keep my mind present and to keep from losing it permanently, I walked the midway and checked on the rides as I passed. They were supposed to run without assistance and maintain themselves, but I refused to accept that any machinery could ever be a substitute for a human eye and hand.

The carousel turned smoothly, its antique alien horses hovering up and down in a synchronized pattern, and the screams echoing inside the spiral slide indicated the movies projected on the ceilings were working. Good. That meant I wouldn't have to go in there and watch it myself; they tricked the brain into believing it was plummeting to the ground from space, a notion that scared the hell out of me.

Lily leaned on the front of her booth, one of many she manned on a rotating basis. "Business is slow today," she said, rolling a ball in her hand. "You want to take a chance, maybe win me a prize?"

I glanced at the rows upon rows of glistening glass bowls behind her and raised an eyebrow at the multicolored betta fish inside them. "I don't know; I hear these games are all rigged."

She batted her long lashes. "Oh, come on, win a fish for a pretty lady, Jack."

"Parthen breeds them; you can have any fish you want. If it survives the trip up to your room."

"I heard that!" Parthen shouted from her concession stand down the midway, and a piece of fried dough flew past my head.

I threw it back with a laugh and listed toward an adjacent booth. "The buzzer game is more my style," I told Lily, but the booth was dark and its proprietor absent. "Did Merulo ever come on board?"

She nodded. "Saw him talking to Cara, and then he left again."

Struck me as odd, but I didn't need anything else to worry about so I didn't think too much of it. As long as he returned before the show.

"Let me know if he comes back," I said, "and I'll win you a prize."

I continued my patrol, weaving through a stampede of toddlers, and ended up at a table shared by Pneuman and Theon and surrounded by another group of kids with unending reserves of energy. If only we could harness those resources, we could light up a galaxy.

Though the boys couldn't access the psychic and empathic powers only the music could give them, they did pretty well with their natural talents for entertaining, passed down from ancestors who thrilled entire villages into believing in the supernatural.

Pneuman entertained them with a plate of molten glass, specially designed to be cold and safe to the touch, that was illuminated from underneath by multicolored lights. He blew into it with a thin straw, daintily molding the shape into glistening animals and flowers before collapsing them into a liquid pool once more.

He spent every spare second staring at Parthen's food stall, his eyes sparkling with passion and desire. He must have really loved fried dough. His brother, on the other hand, didn't so much as glance in that direction, too busy doing magic tricks and using mentalist techniques to convince the children of his nonexistent supernatural abilities.

Maybe there was something to Cara's claim after all.

Pneuman finally tore his gaze from Parthen and smiled at me. "These kids are more excited to see us than most people."

"Always are, on the poorer rocks," I agreed.

"Doesn't hurt that it's free," Theon said, faking a wide grin as he pulled a handkerchief from a tiny hole in an egg before an unimpressed audience. "It's a real egg," he said, his voice slipping toward irritation as he rolled up the sleeves of his navy blue shirt. "I'm not hiding anything." He let them examine both of his hands— seemingly empty but large enough to conceal a balled up handkerchief—and another egg. "So everything's on the up and up, yeah?"

The children just stared in confusion as he pierced the shell with a nail and produced a carnation.

Theon stared back. "Do you guys understand what I'm doing here? At all?"

A girl raised her hand. "You're taking things out of little oval boxes."

Her words hit me like a punch to the gut, and I realized the severity of the town's poverty. "They don't know what eggs are," I said, reaching out to take it from him. I cracked it on the edge of the table and started to explain the absurdity of a chicken laying an egg with anything but yolk inside, but they found amazement in their own way.

"How did the flower stay dry in there?"

"Why isn't the bandana covered in goo?"

I didn't correct them. What did it matter how they ended up in their hushed and reverential awe, so long as they got there?

Pneuman handed them each an egg. "When you get home, have your mothers break these into a pan. Take out all the crunchy bits and cook the goo. When it isn't gooey anymore, you can eat it."

One girl eyed her egg with suspicion, looking like she expected it to explode.

"No flowers or handkerchiefs," Pneuman assured her. "Just yummy protein."

Cradling their dinner in their arms, the kids ran off en masse to the haunted funhouse attraction. I wondered how many eggs would make it home intact, and how many I'd have to clean out of the alien vampire's coffin later.

"We should come back here someday," Pneuman said. "Give everyone on the asteroid a great night."

Theon scoffed. "With what money do you expect them to pay?"

"Well, maybe if we ever have a good run, build up a little extra cash, we could—"

"We could have a night of free admission!" Theon said, mimicking his brother's enthusiasm. He lowered his brow. "Us having money to burn? Not likely."

Much as I'd have liked to entertain the idea of having a free night more often, I had to agree with Theon. I knew more than any of us how unlikely it was we'd ever have that much expendable income, but I knew better than to get between the Fago brothers, even when they looked to me to take sides.

"Merulo's back," Lily called out. "And just in time."

I checked my watch. Music would start soon—if it was going to, I thought with a sickening feeling in my gut. What if something happened to her? We hadn't been near enough to a news satellite to get updates since the previous night on Hodge. Anything could have happened in that time.

I looked at Merulo. He was shaking, his jaw clenched and his eyes wild with rage. A speckling of blood dotted his meaty hands.

I took his arm and drew him away from the children. "What the hell happened to you?"

"Went to find fuel," he said, evading my question. "What they're paying won't get us all the way to Vespi."

By the door, I saw two large barrels of fuel and cages filled with all manner of exotic animals. In the better lighting, the lizard I saw back at the tent appeared to be some sort of monitor lizard.

"Do I even want to know?" I asked.

He nodded to my watch. "Are we putting on a show?"

Anxious uncertainty gnawed at my stomach. He'd killed Orion. I couldn't believe it, but at the same time I couldn't deny it.

No way I could put him on stage now. Hell, we should have been hightailing it off that rock before they found the body. But I'd need him at his best if they gave chase.

"You're gonna go cool down in your quarters. Take the..." I gestured to the animals. "Take the birds and whatever the rest of them are with you."

He looked like he wanted to argue, but just nodded and hung his head. "Are you putting on a show?"

"If the music plays."

CHAPTER FIVE

After my dad abandoned me on her moon, Diantha, being a gracious and sympathetic soul, offered her home to me until I could find better accommodations or a way off-world.

I expected someone like her to live in one of the sculpted towers in the heart of the city, but she led me instead to a shabby village where people dressed in rags and lived in houses built of haphazardly stacked stone. She stood out in stark contrast from the sad, colorless world around her.

Her house was indistinguishable from the others except for the cracklingly dry attempt at a garden out front. Inside wasn't much better, just a single large room full of furniture no one else wanted and wide windows on every wall to let in golden shafts of sunlight. But she beamed with pride for it and I had to smile as she took my hand and gave me the grand tour.

"It's been in the family for generations," she said with a hushed reverence. "Went through war and came out of it unscathed. It's a survivor, like the people who live in it."

She pointed out half a dozen medals in a frame high on a wall, in a place of respect. They were wooden, roughly carved by hand.

"These were my father's, and his mother's. And someday mine and my children's will be among them. Vespi books don't even acknowledge the wars that so define us, but rebellion is etched in our history. Every generation tries to wiggle out from VesCorp's thumb, and every generation fails. Every loss comes with consequences, the stripping of our land and the erasure of our cultural identity. Our moon isn't even allowed to have a name anymore, just a designation." She turned to look at me. "But with every loss, we get stronger. Their sacrifices push us closer to victory." She covered her mouth and laughed. "Listen to me, going on like this."

"I don't mind," I said, and meant it.

"Still, I should make up your bed. It's almost midnight."

The bright sun showed no indication of dimming, but I didn't argue as she pulled sheets from a closet and began folding them into a lumpy shape resembling a mattress. Maybe they had a different way of telling time here.

"We don't have night," she said, noticing my confusion.

"VesCorp won't allow it?"

Diantha laughed. "We orbit the planet in a unique way that makes our side of the moon always face the sun. Eternal day, except during eclipses."

She indicated a clockwork model of the solar system on a bedside table, the sun of which gave off a warm glow. The planets and their moons rotated lazily, and the marble representing Vespi 3-14 did always face the same direction. One larger ball swung on an irregular path that would eventually pass between the sun and planets before going back out into space for, if the speed of the model was any indication, possibly hundreds of years.

"The rebel asteroid," she explained. "It was captured by our sun millions of years ago but makes its own orbit. It'll be coming back in ten years, and I'll get to see the night sky for the first time."

She sounded like a kid counting the days until her birthday, and almost giggled as she pulled a dress from the closet to bundle up into a makeshift pillow. I couldn't help but notice the rest of her clothes looked more suited to the village—faded and torn garments without a lick of ruffle or style.

If she was embarrassed by this, she didn't let it show. In fact, a bit of pride lit up her already bright eyes. "I saved up for a long time to buy my good dress. The city is decent to us—they know we all belong to VesCorp and only serendipity prevented them from being destroyed in the first wars like the cities that used to be here—but they have standards. If you want to study or work there, you have to look like you belong." She smiled. "Do you want to see something beautiful?"

"Always."

She went around the house, dropping heavy curtains over the windows. Darkness took the room piece by piece, until only tiny droplets of light dotted the floor. I looked up to see thousands of stars coating the blackness of the ceiling.

The starlight danced across Diantha as she walked through it, giving her luminous freckles.

"This is what the sky looks like at night," she said, taking my hand. She craned her star-speckled neck to the false heavens. "The holes are drilled straight through the ceilings, so technically it *is* starlight, since the sun is a star."

"What happens when it rains?" I asked, my face growing uncomfortably warm the more I looked at her.

"VesCorp doesn't let it rain," she said. I thought she was joking, but she went on, "They can control atmosphere, gravity, whatever they want. We still have clouds sometimes, but it hasn't rained since I was a kid. Our punishment for the last war, having to live only on the groundwater they allow us."

She pulled me to her bed and my heart leapt into my throat, but she lifted a textbook from her pillow and set it in my lap, open to a dog-eared page about weather modification.

"I have this idea," she began, pointing to a highlighted passage.

"It's called cloud seeding—basically adding chemicals to clouds that condense their water molecules and make them fall as rain."

I could tell she was simplifying her explanation for me. Anyone smart enough to understand the diagrams in the book had to be lightyears ahead of me on the intelligence front. But I didn't care. I could sit there and listen to her spout her beautiful scientific nonsense for hours.

"That's what the propane was for."

I looked up, sure I'd missed something. "What?"

"The crate you delivered. It was a tank of propane. I've been slowly amassing it, in the hopes that I can get a plane and use it to seed the clouds—"

I kissed her. Just a quick peck, and I couldn't explain why I felt I had to do it. I just couldn't go another second without. She was too beautiful, too brilliant.

She smiled and kissed me back, adding, "Talking about cloud seeding has that effect on me, too."

And she was funny.

That settled it; I was gonna have to fall in love with that girl.

***

The music played, and the crowd—the kids and a good number of adults from town who were drawn in by the allure of a show—fell into an excited hush. Though the song echoed inside my heart and filled me with relief that she was okay, something about the music didn't sound quite right. Like she was hesitating on some notes, uncertain.

"Welcome, ladies and gentlemen and variations thereupon, to Jack Jetstark's Intergalactic Freakshow. Our first specimen, or should I say specimens, were born on a distant planet in the Ilex system. Or maybe they were hatched, or created… no one quite knows for sure."

The conjoined triplets incited thrilled shrieks of disgust, but they didn't play up the zombielike expressions or move in sync. Parthen winced for seemingly no reason, looking at the boys as if worried that she had offended them.

"They feel the others' pain, hear the others' thoughts."

That explained it. With their minds connected, she feared thinking about her feelings for Pneuman lest Theon hear, and that Pneuman would feel that fear. And maybe they did, or maybe they only picked up on her attempts at keeping a mental distance and responded in kind. The audience loved it anyway, shrieking in delight at the demonstration of their abilities.

I looked at Cara, who stood beside me above the stage, her electric hands connected to the lighting and effects panel. I hadn't had time to tell her about Merulo. "I'm going to need you to go on next," I said, quietly enough that the audience wouldn't hear.

Panic overtook her face. "I'm not ready," she mouthed.

"Beware!" I called out to the crowd. "For their extrasensory reach is unlimited. They see your deepest secrets, feed upon your most primal fears. Some say they can even implant thoughts, alter the minds of those around them."

I signaled to Cara as the song shifted to the low, rhythmic section, and the lights cut out. A thick mist, illuminated from below by tiny, red lights, took over the stage. Cara's idea, hacking our heating system to add ambiance to Merulo's performance. How could I spin it to fit a robotic act?

My mind reeled, scrambling for an idea, any idea. My patter for Merulo fit the tribal tempo; what could I say about Cara that would have the same effect?

The crowd grew restless, and I had to do something.

"We've all heard tales of Earth, of how its people destroyed themselves in nuclear warfare, leaving the planet a lifeless, radioactive lump of rock. Though these stories are true, the Earth isn't devoid of all life."

Cara looked at me, brows furrowed. Where was I going with this?

"Though primitive beasts still roam its wilds, the real dangers lurk not in our past, but in our future."

The lights brightened a bit and I let the audience wonder and speculate while I told Cara my new plan.

"I don't even have a costume," she protested.

"That's the idea." The words flew from my mouth without thought, fueled by the fire burning inside me. "Allow me to paint you a picture of our future," I said, speaking slowly to set a suspenseful undertone while keeping time in my head. "Mankind is obsolete, on the verge of extinction but kept alive to serve as playthings for a superior race. They won't come from the stars or from the oceans, but from our own minds."

I let that notion sink in, playing on innate fears of advanced technology, before adding a single word, punctuated by a shrieking note in the song.

"Androids."

I flicked on a spotlight behind the audience. They turned as one with a gasp to see Cara standing before them, limbs locked in place and head low in mock sleep mode. As the volume of the singing rose, she came to life, and gave a vacant smile lit from within by LEDs borrowed from the effects panel.

"Once helpful, innocent machines designed to repair our ships and make our societies run smoother, the androids soon developed free will... and weapons."

That was her cue to show off the attachments in her hand, but she froze under the gaze of a hundred eyes. Even from where I stood above the stage, I could see the fear on her face. Damn kid didn't want to show off her arm.

"They seem just like everyone else," I improvised. "Damaged and flawed. But they aren't like you. They have no shame for what they are, for the way they look or the things they can do that set them apart from the rest."

Cara looked up at me, nodded as if she understood, and did something I hadn't planned. Instead of merely showing off, she took a sudden step toward the crowd and put her hand on a man's head.

I could only guess what she intended to do, but a faint glow in the terrified man's back pocket gave me a clue and I continued, "They became one with our technology, turning it against us as they rose to power. Fear not, for this one has not yet developed the desire to enslave. Watch as she—or should I say, *it*—connects with your electrical field and uses it to control your communication devices!"

Cara closed her eyes, rocking to the music as the glow grew brighter.

A quiet voice, a message from within the memory of his phone, said, "It's Orion. Someone attacked him; stole fuel—"

"Damn you, Merulo," I muttered.

Cara tried to hide her alarm as she backed away and found another target.

The crowd started murmuring, conferring with each other and watching the scene with caution, their bodies tense and ready to strike at the slightest provocation. I put a sweating hand on the control panel in case I had to throw on the lights and diffuse the tension.

"Don't be afraid," I warned, hoping she'd take the hint and find a less scary message this time. The thought of a mob descending on her filled me with dread. "It won't hurt you."

Just as the commotion grew to a climax, a child's voice spoke from high above.

"Hi, Daddy," it said with a giggle, throwing the crowd into a dead silence as they craned their necks to search for the source. "Are you still in space?" the girl asked, and the man fell to his knees in tears.

"My baby," he sobbed with joy. "It's the last message she sent before she went missing... I thought my phone had erased it."

The song shifted to the quieter, soft part. Time for Lily's act, but I couldn't end this now, not during what felt like our new headliner. Couldn't tell you how she did it, probably reprogrammed the phone to give her access to deleted files or something, but I didn't care and neither did anyone who saw it.

"Are you coming home soon? There's all these big bugs outside and I can't wait to show you."

As the voice continued to project from the ship's sound system, I snuck down to the stage and brought Lily up to my catwalk.

"Going a bit off script?" she whispered, her beak grazing my ear.

"Just a bit." I looked to the ceiling, indistinguishable from the dark walls surrounding it. "How's your night vision?"

Lily batted her enormous eyes and struck a pose with her wings outstretched. "Fantastic, just like the rest of me."

"Then you shouldn't bump your head up there. Try to time it with the crescendo."

She furrowed her brow, putting her hands on her lightly feathered, bare hips. "I'm afraid you're going to have to be a little more clear with what you want."

"I want you to give them an angel," I said, going to the control panel.

It would have been nice to have some fog, but I'd have to do my best without Cara's help. The message came to a close as the music swelled to its dramatic conclusion, and Lily took flight with a quiet rustle of feathers.

"I can't wait to see you, Daddy. I love you."

The overhead lights flicked on, bathing Lily in a golden halo as the song hit its final notes. The lights went out and the crowd cheered.

And the song continued.

A slow, almost eerie melody that rose in volume and pitch, turning my stomach and sending my heart into anxious overdrive. It wasn't the same song, but it had a similar sound, like a fourth part she'd never sung before. The ending.

Fire ran through my veins, pulsing to the quickening beat. Lily took flight like a startled bird. The triplets, from what I could see in the dark, fell away from each other, and part of the stage turned to shimmering ice as Parthen's bare hands contacted it.

"Show's over, people!" I cried out, unable to find a polite or more eloquent way to say it. When nobody left, still angling for a photo of the angel or obnoxiously wondering aloud about the more personal aspects of the triplets' anatomy, I delivered a stern and final warning. "If anyone's still here in five seconds, I'm letting the wildman loose!"

Even without the crowd having seen Merulo, it seemed to be a good enough threat to get them moving. Most of them left in a hurry, screaming and laughing like it was all part of the show. An eardrum-rattling roar from Merulo—who must have come to check out all the commotion—sent the rest scrambling for the exit, and all was silent save for the music and my own heartbeat.

The song climbed to a high, fast pace, taking my pulse along with it, then crashed down in an explosion of sound, a cacophony of every note at once. If I concentrated, I could make out familiar sequences of notes, like parts of the song being sung over one another.

It went on like that for a good minute before cutting off without warning.

We all stared at each other for a long time, all of them back to their regular selves, no one daring to give voice to the single thought bouncing around in our heads. We were all thinking it.

Our lives as we knew them were over, and the future loomed dark and infinite before us.

CHAPTER SIX

Dust and dirt fell from the ceiling with every quaking blast while Diantha and I huddled together with the rest of her village, praying the thick walls would protect us.

It was easy to lose track of time down there in the bunker below the city. We had electric lights, eerie ones that gave the caverns an unnatural bluish glow, but they didn't dim at night the way they did in my dad's ship. I'd guess two or three days had passed since the rebels attacked the mines and VesCorp began returning fire.

Everyone who had weapons was topside, fighting an intergalactic army with the ballistic equivalent of slingshots and pointy sticks. They were going to lose, no doubt about that, but the mood underground was one of hope rather than despair.

"They've never gone at us with explosions before," Diantha explained with a smile. "They must think we're a threat. We've never been a threat before, more like easily squashed mosquitoes than an army."

I wished I could share her enthusiasm for bombardment, but I did find the atmosphere of optimism against all odds kind of contagious. I'd never really been afraid to die, but then I'd never really been in danger like this, either. No one around me, not even the smallest children, would let on that they were scared. They channeled their energies instead into more productive pursuits. Cooking, sewing, telling stories.

They liked my stories, even if I was making them up on the spot and pulling random facts from books I'd once read. Kids and adults alike hung on my every word that echoed through the expansive system of tunnels, and I must say I enjoyed telling them in a way I'd never enjoyed anything before. And when Diantha listened, she looked like she felt the same way. Like she saw purpose in me.

"Let me tell *you* a story," she said, pulling me down a long corridor to a chamber used for food storage. She held a book of sheet music, the only personal effect she'd brought down. "It's a true story, and I'm telling it to you because I think you need to hear it."

She spoke with gravity and reverence, her voice shaking as if the words were afraid to leave her mouth. I just nodded and let her talk.

"A long, long time ago, the government of Vespi decided that ruling the solar system wasn't enough for them. They wanted more, but their army was weak compared to others in the universe. Vespi had some of the most brilliant scientists and advanced technology, so they decided to turn people into weapons."

Tears welled in her eyes but she wiped them away.

"They took people from the moons, and they altered their bodies at the genetic level. They became more than just human. They had claws and wings and poison spikes, they could turn invisible and use sound to shatter any object. They could infiltrate enemy armies and win the war before it even began."

I felt uneasy at the idea of this being a true story, and had to lean against a rack of canned goods.

"But something went wrong. They couldn't control their powers. What good is a secret assassin if he can't hide his wings? So they called them freaks and hid them away in a prison in the great mountains to the north. But what good is a prison when the prisoners can melt lead? The freaks escaped, and tried to fight back against the people who hurt them. Only a few survived, but they stole the machines that damaged them, and they used the machines to fix themselves. They made the powers hidden, only activated by a certain sequence of vibrations."

I looked at the music in her hands, and she delivered the final line of her story with a whisper.

"They dispersed throughout the universe to hide, and they passed the genes to their children."

She lifted the music and began to sing. A hauntingly wordless melody that I felt reverberate through my body. How had I lived this long without that song, without knowing I had such an emptiness for it to fill? I'd been waiting my entire life to hear it and never even realized.

As she sang, it became obvious she didn't need the sheet music. It was just a prop to help demonstrate her ability to turn invisible.

It started off slow enough, with a gentle fading of her colors as if someone had dimmed those eerie blue lights, that I didn't think to mention it in case I had imagined it. But then I saw the rough texture of the tunnel wall behind her and there could be no doubt.

She vanished and left me with a song coming from seemingly nowhere. The sheet music hung in the air of its own accord. I reached out to touch her. Still there, just invisible—or almost. The image was distorted just enough to reveal her outline.

I leaned in to kiss her invisible lips, but smoke curled from my nose. My chest felt warmer than it ever had, and every heavy breath added oxygen to the burning embers.

I stepped back and, just as she reached the climax of her song, exhaled a plume of flames. It probably should have shocked me more, realizing I could breathe fire, but somehow it felt so *right* that I didn't question it.

"It's called *The Libramo*," she said, reappearing, "and you never sing the ending."

***

The next night I waited, receiver in hand as we continued on toward Vespi, but the music didn't play. Not on time, not late. It just didn't play.

It left the *Rubeno Mardo* and her crew in a silence like nothing we'd ever heard, a dark and meaningless void that nothing could fill.

What happened? Why did she sing the ending? Did she think I wouldn't drop everything and run to her the first time she was late?

I burned with anger and anxiety, cursing the distance between us and Diantha—another full day's flying, maybe two—and spending every spare second listening to reports of violence coming in from all over space.

It started off innocently enough, with a bunch of moons and asteroids rebelling against their planets, against anyone who exploited or oppressed them. Futile effort, I figured, but more power to 'em for trying. We needed more people standing up for themselves, even if they kept getting beaten back down.

The rebellions should have died down like they usually did, but the sheer volume of them all attacking at once depleted arsenals and scattered armies. Something was different this time; they had a unifying reason not to back down—scores of people supposedly getting "disappeared," according to the news. Rising tensions opened old wounds between planetary allies, and an all-out galactic civil war broke out seemingly overnight.

We stayed abreast of the front lines best as we could, but we had to get to Vespi. The music had to be a sign that she was in trouble, and the war only confirmed it.

I guess it was just a matter of time before we ended up somewhere we weren't welcome, but we never saw it coming.

First laser pierced our hull, doing god knows what damage to the crew quarters and blasting a hole through the carousel's pink unicorn. Not that anyone would be riding it anytime soon.

I banged my fist on Merulo's door on my way down the hall.

"Need you on the bridge, Merulo!"

Dust swirled in a vertical beam of light that cut through the darkness, a straight line from the hole in the floor to a hole in the roof through which the atmosphere was quickly escaping. Damn lasers. At least they hadn't hit anything too important. Just my damn ship.

Saw the space bastards the second I stepped onto the bridge, a massive black shape silhouetted against the stars, with cannons jutting out in every direction. It hovered directly overhead, its lower laser turrets aimed right at us.

Lily kept us steady, plunging into the atmosphere of the nearest planet just as the ship shot out another volley of lasers. Some hit us— I could hear the sizzling metal scream as the beams bore through— but most hit other targets as a fleet of ships rose up beside us to defend the city that we had just put in danger. Pleasure vessels and personal transports for the most part, smaller than us by far and hardly a weapons system among them, from the look of it. I had to laugh.

"What's so funny?" Merulo asked as he came to the bridge and sat beside me and Lily. A big-eyed lemur with a ringed tail sat on his shoulder, munching a cracker and dropping crumbs on the lapels of his navy robe. Great. Just what we needed: the animals he liberated from Orion running loose.

I motioned to the armada surrounding us, each waiting for us to make a move. "We're the biggest and most powerful ship here, and they expect us to lead the charge."

Lily thought a moment before responding. "That isn't funny; it's tragic."

Couldn't agree more, especially as my original plan involved speeding away while shooting missiles behind us. Displays on the instrument panels showed we had only a few hydrogen/oxygen projectiles. Just about enough to take out one of the warship's landing gears, assuming we didn't get knocked out of the sky first.

With a look of concern, Lily yielded the controls to me. I put my hand on the throttle but didn't engage, scenarios of death and destruction playing in my mind. A battle between a military aircraft and half a dozen pleasure and cargo ships over a town of innocent bystanders... Nothing good could come from this, yet they all expected something from me, some brilliant strategy to surmount the insurmountable odds.

"What are we waiting for?" Merulo asked with a grin. His round reading glasses with the blue lenses reflected the light of the instruments and displays, giving his eyes that wild glow I missed seeing onstage. "Let's do something ill-advised and reckless." The lemur chirped excitedly.

Sounded like a plan to me.

"All right, guys," I said to my crew over the comm as another round of lasers hit. I tried to keep my voice calm and steady, but I heard it shaking with fury. "I'm not gonna tell you everything's fine, because it isn't. We're being attacked. To tell you any different would be lying, and I make a point of not lying."

Merulo smirked. "Where did you meet me again?" he asked under his breath. "Nuclear wasteland of former Earth, or a forest on Valeo? I forget."

I ignored him. "Everything ain't fine. The universe is at war and it's made its way to us. But we're gonna get through this."

Pneuman's soft voice crackled through the speaker. "I'm down in the carnival; they just blew up the concessions stand. But I liked your speech."

"Well, sometimes that's all a guy can hope for," I said, and cut off communication.

I tapped out a brief message to warn my little militia to stay clear of our weapons, and I gunned it west. Nothing much in that direction except the ocean, according to radar, so no one to get hit by falling debris. Or falling ships, for that matter.

We skimmed hilltops, rustling leaves as we passed mere inches from thousand-year-old trees, the smaller crafts disappearing beneath the canopies. The bulky warship barreled through, unwilling or unable to match our sharp turns, and deforested huge swaths of land with its wide wings, though I saw it falter and slow down slightly at a row of thick trunks.

Something to be said for zipping over the surface of a planet or moon, as opposed to empty space. You got to see things. Landscapes, culture, *life*, all blurring right outside your windows. The bucolic moon Rouze had a lot to offer in the way of scenery, and if we hadn't had a flying arsenal on our tail, I might have taken the time to enjoy its rolling hills and endless patchwork fields.

As we left the farmland behind and sailed out over an ocean that stretched to the horizon, our radar display showed an underwater landscape just as striking, with deep valleys and gigantic stone archways dotting the ocean floor. Must have been a desert at some point.

Now that we'd left the populated areas far behind, Merulo started shooting our arsenal at the enemy ship, with little results. My heart pounded and my palms grew slick as they returned fire, striking us and the other ships.

I couldn't figure out why they all would come along for the fight, as their tiny bullets pinged off the hull without any effect. I understood wanting to protect their homes and their people, but didn't they know it was pointless? Didn't they realize that they couldn't possibly damage that massive thing?

As the thought crossed my mind, the smallest ship appeared just outside our dome. Cute little thing, painted in bright red and black checks, but hardly built for war. Its pilot, a young girl built even less for war, gave me a salute and a grave nod before jettisoning herself directly into the path of the warship.

My heart skipped a beat. Pretty sure time itself skipped some beats, too, or at least went in slow motion as the red and black ship struck the front window of the warship with a sickening crash and went skidding over the top.

I waited, holding my breath and hoping to see her fly up unharmed, but she just plummeted into the ocean and sank from view. For a moment, I couldn't breathe.

Some of the other vessels went down to rescue her, but their attempts shrank from view as we sped away, the metal monstrosity close on our trail. It kept shooting—not at us, but at some nonexistent target above itself. The crew had to know the other ship had fallen; though I couldn't see any windows except the one at the front, their radar had to tell them where—

Unless they didn't have radar. The *Rubeno*'s radar sat at the top of her nose; if they had a similar setup, the collision could have taken out their radar systems.

"They don't know where we are," I said.

In light of the tragedy, Merulo tried harder than usual to suppress his enthusiasm, but he trembled with adrenaline and his wide grin threatened to split his cheeks. "We can use that. Have the others serve as diversions while we swing around and attack from behind."

And put more lives at risk? Not if I could help it. The image of that little ship splashing down echoed across my mind's eye, and I racked my brain for an alternative strategy. An idea came to me. An incredibly dangerous idea, but the only one I had at the moment.

"Hey Cara," I said into the comm, "is this thing seaworthy?"

After a long pause, she asked, "If you mean spaceworthy, her hull's been breached. We would have to use pressurized suits to survive the vacuum—"

"I said seaworthy. Can I take the *Rubeno* underwater? Will we lose the engines or anything important?"

She started to answer several times, but stopped herself. Finally, she said, "I have no way of knowing—"

"Guess."

"Our hull is breached," she said again. "Water will pour in as soon as we go under, but a brief venture at a shallow depth, assuming the more sensitive systems are still airtight…" I could hear the gears turning in her head as she did the calculations. "It *should* be fine?"

I didn't like how much she stressed the word "should," but it was good enough for me. "All right. Make sure everyone's strapped in or tied down."

Lily stared at me. "Why *would* you want to know that?"

"You'll see."

I lowered the *Rubeno* until the sparkling blue ocean just lapped at her underside, our remaining compatriots flanking us. I saluted them each, awed by their courage and determination in a time of crisis, as well as their ill-advised decisions to follow a complete stranger into an unwinnable battle.

I waited, hand tense on the yoke as I watched the radar for the perfect moment. When it came, I told the others to disperse, reflexively took a deep breath, and tipped the nose down.

The water split around us as we dove into a world of shimmering blue light. Didn't look like water so much as the inside of a sapphire, a perfect gemstone world teeming with fish. Merulo's lemur shrieked and scampered off somewhere.

Water poured into the bridge through laserholes I hadn't noticed until now, but we wouldn't be under long if I did this right.

I barely pulled out of the dive before we hit the ocean floor—water being thicker than space, it took more power than I'd anticipated to change direction—and we skimmed along the ocean floor, Merulo and I whooping and screaming all the way. Whether in excitement or fear, I couldn't say. Probably a little of both.

The warship followed close behind, enormous propellers on its tail pushing it through the water with ease. They started gaining on us, and I aimed for a thick curtain of kelp in the distance.

"Jack—"

"Trust me."

Lily glanced at the radar screen and figured out my plan, though by the tone of her voice, she didn't much care for it. "Are we even going to fit?"

Well, that was the question, wasn't it? Radar indicated an opening that left hardly any breathing room between the rock and my ship. Tight squeeze at a high speed. Hell, tight squeeze at any speed.

"Are we going to fit?" Lily asked again.

I pointed to the hulking black mass behind us. "*They* won't."

"But will we?"

"And the best part is that they'll never see it coming."

The emerald kelp swayed in the current, stretching from the ocean floor all the way to the surface overhead and concealing the danger that lurked behind their leafy curtain. The constant movement threw off our radar, making it all the more difficult to see the target, but I lined up best as I could and gunned the engines.

By the time we emerged on the other side of the kelp and saw the enormous stone arch rising up from the sand, we didn't have time to adjust our trajectory.

I released the throttle, trusting the *Rubeno* to fly true as the cold water poured onto my head from a new hole. Last hole they'd ever inflict on us, with any luck.

The arch flew toward us, growing larger until it encompassed our entire field of vision. Bigger than it looked on radar, with two thick columns of blue-gray stone standing like the legs of a giant, the top of the arch so far above that I had to crane my neck to see it. Might have *been* a giant, for all I could prove.

We passed through in an instant, too fast to worry about fitting, and came out the other side with minimal scraping of rock on our hull.

The warship followed a second later. I could only imagine their panic and terror as they left the kelp forest, faced with the image of an unavoidable collision between their wings and solid stone columns almost a hundred feet in diameter.

The catastrophic sound of metal and rock meeting in mutual destruction reverberated through the bridge. I didn't dare look back;

Merulo did, and let out a long, victorious scream.

I pointed our nose upward and brought us back to the surface, where I cut the engines and let the ship float on the water. My hands shook as I watched the radar for any sign of movement, but the warship's blip remained dead still at the bottom.

The smaller ships buzzed around us, all except the little one.

"Damn it," I muttered, stomping my foot with a splash.

The comm system crackled to life. Nothing but static. Must have been damaged in the battle, like god knows how many other systems. I'd have to find a safe place to land, do an inspection of the whole damn ship...

But it wasn't static.

Applause, from my people and from the comms of the surviving ships. I never thought I'd hear it again now that we couldn't put on a show, much less for myself. Didn't realize how much I'd missed that sound, how much I *could* miss the sound of people slapping their hands together like fools.

But it sounded good.

***

Lily came to my quarters in the middle of the night, looking more frightened than I'd ever seen her. Come to think of it, I couldn't recall ever seeing her scared of anything in all the years I'd known her.

"Jack?" she whispered, nervously fussing with the hem of her lacy shawl as she lingered in the doorway. "I have something I need to show you."

I sat up in bed and waved her in. She flicked on the lights and sat beside me, trembling as she started to talk but couldn't find the words; not the brassy broad she'd become but the unconfident shell of herself she'd been when I met her.

"What's wrong?"

She turned her back to me and slipped the shawl off her shoulders. I'll admit, my mind first went to a different place than she had intended, and though I can't say it was an unpleasant place, it gave me pause. She exuded beauty and light, but a captain and his pilot…

And then I saw the reason for her visit, and felt silly for ever thinking of anything else.

Tiny, off-white bumps protruded from the skin on and around her shoulder blades, some tipped in the wispy beginnings of feathers. I ran my hand across her back as if to wipe them away, but they remained embedded deeply in her skin.

Lily turned to face me, her dilated pupils almost eclipsing her gold irises. She tried to talk again, and finally put together the words to ask, in a shaking voice filled with dread, "Jack, am I growing wings?"

I put my arms around her and held her to me, her emerging feather shafts poking at my palms. I wanted to tell her it was all right, but I couldn't bring myself to lie to her.

She had every right to be terrified, but why couldn't *I* catch my breath? Why did my heart beat so hard that it felt like it would come loose from its moorings?

Her body heaved a silent sob and a tear hit my shoulder. I didn't embarrass her by acknowledging it.

"At least now I look the part," she said with a heavy sigh, nestling her head beside my neck.

"What part?"

"A freak. It was always inside me, and I guess it had to come out eventually."

"You aren't a freak."

She laughed, pulling away from me. "I beg to differ." With a sigh, she lay down on the bed and stared up at the ceiling. "You know, I'm smart. I could have done something with my life, but instead I prey on men. Teasing them, coercing them to buy me pretty things with the promise of…"

"With the promise of pretty things?"

She punched me in the arm. "Yes. And sometimes I don't even ask for anything in return. I do it for the thrill of seeing them fall in love, only to snatch it away. I like to see them crumble, and I know it's sick and if that doesn't make me a freak, the wings I'm growing do. Even if I wanted to do something more, go out and become... I don't know, a fighter pilot, or if I wanted to settle down and get married, I'll have wings."

Couldn't argue with that, and she probably didn't want to hear a speech about loving and accepting herself any more than I wanted to give one. I lay down next to her, the cold wall pressed against my side in the cramped space, and I pointed out one of the stars glowing over the bed.

"See that dot?" I asked. "Tiny little one, barely worth the paint it took to put it there?"

"Yeah."

"That's the star your planet calls the sun. From your home, it's an enormous ball of light that takes up the whole sky, so big and bright that you could only survive by putting up shields that blocked it out. But go to a different planet, get a different perspective, and it's not so big or dangerous."

"What's your point?" she asked.

"Who said I had a point?"

We stared up at the fake stars until I lost track of time, the only sound that of our breaths and the occasional clanging metal of Cara working late into the night on repairs. If any moment could last forever...

"People died today." Hard as it was to say, it felt good to finally get the nagging words out of my head. "Because of me."

"Bad people," Lily argued.

"And the pilot of the little ship. Because I was there. Because the warship thought we were bringing supplies to their enemies and because the others thought I was someone worth following to war."

"More would have died if you hadn't been there. And you *are* someone worth following. To war, to anywhere."

Room fell silent again, and I turned to face Lily. Anyone else would want to talk about my feelings, push me to explore the guilt and lack of self esteem or even Diantha. She just answered me, honest and simple answers, and let the matter drop.

"How come you never tried any of your tricks on me?" I asked. "I show up with a big, fancy ship and a broken heart... I was a prime target for your kind of schemes."

"You weren't a challenge," she said without thinking, then smiled and looked at me. "And you were different. I knew it as soon as I saw you that you were my way off that dark little rock, and I..." She moved away, averting her eyes and putting on her air of false confidence as she sat up. "And I'm not foolish enough to piss off the captain of the ship I want a free ride on."

Before I could respond, a figure appeared in the doorway. Theon.

He looked at Lily and I but declined to comment. "Hey. We got a problem," he said, and left without another word.

Lily wrapped her shawl around her shoulders to conceal her wings, and we ran after Theon to his brother's room.

"Heard Pneuman and Par cursing all the way across the ship," he said by way of an explanation, and went back to his quarters. Struck me as kind of odd, him not staying to help his brother and girlfriend. He seemed on edge, but then we all did lately.

I pushed the door ajar, not knowing what to expect. I found Parthen and Pneuman huddled together on the floor of the small bedroom, her wearing his old souvenir freakshow shirt, the two of them stricken with a kind of horror I'd never seen. They looked up at me, then at the glittering glass shards scattered around them. Remnants of a wine glass, judging by its mate on the nightstand.

"Everyone okay?"

Neither knew how to answer, and Parthen held her hands away from her body as Pneuman took her in his arms.

I saw no blood or any other reason for their behavior, and stooped to examine the glass. Among all the clear, jagged fragments, the stem and base remained more or less intact, but it looked different than the rest. It didn't catch the light quite right, with a foggy quality the other glass lacked. I reached for it, and the cold emanating from the glass caught me by surprise. I could only hold it for a few seconds before its bite was too much for me.

"It's ice," Lily said, touching a finger to the wet spot on the steel floor.

"It fell through my hand." Pneuman laughed at the absurdity. "Not out of. *Through*, like my hand wasn't there. And then Par tried to pick up the pieces, and…"

"And it turned to ice." Parthen extended a shaking finger and touched one of the larger shards, recoiling as it turned an instant, semi-opaque green. Jade. She buried her face in Pneuman's chest, careful to keep her hands from touching him.

A change came over the *Rubeno Mardo* that night, punctuated by a primal roar from Merulo's quarters. At the time, I didn't know what kind of change or how much it would affect every aspect of our lives and the lives of people all over the universe. I only knew that I could feel it coming, whatever it was, and that this was just the beginning.

Should have scared me, terrified me, even, but it didn't. Somehow, deep down inside, I think I'd been waiting for this all along.

***

We were only a few hours from Vespi, and deadly glares shot across the table, arms recoiling from the accidental touch of their friends'. I could only guess at the source of the tension—Parthen's feelings for Pneuman, the fact that Merulo had murdered someone—but I, too, fell victim to its ugly influence, finding irritation everywhere I looked.

The way Theon chewed. Parthen sorting her food. The sound of Merulo's fork hitting the plate. Cara's constant apologizing for every little thing.

It had to be the music—or lack thereof. Its absence had turned our lives inside out and I couldn't even consider the idea that anything else, be it murder or infidelity, could ever come between us.

With only hours until we entered Vespi airspace and the ringing in my ears reaching a pitch I'd thought only dogs could hear, I couldn't take it anymore.

"We're going to talk about this," I announced through the ship's speakers. "Meet me downstairs. This is a mandatory meeting."

As soon as the words left my mouth, I felt the sting of panic. What if we couldn't fix things? We couldn't go on like this forever. I waited a few minutes to let everyone decide, then headed to the carnival, usually a source of joy for us all. On that day, you probably would've had better luck finding a friendly smile in the empty space between the stars.

Parthen sat on the ground with gloved hands, plotting our course on a tablet, while Pneuman and Theon stood as far apart as they could, occasionally shooting glances at one another as if in response to insults the rest of us couldn't hear. Cara sat on the broken carousel, watching the scene anxiously, and Merulo leaned on an overturned booth, passive-aggressively stroking one of the many doves he'd liberated from Orion. He was more hunched than usual, his limbs covered in a light coat of fur and his cheeks a little more lean.

That left Lily, and though I stared at the doorway and waited, she failed to appear. My heart sank. I'd thought she, of all people, would have wanted to be here.

Nothing I could do about that now. I stood before my fractured crew and shook my head. "What the hell's wrong with us?"

"People want to leave," Cara whispered, terror lining her face.

I stared at my boots, my chest heavy. "That true?"

"We just..." Parthen struggled to find the words, so Theon supplied them.

"This isn't our home anymore, and you're dragging us along to save your damsel in distress who has an entire army to protect her."

"Look, I don't know what I'm going to find there and I can't make any of you come with me, but..." I left that sentence unfinished. It felt like weakness, begging them to follow me on my personal quest to save a girl who didn't need saving and almost definitely wanted nothing to do with me.

"No," Cara begged. "This is a *family*. We have to stick together, or there's no point in anything."

I nodded, relieved that someone else felt the way I did. "Then we fix it. I'm not singling anyone out. I'm including myself in this. Something's different around here, and I can't fix it if I don't know what it is."

"Why do you always have to fix everything?" Merulo asked.

Theon smirked. "Because when *you* try to fix things, people end up dead and we end up with a metric ton of lizards, birds, and lemurs crawling around our ship."

Merulo raised his hackles in defense. Every cell in my body screamed for me to stop their argument before it started, to keep the peace among my crew, but I resisted. At least they were communicating.

"I'm relocating them," Merulo growled. "They're special, rare creatures who deserve better from life than to be a status symbol in some menagerie or—" He covered the bird's ears. "—decoration on someone's hat."

"Of course," Theon pretended to agree. "Much better to let them run loose on a spaceship. Monkeys totally aren't known for their curiosity and love of pushing big, flashy buttons or anything."

I made a mental note to lock the bridge and take an inventory of just how many animals we had on board.

"Plenty of lush forests on Vespi," Merulo pointed out. "I just want them to live out the rest of their lives in peace."

Pneuman muttered something under his breath, then winced as if instantly regretting it.

Merulo glared through narrowed eyes. "Say that again?" he challenged.

"I... I just..." Pneuman lowered his head and averted his eyes, as one might do when faced with a vicious dog, the brim of his hat hiding his face. "I don't feel peace from you. I feel rage, like I could kill the next person who looks at me sideways, like I feel from you during the shows. I try to send good feelings, but..." He faded a little, something he'd been doing lately. He called it "phasing," and it resembled the way Diantha went invisible, but Pneuman didn't just turn transparent. He became less solid, like a ghost, something he'd never done during the show. Weirder still, he claimed that he could actually phase *into* the mind of someone else.

Freaked me out.

Pneuman had put into words the lurking fear I had been unable to name, and something like relief came over me. I wasn't the only one who felt it, who thought Merulo wasn't quite himself. Or maybe he was too much himself. Maybe we all were.

"I don't understand something," Cara said quietly, breaking the awful silence with words mercifully free of tension. "How can you send him good feelings?"

"Only Theon is actually psychic," Pneuman explained, no longer transparent. "I can absorb and transmit feelings, which sort of spreads his power between the three of us, and Parthen joins our bodies; she can alter the chemical structure of any object or material, our skin and organs included."

Theon turned to Parthen so fast, it's a wonder he didn't need to wear a neck brace afterward. "You can?"

Parthen narrowed her eyes but kept her head bent over her work. "Maybe you'd know that if you ever bothered to talk to me."

"Why the hell aren't we living in a gold palace somewhere?" Theon asked, as if accusing her of some horrible crime.

"Maybe you'd know *that*," Parthen said, slamming down her tablet, "if you ever bothered to talk to me, too." She stood and stormed toward the stairs, stopping in her tracks when Theon made the mistake of calling after her.

"We don't need to talk, Par; I can read your thoughts."

Parthen stalked back in a fury, not saying a word until she stood before Theon, her forehead nearly touching his. "Go ahead, read my mind. You might want to try a little harder because I can think of a few key thoughts you haven't picked up on."

"Parthen," Pneuman cautioned.

She gave him an apologetic smile before turning back to Theon, rage shining in her eyes. "We may be conjoined at the torso during the show, but you aren't the only Fago brother I've shared my body with."

Merulo watched them with a disinterested amusement. Being asexual and aromantic, he probably didn't see the point in all the drama.

Cara broke the deathly silence with a timid statement. "I can't help noticing that everything went wrong when I came on board."

"No," I said. "We've been together for too long, been through too much for it to fall apart just because a new person gets thrown into the mix. It's just a weird couple of days and it'll pass."

Merulo chuckled to himself.

"What?" I snapped.

He shrugged. "It all went wrong when Diantha was in danger. You haven't been the same since."

"I'm fine—"

"It's the music, for god's sakes!"

All heads swiveled to the stairs, where Lily stood in a long-sleeved shirt with a high neckline I didn't know she even owned, with layers of gaudy jewels on her neck. A cloak covered her back and bulged oddly.

Wings, I realized with a start. And feathers she was hiding on the rest of her body. She stayed up on the stairs but I could still see a change in the shape of her face. Flatter, rounder.

"What about the music?" I asked.

"It changed us, her singing the end. We're all turning into our freak personas."

Diantha had told me you never sang the ending. Was this why? Because the changes would be permanent? Had our ancestors programmed this into our genes, keeping us more or less dormant until it was time to trigger the transformation into supersoldiers? I did feel that same burning in my chest, like my lungs could catch fire at any moment.

"But we were fine the last time it changed," Lily continued, "so we'll be f—"

"What?" I interrupted. "It never changed before."

"An owl can pinpoint the location of a field mouse under the snow using only its sense of hearing," she pointed out, "and an owl that's been dancing to the same song every night for years can pick up on minute variations in the music. You may not have heard it, but it changed a few months back. But we're okay."

"She's right," Cara said, nodding with enthusiasm. "I can feel it, too. This is a good thing."

I think we all liked that theory. Meant we could go back to our quarters a little more at ease. The news talked of rising tensions and rebellions on more nearby moons, but inside the *Rubeno Mardo*, tensions had fallen somewhat and all seemed more or less okay. It wasn't, but it seemed.

CHAPTER SEVEN

I sat in the empty bridge, grinning like a fool as the automated drones inspected every inch of the *Rubeno Mardo* for weapons, contraband, and anything else they could possibly consider an act of war.

The capital hung above the distant horizon, a shining city hovering on a plate as if suspended from wires anchored in the heavens. No reason for it, as the surface of Vespi was perfectly hospitable and plenty of cities dotted its mountainous landscape; just a needless show of power. I'd have despised it on principle if I didn't know Diantha was up there waiting for me.

Yeah, so maybe I was a little naïve to think I could waltz onto a planet sieged by war, sweep their queen off her feet, and single-handedly protect her from assassins, but she did change the music, and hadn't sung it since. Lily disagreed, but if Diantha didn't mean it as a signal to come rescue her and finish the rebellion our ancestors started, I couldn't think of another reason for it.

A flying drone swept into the bridge with a bird held gently in its grasping claws.

"That's one of mine," Merulo said, following the drone up the stairs with a handful of squirming lizards. He was growing more beastly by the day, a little more stooped in posture, but still human. Lily was right: hearing the new ending of the song was changing us. I'd noticed my breath feeling hotter sometimes, but so far had managed to keep it from igniting.

The drone held the dove out to me, though I couldn't tell what it wanted me to do with it. Not the most expressive machines in the universe, just metal bodies the size of a toaster, with a couple arms and propellers.

"That would be a bird," I said. "What about it?"

"Please state the nature of the bird," it said in a crackling, pre-recorded voice. "Companion? Food? Surveillance? Explosive device?"

I refrained from making a smartass comment about how hard it would have been to stuff a bomb inside a bird, as I doubted the drone could take a joke and I didn't have time to get arrested. "It's just a bird," I said, stroking its silky little head. "And not even mine, so I guess 'none of the above.'"

The drone stared at me with its flashing red eye, scanning my face or computing my response or something. "That is not an acceptable answer. Please state the nature of the bird."

The bird tried to wriggle free. I took it from the drone and shrugged. "I don't know what to tell you. It isn't my bird."

"Who is the owner?"

Merulo started to say something but I released the airtight seal on the bridge's windows and opened an air vent, nudging the bird toward the opening. "No one. You can't own another creature, not one wild as this. You can keep it in a cage, but that doesn't make it yours."

The bird tilted its head and peered through the vent before hopping out of my hands and scurrying through to the freedom of the wide open sky. It skirted around the *Rubeno*'s dome, scrambling for traction on the glass, then fluttered off and disappeared.

I wondered if, when it was captured and shoved in a cage, it ever thought it would fly again. Must have felt amazing to stretch its wings, feel the breeze, and know it was bound only by its own limitations and no one else's.

I elbowed the inspection drone. "Beautiful, isn't it?"

"Extremely."

I could have sworn that little bucket of bolts was mocking me. Who knew they could program in sarcasm?

I frowned. Was that offensive? Cara played a robot in the show; it stood to reason the change would affect her like it affected the rest of us, and while she'd gone out of her way to pretend all was well, I wanted to make an effort to strike any robot hate speech from my vocabulary just in case.

"So we're good here?" I asked.

"No prohibited items or materials on board," the drone confirmed. "We are indeed good here." It zipped off with its buddies to inspect the next ship waiting for permission to enter capitol airspace.

Lily came to the bridge and started up the engines, their low purr rumbling through my body alongside the electric excitement as the *Rubeno Mardo* lifted off. The flight passed by in a blur, and we soon rose above the level of the antigravity plate to see the technological wonder of Vespi's capital city.

When kids on poor, rural moons laid in bed thinking of the amazing planets we'd never get to visit, we dreamed of places that looked like this. Rivers of hovering cars winding around a forest of glassy skyscrapers, fancy people draped in silks and fabrics that changed color with every step, and an enormous castle in the center that dwarfed and outshone it all.

The center of Vespi government and VesCorp headquarters comprised a palatial building made from the finest marble that gleamed a sunny pink, with a solar system of orbiting gunnery turrets and its own levitating plate that separated it from the rest of the city and created something of a moat through which you could fall miles to the planet below. A shimmering forcefield and an army of footsoldiers and triangular Vespi ships served to further deter anyone foolhardy enough to attempt to enter the property without permission.

We landed and disembarked in a crowded airfield a good ways away from the Castle, walking on what felt like solid ground, though Pneuman watched it suspiciously the whole way.

"It's so thin," he whispered. "You saw it on approach, right?"

I nodded. The plate beneath our feet, the plate holding up the entire city, was less than an inch thick.

"It's the artificial gravity." Cara skipped alongside us—actually skipped. I'd never seen her looking so at ease, like she belonged here. "I've been reading the specs. There's a huge power plant in the Castle that generates a strong enough field to support the city's weight. Theoretically, we don't even need the plate to hold us up, if they just generated a field in mid-air."

That thought turned my stomach something violent. I would have felt better if the plate was a little thicker. Thick enough to reach the ground, maybe. Pneuman looked like he shared my sentiments.

"You can always go back to the ship with Merulo," Lily suggested.

"And Parthen and Theon," he added.

They'd stayed behind, Theon because hearing all the thoughts of the city was too much for him, Parthen because she was afraid of accidentally touching someone and turning them to glass. I rubbed my face in frustration. What the hell was happening to my crew?

Still, Pneuman going back might not have been the worst idea, as he started to fade before my eyes.

"Go," I ordered. "Help Merulo find new homes for the critters. She's a big ship; you'll find a way to avoid each other."

He dipped his hat and turned back without argument.

I noticed only a slight increase in security measures from my last visit a decade ago. With the place already more secure than a bank vault, I guess they couldn't have done much more unless they encased the entire building in bubble wrap and denied all outside access to the countless dignitaries and representatives from allied systems who were inside the Castle at any given time.

We walked the crowded streets, jostling for position with people in fancy dresses and elaborate suits that had never seen a speck of dirt until they brushed against my clothes. Easy to assume they'd all be snooty, high society people on the way to balls and art galleries, but a few surprised me with polite apologies for bumping into me. One man, a proper gentleman in a flashy jacket and pretentious top hat, went so far as to joke about his clumsiness and proceeded to call himself every vulgar name in the book—and a few he must have added—all while grinning the biggest, most honest grin I'd ever seen. Just goes to show there were good people all over, even on planets home to the worst corporations.

Grand, steel archways stood at seemingly random intervals along streets lined with shops and restaurants. Scanners, if I remembered correctly, designed to detect anything that could be used as a weapon or act of war. Whole city served as a neutral zone where higher-ups from all corners of the universe came to make and break deals, and they expected a certain degree of safety that Vespi had strived to provide even before Garon's assassination.

And yet someone had assassinated him. That seemed unlikely, and an inkling of dread seeped into my heart as I considered all the security measures the assassin would have had to pass through in order to poison Garon and Diantha's family.

No way I or anyone else could have smuggled poison—whether pure, diluted in a beverage, or in plant form—past the drones or any of the myriad guards that stood between me and Diantha. Not like I had a realistic chance of seeing her; that privilege would be restricted to those closest to her, whom she could trust with her life and the lives of her family. Maids, political advisors, cooks…

The answer hit me without warning, leaving me gasping for breath and wondering how I hadn't seen it sooner.

The staff lived there, alongside the leaders of arguably the universe's most powerful corporation—and, at any given time, scores of their influential guests—and though someone undoubtedly checked and double checked them a dozen times a day, I'd bet my ship it was an inside job.

I stopped dead in my tracks, forcing pedestrian traffic to divert around me, and stared up at the shining Castle. She was in there, hidden away from the people who would do her harm and never knowing her assassin may have been in there with her.

"Jack?" Lily asked.

"Everyone took it as a declaration of war," I said, my eyes never leaving the Castle, "but for all we know it was a personal vendetta by a scorned mistress or the lone survivor of a moon poisoned by VesCorp's mining operations."

Maybe I hadn't had much of a plan for once I got to Vespi, but I did now. Somehow, and I hadn't figured out exactly how, I had to find a way to warn her.

***

The forcefield shimmered in the last rays of evening sun, its billions of microscopic metal flecks catching light particles and throwing them in every direction. Almost looked like a rippling sheet of water, but signs posted every few feet warned against touching it, as between the levitating metal pieces surged a powerful electric current capable of knocking a grown elephant on its rear (paraphrasing, of course).

Reporters crowded around us, each reaching a microphone or hologram recorder through the forcefield, trying to be the first to transmit Diantha's address to the universe, and my hope for getting a message to her dwindled as the media swarm grew in size.

When they announced that Diantha would appear that evening and make a statement about the war, her first public appearance since the assassination, I thought I'd be able to stand there at the perimeter and either shout or signal to her in some way. But now, with her on a balcony some four hundred feet up on a floating castle that touched the sky and me lost in a crowd of thousands, I'd have been lucky if she saw me as anything more than an ant. And forget about hearing me.

I considered, if only for a moment, whether she'd want me standing around waiting while I could have been helping her take down VesCorp. Getting an army together, drawing up plans of attack on all their operations and outposts… But I knew precious little of what had happened last time, or what the plan had even been. People with special powers took on the government and lost. The end.

No, I needed to talk to her, maybe get her somewhere safe. As secure as the Castle might have been, it brimmed with people who wielded insurmountable power against a lot of people on a lot of moons, and I didn't want her anywhere near them when they realized she wasn't on their side.

Time passed at an excruciatingly slow rate, letting all manner of unpleasant thoughts pass through my mind. What if the assassination was someone's attempt to start an intergalactic war? Or trying to loosen VesCorp's grip on the economy and people of the universe? What if—and the irony sickened me—someone from down on Vespi 3-14 felt that Diantha had betrayed them by becoming part of the entity they despised most, and had tried to exact revenge?

I took Lily and Cara's hands and we waited. Wasn't their battle, but they stood by my side anyway.

The sky gradually darkened, and a familiar pattern of stars revealed themselves behind the Castle. First time I'd seen them in person, and the bright lights of the city made them a less than spectacular sight, but I'd know them anywhere. I could still hear her telling me about all the constellations and the myths they had inspired.

My gaze fell upon the king, represented by a cluster of stars in the shape of a crown. According to traditions down on Vespi 3-14, he had been killed by a trusted servant.

A voice booming from an unseen speaker announced Diantha's imminent arrival, a door opened on a high balcony, and, after years waiting to see her again, I turned around and ran back to my ship, Lily and Cara struggling to keep up.

I flew as close to the Castle as the security drones would allow, and hovered between two massive skyscrapers encrusted with lights. Not the ideal location, with the gap between the buildings barely wide enough to let the *Rubeno* pass, but the angle was right and I hoped she'd take notice.

The crowd stirred below, a mass of indistinguishable people surging forward at some unseen stimulus. Diantha, I assumed, but I couldn't make out any detail at this distance.

Angling my ship so that her hull just scraped the corner of one building, I said a silent apology to the people inside and prayed for no sudden gusts of wind. I turned my seat backward and watched the top of the *Rubeno*'s mirrored tail fin sweep from side to side.

Did my best to put it at just the right angle to reflect the constellation into Diantha's eyes, but I was basing my attempts on my knowledge of physics, which, if I'm being honest, left a lot to be desired. I could only hope she saw it and understood its meaning.

***

I thought about sleeping under the dome in the bridge, with the stars of Vespi sparkling overhead, but even though they were arguably more real than I'd ever seen them, they just felt wrong somehow. I'd spent so long wanting to see them in all their glory, instead of as holes drilled in a ceiling, but I couldn't look at them, couldn't pretend they meant anything without her by my side, and I retreated to my quarters and the stars painted over my bed.

I waited for her address to appear on my tablet, but other stories dominated the news. For all the excitement leading up to it, she must not have said anything too interesting.

Not that she could have if she wanted to, politics being the volatile minefield they were. If she admonished the war and pulled out her troops, they'd have called her weak and those that opposed VesCorp would have taken the opportunity to target her planet. And she'd never actually condone her armies going after anyone else.

So it was probably just a general statement of strength and courage and all that stuff that paled in comparison to graphic depictions of violence and personal pleas for mercy. Couldn't blame the media for choosing to run stories that pulled on heartstrings already stretched beyond their limits, only to give them a fleeting, hopeful reprieve in the form of a smiling orphan or a truce between brothers fighting on opposite sides, all to get viewers and sell advertising. It was despicable, it was exploitative, but I couldn't blame them because it was exactly the kind of pageantry I'd have used.

The news finally ran out of violence, and Diantha's face appeared. I sat up straighter and turned up the volume.

"Good evening, Vespi," she said with a smile.

It looked genuine enough, but she held herself with the elegant poise of a queen and had herself draped in so much finery and unnecessary embellishments that I almost doubted her sincerity. This wasn't the Diantha I'd fallen for.

"I extend my greetings to all reporters from foreign systems, and to all those watching in every corner of the universe. We may look up at different skies, but in our hearts we are the same. We are human, with the same basic needs and desires. We want to be free to eat, sleep, love, and live in a manner of our choosing. Some believe our own desires are more important than those of our neighbors. This way of thinking can easily escalate into war. It has always happened this way, and it always will."

Her smile faded, and she didn't strike me as particularly sympathetic. Almost sounded like a general, cold and uninterested in the words that had been written for her.

"Since my husband's death, I've hidden myself away for my own safety and the safety of my daughter, but I can remain quiet no longer." She cleared her throat, brushing a strand of straightened and styled hair from her face. "I never intended to become the leader of an organization that destroys moons and ruins the lives of their people. I was born on one of those moons. I am one of those people. But this is the hand life has dealt for me, and I—"

Something caught her attention and she turned, the camera zooming out to show the room behind her. Extravagantly decorated, as was everything on Vespi, but in understated colors that reminded me of her house on Vespi 3-14.

A child stood in the doorway. The girl, about ten, might as well have been a younger version of her mother, with frizzy black hair and a smile that could melt hearts. One of her arms was supported by a cybernetic brace.

She was beautiful.

I couldn't remember ever seeing her face before, Garon and Diantha having gone to great lengths to keep their daughter out of the scrutinizing public eye, and I found myself searching for any resemblance to myself. The timing didn't preclude the possibility; her skin was certainly a few shades darker than her mother's, and I'd nearly convinced myself she had my cheekbones when Diantha turned back to the window and resumed her speech.

"It pains me to lead VesCorp, a corporation so infamous for its treatment of natives that many rebellions have been fought against us. This war began as one such uprising, and it is unfortunate that it has spiraled out of control. I used to dream that I might have some hand in the end of VesCorp, but now that I stand at its helm with every opportunity to sail straight into the jagged cliffs, I cannot let it crash."

I shook my head. What did she have planned?

"The minerals we extract from the moons are an invaluable resource that many people depend on, and though I would love to phase out operations, rest assured that any changes will happen far in the future."

I sighed as she tilted her head down in a slight bow, signing off after saying a whole lot of nothing. I'd expected as much, but something in the way she said it didn't sit right with me.

In saying that she wanted to shut VesCorp down, but not anytime soon, she—or, more likely, her speechwriters—had probably meant to sate the people who gained from the mining as well as the people destroyed by it, but I feared she had angered both. She'd effectively threatened the miners' and governments' way of life while at the same time pretending to care about the natives' well-being yet doing nothing about it.

I couldn't claim to know a lick about politics, but that sounded like a quick way to make a shipload of enemies.

I reached up to shut off the screen, but Diantha said, "Wait a moment, please."

Talking to an attendant, I realized, someone trying to close the doors on the balcony. For a second, it felt like she could see me.

Diantha squinted past the camera, at some unseen object in the distance that caught her eye. The *Rubeno*. She smiled and looked to the camera again. Maybe I was just seeing what I wanted to see, but I thought she let a bit of her façade fall away.

"These are challenging times," she said, speaking only to me, "and we must find comfort wherever we can. I like to remember the legends my mother taught me, ancient stories about the heroes hiding among the stars. Heroes like the king, whose legend has become increasingly relevant in my own life."

I laughed as a knot of worry came loose in my stomach. She got my message.

"The worlds are full of violent people and armies searching your beliefs and ways of life for anything contrary to their own, for any reason to hate. When we go to war just for the sake of war, when we get so wrapped up in hate that we forget what we're fighting for, we lose ourselves."

She spoke without any semblance of rehearsal, an improvised plea straight from the heart.

"It can be hard to find ourselves again. Some of us never knew who we were to begin with, but we can start by finding the people

JACK JETSTARK'S INTERGALACTIC FREAKSHOW

who accept us for who we are. In being with them, we can discover both our purpose and the means to achieve it. Stay strong, brave travelers of the stars, and trust in your true self."

Here the video ended, with a final shot of her smile that stayed with me long after the news ended.

It wasn't hard to decipher what she wanted me to do.

"She wants me to protect her."

"She has an army."

I looked up to see Lily standing in the doorway, arms crossed.

"Her army might be in on the attempt on her life," I explained. "The king is a constellation—he was killed by someone he trusted—"

"So you're going to… what? Storm the Castle? Hoist her over your shoulder like her knight in shining armor and rescue her?"

I narrowed my eyes. "Why not?"

"Because she has an *army*. And it isn't like you have blueprints to the Castle."

No, but I knew someone who might. "I have to protect her, Lily."

She fluffed her wings, stared at her feet for a moment. Then she nodded and left without another word, and I settled in to sleep under the painted stars, wondering if Diantha was doing the same.

CHAPTER EIGHT

Last thing I ever thought I'd do, set foot on Stoval again, but desperation leads otherwise level-headed men to do some really unwise things, as Theon took delight in informing me.

We left the *Rubeno* in the only clearing large enough to land a ship her size, a swampy patch miles from the nearest town and surrounded by thick stands of cypress, and began the trek to the place I used to call home. Not exactly a big spacefaring culture, Stoval, and not a place people went out of their way to visit. But like I said, desperation.

"I still don't understand why you think he can help," Parthen said, tugging her gloves on tighter. She had her hair pulled back in a single purple braid, not a bad idea in the humidity.

"He delivered things to the Castle," I said. "Back when he was legit. Companies sometimes make delivery people wear cameras at secure places to guarantee they don't steal stuff. The data should be in the *Rubeno*'s databanks; I just need his biometrics to get in."

"Because you stole the ship from him."

I glared at Theon. Gorgeous bastard. I really hated him being psychic sometimes.

JACK JETSTARK'S INTERGALACTIC FREAKSHOW

Insects swam through the humidity, on the prowl for some poor sucker they could drain of blood. A guy could get anemia living there, assuming he didn't drown in the air first.

We walked along a vague suggestion of a path, and with every step I tried to convince myself not to take the next, to turn back and find another way. But none were out there to be found.

Cara had tried to hack the biometric lock but it resisted, and she'd asked—begged—to stay back on Vespi to watch Diantha. Lily had stayed to watch Cara. She didn't say so, but I think it bothered her, my wanting to protect a woman I hadn't even spoken to in years.

But even if I could forget everything and start the carnival up again, I couldn't guarantee my crew would go with me. I couldn't get Merulo to leave the ship, and the tension between Parthen and the boys was thicker than the air here. Pneuman kept fading, I think just to avoid the glares.

I couldn't run the carnival on my own any more than I could trust anyone else to help me, and no one would come to see a show featuring one miserable firebreather.

I'd forgotten how little I'd missed Stoval, with the ground sucking at my shoes and hanging vines slapping at my damp hair. Long shadows snaked through the swamp, playing tricks on the mind. You could almost see monsters lurking behind every mossy cypress, feel the giant birds about to swoop down and snatch you up. Imagination ran wild in a place like that, but it ran alone, as no animal had lived there in generations.

The first settlers worried the cats and gators would eat their livestock, so they killed and shipped them all off, only to realize later that the waterlogged ground couldn't sustain any sort of farmland. Rather than waste time and money terraforming the moon into something useful, the people up on the planet decided to waste time and money importing massive amounts of insects to pollinate the plants and keep alive the swamp no one wanted.

Bureaucracy at its finest, and to top it all off, they chose insects that needed to consume blood to complete their life cycle. If you ask me, that's why they made it so cheap for people to live there—to feed the mosquitoes.

The tangled trees opened onto a village of houses on stilts, a heavy netting tented over each thatched roof. They stood in staggered rows, some taller than the others but overall pretty identical except for the rustic furniture and wood carvings on the porches.

A few people called out to me but I ducked my head and quickened my pace. I found the building with the highest concentration of broken bottles underneath, and climbed the ladder to the dim, stagnant bar.

I stood in the doorway, trying to breathe through my ears as my eyes struggled to adjust, but he saw me first.

"Well, well, well." His raspy, cackling voice cut through the boisterous din of the other patrons, and my skin crawled. "Get out your sunglasses, boys! The sun's gonna explode! No other reason Jacky'd come here unless it's to see me die a horrible, fiery death."

His buddies let out a round of hooting laughs, and I locked onto his hunched, bearish form in the back of the bar.

Parthen and Pneuman stayed by the door while Theon and I elbowed our way through the raucous crowd, with me making a conscious effort to keep my hands from becoming fists. I liked to think I wasn't the kind of man who would punch his own father, but he knew the location of every one of my buttons and pressed them like they dispensed free money. Better safe than thrown out of the bar.

Found him at a card table, playing a game called Arlekenon with a handful of his grungy friends who had more teeth than manners. Which is saying something, because they didn't have a full mouth of teeth among them.

I pulled up a chair and grabbed some dice from the pile, ignoring him entirely. "Deal me in," I said, tossing the last of my spare money on the table. I glanced at Theon, who positioned himself at my right ear.

Maybe it won't hurt to have a psychic, I thought with a grin.

If they minded our intrusion, they didn't say anything, and one of them dealt me five cards. I pretended to study my hand while trying to remember how to play the convoluted game. Something about matching the symbols on the cards with the ones on the other players' dice while trying not to match your own... but what did they use the little pegboard for again? I never could grasp the rules. Mostly because they made them up as they went along, but that didn't stop them from coming to blows over accusations of cheating.

"Come all this way to play games, then?"

I kept my head low. I'd never been particularly good at Arlekenon, but I threw out a card. "Squares are wild, right?"

One of the men grunted. "Until someone plays an arrow on the same turn as he rolls a seven or the men on either side of him both play something blue."

Another man took a swig of his whiskey and added, "But if anyone plays a red dragon while squares are wild, *everything* is wild for three turns, *except* the queen of spades. If you get her, you're out of the game and the guy to your right gets to live in your house for the night."

"Unless you can beat him in a footrace, in which case you get to keep his shoes."

Yep. Definitely just an excuse to drink and get into fistfights. Like they needed an excuse.

"This level of flippant bullshittery explains so much about you," Theon whispered.

"Never were much of a talker, were ya?" my father asked. "Always brooding in that shaggy head of yours, nose in a book about where you wanted to go instead of noticing the beauty around you."

I rolled my eyes. For most of my childhood, the beauty around me looked a lot like my current situation. Old guys that smelled of stale liquor, shady places and shadier business deals, that anxious feeling of waiting for laughter to turn to shouting, always on the lookout for the glint of a blade in the darkness. Shame on me for ever wanting to leave this place.

"Then I finally let you come along on a run and you don't say a word that whole trip, while we unloaded the crates. Almost makes me think you didn't like me."

He poked me in the arm. I shook him off and considered my next move. "Is it still legal for me to get rid of my best card and risk everything on a dice battle?" I asked, making it up off the top of my head. "They used to call it the old 'abandon your kid on a distant moon' strategy, right?"

They all nodded, and I stacked my dice with a smirk directed at my scowling father. I was beginning to realize the only goal of the game was to hide that fact that no one knew how to play. Confidence and BS; no wonder my father was such a pro.

"My ship still flying, or did you have to sell her for scrap?" He wagged his eyebrows at a friend. "That's how my first marriage ended, you know. Real tragic. Got a few bucks out of her, though."

"Jack," Theon warned, alarmed at the violent images flashing through my mind.

It took all my good judgment not to beat my dad to a pulp for talking about my mother that way, but I couldn't keep my mouth shut anymore. "Still flying. Few hiccups now and then, but she's a good ship."

"*My* good ship," my father corrected, rolling his dice and snatching some money from the pot. "And don't think I've forgotten how you stole her from me."

"I thought you were dead, making her my inheritance."

"My body wasn't in the ship. You just didn't look for me."

"I liked thinking you were dead." I tipped my dice tower in his direction; one skittered off the table and landed in his lap, eliciting a hushed silence from the other players.

"That's Krono," one announced.

"Yep. Now you draw cards; first one to get a hand that adds up to more than thirty-seven buys the other guy a drink."

I leaned back in my chair. "Rather have her registration put in my name."

"You did just fine without it all these years," my father pointed out. "The carny game tightening restrictions, or are you wanting an honest job for once in your life?"

I shrugged. "Maybe I want to leave my kid on Vespi 3-14 and go fight in the war. Does it matter?"

A wave of uproarious laughter swept through the bar at my mention of the war, and a flood of cherished childhood memories came rushing back to me. Helping Dad install radio wave blockers on the roof and making medicine from roots we found in the swamp because "pills are designed to make ya sick so ya gotta take more pills."

Not exactly the most trusting people, the Stovalians.

"What?" I challenged. "What's wrong with the war? Is it a front to install mind-reading satellites? A ploy to reduce the population of certain strategic moons?"

"Nothing wrong with the war," my father said, for once in his life sounding like a reasonable person. He should have stopped while he was ahead. "Only it isn't real."

I stared at him, scrutinizing every inch of his sun-damaged face for signs that he was messing with me, that this claim was just his latest move in Arlekenon. I found none, and looked to Theon, who nodded in confirmation. Dad actually believed what he was saying.

"Well, I got a ship riddled with laser holes says otherwise."

Everyone in earshot corrected me en masse, a wall of hurled insults and indecipherable shouts.

"But you survived," my father said, pointing his gnarled finger in my face, "and that's how you know it's all fake. They could kill ya. They could kill everyone on all the rebel moons, but they don't. They're just doing it so we won't think it's suspicious for 'em to send soldiers to muck with the ecosystems of far-off planets."

I didn't have a response for this. Not one that wouldn't get me thrown out the door and all the way down to the ground, anyway, but his buddies called out their slurred additions to the conspiracy.

"They're all in on it!"

"Fights are all staged!"

"They kill just enough people to make us think it's a war!"

I tried to wrap my mind around their theory. Truly, I did. Finally, I just had to shake my head. "What kind of plant you guys been smoking, Dad?"

He just grinned. "You go up to the levee, you tell me something weird isn't going on up there. People coming down from the planet, catching swarms of bugs... What, their remote spy cameras stop working all of a sudden? You can't get a planeter to set foot on Stoval if his life depended on it! And let's not forget your second cousin Jim disappearing in the middle of the night."

Go traipsing through miles of muck and marsh to chase down an old man's delusions? Not in my good boots. "Yeah, think I'll pass on that."

He stared, sizing me up with his beady eyes. "Scared of the truth? Of having to admit I was right for once?" Before I had the chance to answer, he said, "You go up there, come back here and honestly say there ain't nothing going on, and I'll transfer my ship over to you. Swear."

What the hell. Couldn't take more than a few hours, and I still had a few patches of skin the mosquitoes hadn't discovered yet.

I took a card off the table and flipped it over as I stood. "Seven of stars on the seventh day of the month, played by a man whose age is divisible by seven," I said, pretending any of that meant anything. "*That*, boys, is Krono."

I reclaimed my money along with a little extra—I did get Krono, after all—and we headed out.

***

JACK JETSTARK'S INTERGALACTIC FREAKSHOW

The levee sat on the other side of a long, tedious walk through a thick and humid silence, a natural embankment that caught vast amounts of rainwater upriver and kept the swamps only slightly flooded.

My father claimed the medicinal roots that grew up there were the best, owing to their proximity to the fresh water that burbled over the top of the levee. I couldn't say for sure if that was true, but the sickly green sludge that stagnated and bred insects near town never looked quite safe to drink, and so I'd made the trek uncountable times in my childhood.

The trail had barely changed in all the years since I'd left, just a monotonous path cut through the sedges and cattails. Every so often, I got to see a pitcher plant fight back against the mosquito scourge and devour one of the little vampires, but those moments of entertainment came few and far between.

Long walks like that might make a man ponder his path in life. Itemize his past mistakes, find ways to put right the wrongs he'd done and repair relationships that had crumbled so he could come out of it a better man.

I didn't do any of that; maybe that says something about me and maybe it doesn't, but the future occupied my every thought. The future, and Diantha.

Wish I could say I had a plan once we got back to Vespi, but I didn't even know what I'd find when I landed. Was her planet under attack, or defended by a fleet of the biggest and best ships in the universe? Had she identified her would-be assassin, or did she need someone like me to track him down and deliver justice? Would she even give me the time of day?

I wasn't so delusional to think she'd be waiting for me with open arms and a royal procession of flying elephants—or whatever they trotted out for special occasions up there—but I had to think she still held a candle for me. She played the damn song every night for ten years so I'd know she was safe. She wouldn't have done that if she didn't care, if she didn't still love me in some way, however small.

I'd win her back. Maybe she wouldn't fall wildly in love right away, not like we did the first time—that kind of love was meant for naïve kids who didn't know better. I'd do it right this time, take it slow. Show her the stars.

"Aw, you really love her."

I looked at Pneuman, who materialized next to me on the path. "Were you in my head? Don't do that."

His gaze dropped to his feet, but a mischievous smile played on his lips. "I can't help it."

Parthen smiled, too, but hers was faint and tight. "I can't speak for everyone," she told me, "but I wanted to let you know I'm grateful for the distraction of fighting your battles with you. If we had nowhere to go, if we went home…"

She let the sentence trail off, but I knew what she meant. There wasn't much left for them back on their home planet but misery and quite possibly a trial for witchcraft and murder.

I'd found her in something like the offspring of a monastery and a group home, tending to the survivors of what used to be a royal family but was now the "unclean" native population of Ilex. They'd been pushed out by settlers, living only on the charity of people like Par.

Took a lot of convincing to get her to come to the show, but I saw something in her eyes. She was one of us.

When the song played, her arm had been touching that of the man beside her. He was a pile of sand a second later.

Turned out that people on Ilex were a superstitious bunch. Parthen showed up just before takeoff, her unclean boyfriend and his brother in tow, saying that people were after them.

"I still want to go back someday," Parthen said, shooing away a mosquito. "When I have the money to help them buy back their sacred land."

The mosquito came back, and touched the exposed skin of her face. I didn't see what substance it turned to, only that it plummeted like a stone.

With the power to change things at an atomic level, she could make unlimited gold for the people of Ilex. But if it were me, I'm sure I'd want to get as far away from any reminders of that poor man as I could, at least until I could control the power.

The air was thick with bugs, growing thicker the farther we went until we had to do an elaborate, slapping dance just to keep from being devoured. The swarm narrowed to a buzzing ribbon moving toward the levee.

A shout cut through the air.

We froze, pressing ourselves against mossy tree trunks and concealing ourselves behind their long curtains of gray-green leaves. The swamp fell back into a calm serenity broken only by the wind in the foliage and the buzzing of insects.

It was all probably just one of my father's cohorts trying to scare us. It wouldn't have surprised me if the whole bar was in on his hoax; one big game of Arlekenon at my expense. I let out the breath I'd been holding.

And set a leaf on fire in the process.

I stamped it out and we walked with caution, senses on alert for any movement or sound, but I was already planning my counter play. Staggering into the bar, eyes wild with fright, stammering about some government conspiracy. Screw the registration; I'd find another way to get into the *Rubeno*'s memory.

I slapped a mosquito off my neck and wiped the blood of its previous victims on my pants. Didn't remember there being that many of the little buggers when I was a kid.

The green-brown sludge grew thinner as we neared the levee, and something almost resembling clear water surrounded the long grasses that waved and bent in the breeze. It must have been a sight before the people came. Whistling birds flitting from bush to bush, floating logs that became gators when unsuspecting deer ventured too close to the shore…

I used to spend hours out there as a kid, making up stories about the beasts that once lurked in the shadows and pretending a small group of them remained somewhere, waiting to be discovered. Just trying to add some excitement to an otherwise uneventful life, I suppose, create a little mystery.

Something moved up ahead, a flash of black that disappeared into the green. I knew it was a joke, just my father being a prick, but I couldn't convince my body.

My heart trying to escape my chest, we waited. When I neither heard nor saw anything except a steady stream of insects, and when Pneuman confirmed that he felt no presence in our immediate vicinity, we continued on, choosing our steps carefully to avoid snapping twigs that would give away our position.

The steep slope of the levee came into view through the foliage, with three men standing beside it. We crouched behind a tree and observed them.

They were skinny; far too thin and gangly to be my father's drinking buddies, and dressed in black uniforms with red trim. I couldn't tell for sure, but they looked blond and fair-skinned beneath their netted hoods. Not exactly the dark hair and ruddy complexion typical of us Stovalians.

Two of them took samples from the swarm of mosquitoes and collected them in large tanks while the third kept watch. I tried to shrink myself, to see without being seen.

Much as I hated to admit it, nothing about this struck me as normal. The way they moved, always looking over their shoulders as they vacuumed up bugs, made it seem like they knew they shouldn't have been there and didn't want anyone to see them.

I couldn't find a link to my father's claims of someone staging the war—he always did like a good conspiracy theory—but I couldn't deny something weird was going on. Why would anyone want to study our bugs, especially when no one on the planet gave a single crap about us and our environment?

Didn't see any weapons on them, and as they started to leave, I decided to go after them, to confront them and figure out what was going on.

They headed along the embankment in single file, carting the tanks on a large dolly. I moved from tree to tree, keeping behind cover as much as I could manage, but the men looked back so often that it limited my opportunities to advance and they soon disappeared from sight.

"What'd you feel?" I asked Pneuman.

"Accomplished. They… they found something. I don't know what. And dread. Guilt. They feel like something bad is going to happen because of what they're doing."

He looked shaken by the experience, and reached for Parthen as we headed back. Even with her thick leather gloves, she didn't dare hold his hand.

***

My father must have drained the bar of alcohol, as I found him sitting on the porch of the same old stilt house I'd grown up in. I climbed up the rickety ladder (which I'd fallen from more than once during my childhood) and leaned against the door.

"Something weird going on?" he asked after a moment.

I nodded reluctantly. "Something weird going on."

"Told ya," he said with a smirk.

"Any clue why they're collecting our bugs?"

He chuckled and corrected me. "They haven't been *your* bugs since you ran off with that pretty little princess of yours." He paused before adding, "Yeah, I checked up on you. How are things going between the two of you? Don't see you bringing her around for a visit very often. I haven't even *met* my grandkid."

I stopped myself from giving a biting answer riddled with expletives and instead tilted my head skyward. Somewhere far away, a ship blasted through the atmosphere, and the first stars pricked holes through the blanket of night.

As a kid, I'd look up at those tiny, meaningless points of light, never knowing they meant everything to the people who lived by them. Hell, until my dad brought home a spaceship, I never knew there were even people up there, that men lived on the planet that rose like a second, dimmer sun in the mornings or that there were kids out there in space, looking at my sun and not knowing I existed.

My life changed forever the day my father bought that old ship and announced his intention to be an intergalactic cargo hauler. I'd never heard the word "intergalactic" until that moment, but it soon became my purpose to get off that rock and go as far into the void as I could.

"Mind control," my father said out of nowhere.

I looked at him. "What about it?"

"I think that's what they're doing up there, taking away our mosquitoes and implanting 'em with nanobots or something. When they bite us, they take our blood and replace it with a solution of nanos that get in our bodies and let people control our minds."

Not the weirdest idea he'd ever had. Not even the weirdest idea *I'd* had to explain what anyone off-world would want with the bugs. "To what end, though?"

He shrugged, throwing his hands up in the air. "I'm supposed to know everything?"

"You always pretended to."

We stared up at the stars for a long while, neither of us knowing what to say and neither really trying to figure it out.

Maybe I could have handled things better way back when, gone looking for him instead of running off with Diantha. Definitely should have gone home as soon as I learned he hadn't died. I couldn't remember my reasoning for why I did or didn't do anything—assuming I even had reasoning—but it probably boiled down to avoiding a confrontation with my father.

But this wasn't completely awful. Almost nice, actually.

"You got the *Rubeno*'s registration?"

His question came out of nowhere, but I didn't say anything until after we'd both put our thumbprints on the scanner and it recognized me as the owner.

"Never thought you'd actually do that."

He scratched at a bug bite. "Mind control."

"Right," I said. "Has to be."

CHAPTER NINE

The *Rubeno*'s memory stores did have pictures of the Castle. A few decades old, but better than nothing. Theon and I stayed up late into the night, sprawled on the floor with tablets and paper, translating the images into a rough blueprint.

As a lowly delivery person, my dad had only been to the lower levels, but the photos gave me some idea of what to expect. Soldiers and weapons, mostly.

"These might not be accurate," Theon pointed out, sitting up to stretch his back. My eyes briefly dropped to his tight black t-shirt and I remembered too late that he could read my mind.

"Shut up," I said as he smirked.

"Diantha will be jealous."

"The pictures were taken around the time of the last uprising," I said, returning to the matter at hand. Diantha had no reason to be jealous; I was bi, but that didn't necessarily mean I intended to do anything with Theon. I just loved to look at him. "Might not be exact, but the level of security is probably the same."

"You said your dad fought in the last one?"

I nodded. He'd never struck me as the type to fight for anyone but himself; all the more reason I thought he was dead. I guess maybe he thought leaving me on a distant moon with my own ship would give me a chance at a better life, but I can't say it didn't bug me. Word comes of an uprising against Vespi, and he just up and leaves everything to fight with the rebels?

"Maybe he knew something about Vespi that sickened him," Theon said suddenly.

I looked up; his dark skin had gone a little pale. He passed me his tablet. The screen was blurry but showed what appeared to be a laboratory, glimpsed through an ajar door.

Tanks. Huge ones, each with a person suspended in it. The people were freaks—some winged, some glowing…

My body went numb.

The experiments had still been going on. They were still genetically modifying people as recently as ten years before.

Dad couldn't have known that his ancestor had once been in one of those tanks, but I was willing to bet the same rage coursed through him as was coursing through me.

The picture faded abruptly as a news alert popped up. Diantha was making an announcement.

She stood on the same balcony, hair done up in piles of braids, her dress a subdued ivory and red number with a high collar. She glared down the camera lens and began with a stern warning.

"This has gone on long enough. It is simply unacceptable."

I smiled. Announcing the shutdown of VesCorp would make more enemies than any one person deserved to have, but it must have been a weight off her shoulders to finally be able to follow through on the promise she'd made to her people. I don't think I'd ever been more proud of anyone in my life.

But then she kept talking.

"The rebellions consisted of a few dozen technologically deprived people with meager weapons, going against armies with lasers and rockets. The odds were against them. And yet, through coordinated efforts that took us by surprise and stretched our fleets thin, they lasted longer than we ever accounted for.

"And now they have turned us against each other. They have started a war, and worse, they expect to win. I can stay neutral on the matter no more. Now I speak directly to the rebels."

"Don't," I pleaded.

"I know your struggles," she said, almost managing to sound sympathetic. "Once upon another life, they were my struggles, and I understand the need to rise up and take back what was yours, but this is not the way to do it and we will no longer tolerate this."

The ship faded away, leaving me alone in a void with her serrated words that ripped apart the picture of the perfect future I'd had for so long.

"This war ends now; whether by surrender or crushing defeat is your choice. The resources gained by mining moons are too valuable to far too many people. Gold and copper make nanochips that cure diseases and heal the injured, iron and aluminum make our ships. Lives are improved because of mining in ways you can never imagine. You may be suffering, but billions more will suffer if we cease operations. We are doing far more good than bad."

She didn't believe that. She could never condone the system that she'd spent her entire life fighting against, even as part of some scheme to ultimately end it.

"What are you doing, Diantha?" I muttered. "This isn't you."

But then, maybe it was.

What did I know about her, really? She adapted and changed herself to blend in with any environment, from the erudite academies of the marble city to the iron-fisted aristocracy of VesCorp. Could I say with absolute confidence that the simple girl with the beautiful smile I'd fallen for in the village wasn't just another one of her personas? For all I knew, I was just a cog in some plan and she purposely became the exact type of person she needed to be to lure me in.

JACK JETSTARK'S INTERGALACTIC FREAKSHOW

"If those on the side of the rebellion deliver to me a statement of full and unconditional surrender," Diantha announced, "no more lives will be lost and you all may go back to the way you were before with no repercussions." Her eyes flashed with an intense fire, and any vestige of humanity left her face. "I encourage you to take that option, as I will not have an endless war in my universe. It *will* end, but I will leave it to you to decide how violently."

The transmission ended, the pounding in my ears drowning out the sound of a news anchor trying to understand the motivation behind this sudden upheaval in strategy. Good luck to him.

I couldn't believe she would turn against everything she had ever fought for, but something nagged at my mind and I had to rewind the video to check.

Yes. There, in the room behind her. Screens showing security footage.

It was small and blurry, but one of them looked like the lab. She was still experimenting on people.

***

Space ran thick with ships in the wake of her ultimatum. I liked to think some were on humanitarian missions, bringing supplies and aid to the moons or maybe ferrying people to safer havens, but most likely, Diantha's decree had set a fire under tensions already on the verge of boiling over.

Stray bullets and bits of space junk hurtled through major throughways, having missed their targets hundreds of miles away and continued on undeterred. Weapons turned in our direction as we passed, the ships unwilling to incur any more damage than they had already sustained.

With every planet, moon, and unaffiliated space station on the highest of alerts, and with a million unsteady fingers resting on a million triggers, tensions ran higher than they ever had. If you scoured every history book ever written, you'd be hard pressed to find a more dangerous day to take a heap of rusted metal on a cross-universe journey, a fact Theon delighted in reminding me.

"I don't mean to be a jerk," he said, breaking a heavy silence on the bridge, "but what do you expect to happen when we get there?"

"I don't know," I admitted. "Our plan was always to get some freaks together and take down VesCorp. I don't know if she still wants us to do that, but I don't know what else to do. And now she might be making more freaks, so I don't know if I can even trust her. You can't read minds through video, can you?"

"Even if I could, you wouldn't believe me until you dragged us all the way to Vespi and saw it for yourself."

I laughed. As hostile as his words sounded, he didn't give an impression of being overly critical. Pneuman's calming presence must have been in his head again.

Pneuman had been struggling to stay in his physical form. More often than not, he retreated into his brother's head. Maybe there'd be a way to reverse the change in the labs. A different song to play. I just hated that I couldn't help them, but there wasn't much good I could do with the power to breathe fire.

"It isn't that bad," Theon said. "We *are* identical twins. Maybe we're just… un-splitting. Besides, Pneuman says we shouldn't want to be fixed. This is the way we're supposed to be. And it isn't like firebreathing is your only power."

I looked at him, expecting some sarcastic comment to follow, but he said nothing further. "What's that supposed to mean?"

He didn't answer, frowning at something in the distance. "You think they're from Lignovalo, or McKinley 3?"

I squinted at the dim shape ahead. Shiny, with sleek wings and a domed bridge like the *Rubeno*, but I had trouble differentiating between the silhouette of the peaceful Lignovians and the bloodthirsty warriors from McKinley 3.

With the former, no problem crossing paths with them, but the latter would take us for the cargo vessel we appeared to be, skyjack us, and turn us into little more than a wet mass floating in space.

"And we can't just change course and avoid them because...?" Theon prompted.

I motioned to the ships above and on either side of us, packed twenty or thirty deep in spots and so close to the ones beside them that their wings almost touched. We'd fallen into the improvised fleet of mismatched pleasure vessels and cargo haulers a while back, cruising in relative safety in numbers though none of them had much in the way of weapons, and I'd seen the panic that ensued whenever someone tried to peel away.

Not a situation I liked being in, but if we left the pack, we'd have to let the rest know about the potential danger and coordinate efforts to get them all out of harm's way. My hand rested over the comm panel as I studied the radar display, waiting for the mystery ship to come far enough within range to reveal its shape.

Yet as I stared at the sweeping lines, something unexpected flashed on the screen. It vanished as fast as it had appeared, and long before I had the chance to point it out to Theon, but I would swear on my life that I saw it.

Diantha.

"Wait. *What* do you think you saw?" Theon asked.

I pointed to the display, and her face reappeared after a moment, this time moving, mouthing the words to her speech from earlier in the day. The image bounced from the radar screen to our fuel gauge, then finally to the comm panel that was capable of playing the accompanying audio.

"No more lives will be lost and you all may go back to the way you were before."

Nothing I hadn't heard already, and nothing I needed to hear again. The mystery ship lingered just out of range, almost keeping pace with us but inching ever closer. Normally, I'd have assumed its route happened to coincide with ours and it chose a slower speed to conserve fuel, but a certain glint of steel when its rear reflected in the light of a passing comet gave me an uneasy feeling.

"Do you think—"

"That shiny part is its cannons aimed right for us?" Theon asked. "I don't know anything about that, but you do, and that's enough for me."

Why wouldn't they just fire at us? Why wait, having all of us in their sights, when they could just as easily blast the front rows and let their wreckage take out the ones behind them? Hundreds of ships ripe for the picking.

Unless they didn't know we were hundreds of ships. Packed together as tightly as we were, we might have shown up on their radar as one enormous mass. Whatever their affiliation and proclivity for violence, they would have to wait for us to get closer before they determined how much of a risk we posed.

Our own radar still refused to show the ship in any more detail, but I didn't want to waste time that could have been spent coordinating the rest of our fleet. The majority of the ships around us, though capable of evasive maneuvers in a technical and mechanical sense, tended to be flown by retirees and people who bred show poodles. Not the type to know how to move in sync with a hundred other ships at a moment's notice; not without a good amount of scraping metal and smashing wings.

"I'll start prepping them," Theon offered. "Want us to go up or down?"

"Down," I decided, seeing a shimmering cloud of oil, probably ejected by a polluting junker, looming above a little ways ahead. "We'll go below, staying out of range, and floor it until we're a good distance past."

As he started giving instructions to the others, I tried to visualize the layers of vessels in our fleet and the relative blindness of those in the middle. I could only pray we executed this precision move without any casualties.

The video of Diantha appeared on every display capable of transmitting it, this time a different segment of the speech, the part where she discussed the need to rise up and take back the moons.

The door to the bridge opened a moment later, and Parthen and Merulo stuck their heads in.

Merulo.

Where he had once resembled a vicious, apelike creature with some human features, he had become something more since I last saw him. A savage beast with a flat, ape-like snout and clawed hands. He stood on his toes like a wolf, and the charcoal fur stood up along his spine in matted spikes. He wasn't wearing any clothes. A creature made of recognizable parts but on the whole unrecognizable as anything, least of all my best friend.

But he was here.

"Something weird is going on with the ship," Parthen said.

"Diantha?" I asked.

She nodded. "The video is playing on every screen. There isn't anything wrong that I can see, but then I'm not exactly Cara."

Cara. Hadn't she spoken to the ship before? And if her powers were escalating like the rest of ours, I saw no reason she couldn't connect to us over the airwaves.

"Creepy," Merulo added, eyeing Theon in the co-pilot seat. His lip curled in a show of aggression, but he made no move to avenge this perceived affront.

"You got that right." Theon rested his finger over a comm button and looked to me for confirmation. "Ready to do this?"

I nodded, and the clip played again, choppy and fractured but put back together in such a way as to make a new message.

"...lives will be lost... rise up..." The last part repeated, growing louder and more rapid until the syllables morphed into a single, shouted word. "Rise up. Rise up. Riseupriseupriseup UP UP."

"Up!" I shouted, scrambling for the comm. "Ignore previous transmissions! We're going up, not down!"

Though he stared at me with wide, concerned eyes, Theon took over communications. "Alpha group, up at the designated angle.

Beta, follow after ten seconds. Gamma and so on, same intervals please." He cut off communication and shook his head. "*Through* the oil. Because you think she told you to?"

"She did. Not Diantha. Cara."

Our fleet lifted up layer by layer without incident. Far from perfect or even pretty, and one cruiser did get flipped over by the wings of the overeager pilot next to them, but everyone survived and returned to formation just as we entered the oil cloud.

What I had first thought to be the expulsion of a single tanker ship turned out to be more of an ocean, the illegal dumping ground for hundreds, maybe thousands of ships purposely leaving their payload behind, possibly so they would be less likely to explode if hit by enemy fire.

Not the easiest environment to fly through, and god knows what kind of mess it would make inside our engine, but as we came out the other side, one of the ships on the lower levels reported a massive fleet of McKinley 3 warships lurking, cloaked, beneath the mystery ship.

They hadn't been waiting to see if they should attack or retreat; they'd been keeping an eye on us to make sure we flew straight into their trap.

Diantha's face lingered on all the screens and displays of the bridge just long enough to deliver a long, knowing gaze. I knew it was recorded, I knew she was only looking at a camera, but I could have sworn she was making eye contact with me no matter which face I looked at.

At one time, I'd have found that comforting. Now it just unnerved me. Could she really have started the experiments up again? Had the power gone to her head?

I turned on the comm and broadcasted on all frequencies used by the ships around us.

"I want to applaud you. You all aren't captains of big, fancy ships armed to the teeth with every weapon ever developed. You're just ordinary people with ordinary ships. I bet some of you have never been off your worlds before now. I don't know why you left—I'm sure you've got plenty of reasons—but you did so knowing you'd be among the most vulnerable out here. You did it anyway, and found strength with others like you. This may be your first journey into the great void, but you've already mastered the most important rule of space travel: find people like you and stick with 'em. You'll go far."

CHAPTER TEN

The last rebellion on Vespi 3-14 lasted four days, surpassing the previous record by almost three days, which excited Diantha for reasons I couldn't begin to comprehend.

"We had explosives," she told me as we lay in bed. The sky might have had a few new stars shining in its roof, but the house had survived.

"Explosives?" I murmured into her hair, wrapping an arm around her shoulder and pulling her close to me.

"So they say. I don't know how we got hold of them but apparently we dropped them down a VesCorp mine. That's why they didn't destroy us right away like they usually do—they thought we had an alliance with a real army and they were just trying to scare us into surrender in case there were lasers pointed at the Castle or something."

All this was said with a profound level of pride that I admired deeply, but was that really any way to live? Hoping that you lose the next war less catastrophically?

"Is there an endgame?" I asked. "Or do we just keep rebelling until they win once and for all?"

We. I don't think I meant to say that, but I liked the way it sounded.

Diantha hesitated, then turned to face me. "There's an old story, a prophecy, my mother used to call it. She said there's a fleet of ships hidden in the bunkers, and that the descendants of the original freaks will band together and use them to defeat VesCorp."

"How many of us are there?" It felt alien, being part of an "us," of something larger than myself, but I liked it.

"Depending on how many children each of the originals had and the odds of the genes being passed down?" She did the math in her head, a process that apparently involved quite a bit of humming and chewing her lip. "Hundreds, maybe more."

"And we're supposed to go find them?"

"I think we find each other. It's our destiny."

Destiny. Right.

Diantha saw my skeptical face and gave a knowing smile. "It doesn't matter if you believe or not. We have a great deal of freedom in how our stories turn out, but the really important ones—the ones about heroes and villains and people who make a difference—those are already written in the stars. We just have to discover which stories are ours."

I looked up at the stars drilled in her ceiling and tried to find shapes in them. Nothing looked familiar. It's funny. The books told me everything about other worlds—the people, the geology, the wildlife—but none of them warned me the sky would change.

We had stories about the constellations back home, but nothing fancy. Just "That one's a king. He's always watching you, so don't go stealing or killing nothing." There were others, about dragons and panthers and alligators, but they all ended the same way.

"So tell me some of the stories."

"Well." She rolled onto her back and pointed to a cluster of four stars. "Those are the Four. The only freaks who died in the first war against VesCorp." Her outstretched finger danced across the night sky. "There's the two-faced blackbird, and the phoenix who sacrificed herself for her mate, and you see the group shaped like a crown?"

"No," I said truthfully. None of them looked like anything to me.

"It's there, next to the judge's gavel."

"I'll take your word for it."

"That one is the king," she said. "He was a good king. He made some mistakes but was mercilessly vilified by his enemies. He was poisoned by a servant and given a place in the heavens so he could continue to watch over his people."

"And all of these really happened?" I asked, trying to grasp how their legends related to our supposed destiny.

"Some of them," she said. "Others haven't yet but will someday, and a few stories are so good that they keep happening over and over again."

I pointed to a shape that, if I squinted and turned my head, almost looked like a flower. "What about that? Is that anything?"

"That's the queen. She's the one who poisoned her husband and blamed the servant."

"Why'd she do that?"

"Simple," Diantha said, smiling at me. "He had all the power, and she wanted it."

"What did she do with the power?"

"That depends on who you ask. The queen would say she bettered the lives of her subjects. No more hunger or thirst, no more war."

I sat up and looked at her. "What would the subjects say?"

"That she turned them into monsters who didn't *need* food or water, and made them into weapons so terrifying that war against them was pointless."

***

The stage where once danced the sights and sounds of mystery and wonder now entertained a dark, motionless silence. No gasps or laughter, no fluttering wings or glimpses of a vicious beast.

It was all a lie.

Always had been, except I used to think I was the one telling it. Sitting up there on my platform night after night, telling tales of the impossible, just to give people hope of something more, of something beyond their sad little existence hauling cargo with their father.

I looked up at the empty stage. I belonged down here, among the naïve crowd, being fed stories I wanted to believe.

"It's our destiny." "You can come and rescue me." "I love you."

Lies. All lies.

I leaned against the stage, putting my full, exhausted weight on the boards I'd nailed together and despising every moment I had ever wasted on the damn show. Hours spent perfecting the timing, losing countless nights of sleep obsessing over lighting cues and whether the triplets should act more violent or if they would scare the children too much. All that time and energy, and to what end? Broke and drifting through a warzone in an obsolete carnival ship.

I could have been something, done something with my life. They all could have, and they deserved better than this, better than being out-of-work space carnies fighting someone else's battles.

Two blue eyes pierced the darkness. Merulo.

"Can we talk?"

"I don't want to."

He walked up onto the stage and lay on its edge, his massive, hairy face hanging just in front of mine. "I do," he said in a low, pitiful growl. More of a whine, really.

A mutant, more creature than human, in a constant battle against his violent instincts. Was that any way to live?

I stroked one of his ears. Pointed, like a wolf's, but at the side of his head and made of all the curves and folds of cartilage of a human's. His short muzzle twitched, curling into a smile below his smushed, ape-like nose.

"Look at what I did to you."

He nuzzled my head, snorting and snuffling. "What I did to myself," he corrected.

"If I hadn't found you, hadn't dragged you along—"

"*Saved* me," he insisted, his voice growing louder and more raspy as he struggled to form the words with what had to be one complicated set of vocal cords. Who knew what the transformation did to his internal anatomy? "My world is poisoned. Everyone dies young there."

"But you weren't…" At a loss for words, I simply motioned to him. "You weren't like this."

"I was worse."

I opened my mouth to argue, but Merulo lowered his brow and bared his teeth as if daring me to speak.

"I was worse," he said again. "We all were. You saved us. Now it's our turn."

Parthen and Theon emerged from the darkness and came to sit on either side of Merulo. Great. Just what I needed; all my friends gathering around to tell me all the wonderful things I've done for them.

"Trust me," Theon said, "we don't want to do that any more than you do. At least I don't. Pneuman does, but he's trapped inside my head and can't speak, so sucks to be him."

I laughed. Didn't want to, but I did.

"We aren't here to convince you that you're a good person," Parthen added, casting a dirty look at Theon. "And we aren't going to tell you how naïve you were for falling in love at first sight and dedicating your life to the grand scheme of a complete stranger."

I stared at my boots, knowing what she would say next. Same thing I said to each of them when they came on board.

"You can't make a person change by pointing out their flaws—"

"But you can be the one person who doesn't try to." I nodded. "Yeah, I know. So what do you want?"

They stepped down off the stage one by one and came to stand beside me in a crowd of foolish people.

Theon didn't waste words. "The girl you loved has gone bad with power, and we want to know what we're going to do about that."

Had to love his choice of pronoun that didn't give me the chance to decline their help. No matter what the problem, no matter the risk, we solved it together. Always had. Just had to figure out how, or if I wanted to.

Everything in me wanted to believe Diantha had a plan, that all the things she said were meant to lead to the downfall of VesCorp like she always intended. I hardly knew her, and maybe she had duped me into being part of her plan, but she just seemed so innocent, so pure in her intentions. Could that person, that kind and brilliant person who only wanted to take back her ancestral home, really have been scheming all along?

I *really* didn't want to believe it. For maybe the first time in my life, I wanted to curl up in the comfortable darkness and lie to myself. Anything was possible in the vastness of space, up to and including Diantha being the good person she had once pretended to be.

My crew—my family—waited for a response, and I knew what it had to be. I could lie to myself, but not to them.

"We're going to take down VesCorp," I said finally, "like she always wanted us to. And we're going to take her down with it."

CHAPTER ELEVEN

As the security drones passed over and through the *Rubeno Mardo*, we could only hope that Cara and Lily got our message.

And that Merulo really had released all the animals like he'd claimed to.

My stomach twisted, knotting and tangling with every sweeping beam of their scanners and whirr of their propellers. With the universe plunged deeper into the bottomless pit of war, it took longer than before as they searched every inch of the ship with increased scrutiny.

If I hadn't been so on edge, I might have found some humor in the circumstances. Never in my life did I think I'd find myself at the helm of a ship full of genetically engineered freaks, about to lay siege to a floating castle while hoping a fleet of flying toasters didn't find the caged beast in my cargo hold.

Merulo. It was his idea from the start, but now I wished I'd fought back, found another way. Some days he struggled to keep his violent side in check; what would it do to him, being locked behind iron bars all day? And why the hell hadn't any of the drones asked about him yet?

"They've been down there," I whispered to Parthen and Theon, crossing my arms as we stood in the hall, watching three of the drones examine the obviously toxic and extremely dangerous throw rug on the floor of Merulo's quarters. "Something isn't right."

Parthen tried to sound positive, but doubt crept into her voice. "Or Cara *did* change their manifest so they don't think it's illegal to transport exotic creatures."

"You don't know these things," I argued. "Just about arrested me over a bird. A perfectly legal bird that wasn't an explosive device, I might add."

Parthen stared at me. "Why would a bird be an—"

"I don't know; ask the bots."

"I can't read them," Theon said, not bothering to lower his voice. He snapped his fingers at the drones. "Hey, you! You find anything, or can we go?"

One of them flew over to us, holding something in the pincher at the end of an extendable arm.

"We have discovered a natural fiber," it said. "Fur, bearing the genetic code of human."

"Hair," Theon corrected. "People have hair, not fur."

It turned to examine his face, then ignored him. "It matches the peculiar creature you have in a cage downstairs. Does someone on your crew make a habit of letting the creature accompany them to bed? Perhaps in a romantic capacity?"

Merulo? Romantic? Not a chance, but no one answered. The drone hadn't made any indication as to whether they would allow us to bring Merulo in, and I couldn't count all the categories of illicit goods he fell under. Weapon, exotic animal, possible radiation hazard… At least they didn't suggest he was explosive.

If Cara hadn't received our transmission, hadn't been able to hack into the drones' database—and I had to admit that I knew next to nothing about her abilities at this point, so she might not have—they'd turn us away. Or worse. Would his being on the ship in a "romantic capacity" make a difference in their little metal brains?

"It was me," Parthen said, staring at the ground to avoid the drone's facial scans. "I love him. He isn't a beast. He…" Girl couldn't lie to save her life. Or ours, in this case.

Theon shook his head in disgust. I couldn't tell if he was acting. "What a surprise."

"He and I…" She turned to him, and she wasn't exactly lying anymore. "He was there for me when the person who should have been there couldn't be. Or wouldn't be. I don't know; I'm not the mind-reader. He understood me more than anyone ever had, and I didn't mean to fall in love, but I'm not going to apologize for it, either."

Theon's face, previously screwed up in thinly veiled fury and resentment, softened. "He loves you, too, you know. I want to hate you, but I think someone's messing around in my head, because I'm hating myself, too."

The drone looked at each of them, then at me. "You run a most peculiar ship, Mr. Jetstark."

I grinned through the pounding anxiety in my chest. "Wouldn't have it any other way," I said, putting my arms around my crew. "So, can we come in? With the creature in the cage?"

"Our manifests show no reasons one cannot import such a beast." It stared at us for a moment, then departed with the others without another word.

"This stress is gonna kill me," I said with a laugh, pulling Parthen and Theon closer.

Our relief evaporated as quickly as it had washed through the hall, forcing us to face the looming task ahead.

"You think it'll work?" Parthen asked as we headed for the bridge. "Has to."

"Because it's our destiny?"

I didn't appreciate Theon's mocking tone, but I ignored it. "Because it has to. I don't know what she's up to, but I know what her plan used to be, and it will get us inside. Beyond that, it's a matter of using our powers and our natural-born intelligence. Maybe it's written in the stars, maybe it's in our genes, and maybe it's all a blank page and we're making it up as we go. Whatever the case, we have all the parts needed to make it work, so it will. Has to."

I took a deep breath and gazed out at the city floating high above the planet, secure and surrounded by a swarm of warships, and prayed with all my heart that it would work. It had to work.

***

I'd been inside the forcefield exactly once in my life, to attend the wedding where Diantha abandoned our plan to kill Garon and decided to marry him instead. Should have been my first clue, but I guess I'm a little denser than most.

We stood on the edge of the moat between the floating plates of the city, watching a pair of armed guards extend a drawbridge across the gap.

"Thank you, Cara," I muttered, gripping the covered cage tighter as the portion of the forcefield directly in front of us was deactivated. I looked to Parthen and Theon, dressed in plain gray work uniforms matching my own.

This was it, the last moment before we embarked on the siege. Once we passed that threshold, every millisecond had to go as planned. If any of us made a wrong move, said a wrong word...

The consequences of failing made me want to back out, and if it'd only been about me, I'd have turned tail and ran back to my ship. But it wasn't about me.

A small group of people crowded at the forcefield, fewer than before but still a good number. The sky ran dark with ships, nearly blocking out the sun at times, but people still came out to shop and to gawk at the majesty of the Castle. The war didn't get in the way of their lives, and everyone deserved that basic right.

"We're doing this for them," I said, more to myself than to anyone else. "For them and for everyone who dreams of living in this kind of safety."

We stepped in sync onto the hovering platform, pushing Merulo's cage between us as the few children in the crowd pointed and wondered aloud what the cloth draped over it concealed.

As did I. If all went right, his only contribution would be as our ticket to the laboratory, as the ape listed on the guards' manifest and labeled for research purposes, but what if all went wrong? Could I ask him to call upon the rage he tried so hard to repress, if it would save us?

I glanced down at the planet far below, just a grassy continent surrounded by a royal blue ocean. Long way to fall.

After what felt like forever—who'd have thought a man who made his living flying around space would be afraid of heights?—we reached the other side and the semblance of solid ground of the inner ring.

As much as the Castle, with its gleaming towers and arched doorways, resembled an Old Earth medieval fortress from afar, the view from within its forcefield amplified that resemblance tenfold.

It erupted from the ground like a mountain, with cylindrical peaks of marble jutting into the sky to end in massive flags that snapped in the wind. Its orbiting gunnery turrets that floated at different levels matched its aesthetic, with conical roofs that caught the light on each of a thousand faceted stones.

A guard, wearing a black tunic with red trim and with a laser pistol strapped to each ankle, leered at the cage, walking around it with his nose in the air. "And this would be the…" He consulted his tablet.

"Gorilla, sir," Theon answered. "Male, captured in the jungles of Valeo, for display in the menagerie."

"Menagerie," the guard repeated calmly, and Theon froze. "There isn't any menagerie on the premises."

I shared a look of concern with Parthen. Why did he say that? Why didn't he say "lab" or "experimentation"? Must have read the guard's mind wrong, or maybe Cara put the wrong word in the document.

"That's what our orders say," Theon said with a shrug, sweat beading on his forehead. He took a moment to compose himself and continued with his usual air of confidence. "I mean, you can see why they might be reluctant to put its real destination on there, what with the political unrest and the constant threat of espionage. You don't just come right out and say the gorilla's headed for the lab on the..." He scrutinized the guard's face. "On the fortieth level, third door on the left, security code one nine five—"

The guard widened his eyes and held up a hand. "You're good," he said, motioning toward a smaller, less-than-grand doorway nestled in a dark alcove on the building's side. We nodded our respects and hurried along.

"I *am* good, aren't I?" Theon whispered.

I didn't answer, focusing on taking deep breaths to calm my racing heart. So many pieces had to fall into place at just the right time, and no matter how many times I went over the plan, I couldn't help but think we were forgetting something.

Merulo would get us to the lab where, assuming they ran a paperless operation, Cara would have updated their schedule to include our delivery. Arriving at the end of a long shift, Theon and Pneuman would play off the thoughts and feelings of the guards and convince them to leave their post while I waxed philosophical to anyone who needed distracting and Parthen filmed what was going on in the lab. If it was still operational, we'd shut it down and have video proof to show the public.

It all worked out in theory, but a feeling of overwhelming dread came over me as we entered the Castle.

The building opened around us in shining steel and industrial iron. Lights hovered in the air, spiraling upward toward the nearly invisible ceiling over a hundred stories overhead, and dozens of automatic stairways and lifts moved people from balcony to balcony around the edge of this hollow tower. Everyone wore a black soldier's uniform with the color of the trim varying by rank, and carried at least one firearm, marching across the tiled floor with precision and poise. Cannons sat at the ready in the few windows on the higher levels.

They must have molded the public image of this place to serve their purpose and hide its true identity, dressing up the grand hall for events and filming Diantha in the only room that had been done up all fancy. Maybe other parts of the building, the living quarters and whatnot, looked different, but I doubted it. From what little I could see, it all seemed like lies, a façade covering the truth.

This wasn't a company or a kingdom, but a military base, with guns and trained security literally everywhere I looked.

"Fortieth floor?" I asked Theon, refusing to let the others see my doubt.

"That's what his orders said."

The glass elevators looked too small to fit the three of us and the cage, so we opted for the long walk up the spiraling ramp that wound its way around the outer wall. Long, exhausting walk. Should have put better wheels on the cage we cobbled together from stairway railings and sheets of metal.

Scrutinizing eyes followed us from down on the main floor, peering out from below lowered brims as we passed. Just keeping watch on the civilians, or did we strike them as suspicious in some way?

I looked to Theon.

"Lot of thoughts," he reported, "but nothing stands out."

"Pneuman, are you sensing any hostility or—"

"Tons," Theon answered, "but not directed at us as far as he can tell."

I considered lifting a corner of the sheet to check on Merulo, but the constant observation gave me pause and I tapped a finger on the top of the cage instead. "You doing okay in there, Merulo?"

"Fine," he whispered, though a faint whimper betrayed his bravery.

It hurt, hearing him in such misery, and the sight of him cramming himself into the cage would steal sleep for years to come.

I looked at Parthen. "You okay?"

She shrugged. Her gloves were in her pocket, her hands bare. Good; she was more confident in her control of her power.

The ground floor, and our one escape route, shrank as we trudged up the ramp, and though I reminded myself that no one would discover what we were planning to do until long after we were back in the ship, the thought of getting trapped weighed heavily on my mind. In a worst case scenario, with Merulo unleashed and Parthen turning the floor to lava in her wake, would we even be able to fight our way to an elevator, or would the army surrounding us take us out in a matter of seconds and go on with their day?

As I examined the soldiers in more detail, noticing the defined muscles on even the thinnest among their ranks as well as all the guns and grenades strapped to their legs and chests, I wondered if it was arrogant to assume we'd survive even a matter of seconds.

"Here," Theon said, jerking me from my reverie.

We stopped at an unmarked door, a solid sheet of steel without a guard posted beside it. Shouldn't have struck me as suspicious since most doors in the Castle didn't have security personnel, but I'd have wanted better protection for my secret laboratory. Maybe that's just me.

I turned the cool, metal handle, and the door swung open without much effort. Not even locked.

Theon echoed my thoughts. "It's too easy."

"Then we go back. Find another way to do this." Parthen started pulling the cage down the ramp, but I reached out to stop her.

A soldier, on a higher level across the way, leaned on the railing, making no attempt to hide her fascination with us. She stared, daring us to do anything but deliver the subject to the lab.

"We're going in," I said. "I am, anyway. You can—"

"Abandon you?" Parthen pushed the cage through the door. "Not a chance."

I think we all knew it was a bad idea, but we went in anyway. Call it bravery, call it foolishness... I called it duty. We had to shut down the machines, had to put a stop to VesCorp's plans. Whatever they were.

The door closed and we found ourselves in an all-encompassing darkness devoid of any sound except a steady, mechanical breathing somewhere in the distance. A pang of doubt and panic hit me, and a fleet of overhead lights flicked on, flooding the spacious room with a retina-scorching glow.

Every surface gleamed with a clinical whiteness, from the floors and walls to the hulking machinery that stretched high toward the vaulted ceiling. Tubing, ducts, and vats of tinted water crowded the laboratory like trees and vines, but not a single person. No guards, no scientists... no one.

"*Someone*," Theon corrected with a catch in his voice, and took off into the tangled, medical forest.

"Watch the door," I told Parthen, taking her camera, and went after him.

The place was enormous, with the walls curving around the tower. Probably took up most of the building's floorspace, and on multiple levels, judging by the balconies barely visible beyond the lights.

I couldn't begin to identify any of the machines or apparatuses I passed. Centrifuges and brain scanners and things like that, probably, but I paid more attention to the space between them, always on alert for someone lurking behind them.

I saw Theon before I saw the woman.

He knelt on the floor in front of a glowing tank of water equipped with some valve that hissed every few seconds. The gentle blue light from the tank glinted off the tears on his face.

Theon didn't cry. He got angry, threw things, shouted at the top of his lungs until the nuts on the *Rubeno Mardo* threatened to vibrate from their bolts, but he never cried. I'd seen him break his wrist and smirk through the pain.

Devastation lined his face, and though I couldn't imagine something awful enough to reduce my most emotionally stable crewmember to a sad, wet pulp, I didn't dare look.

"You have to," he said, wiping his face with his sleeve. "You have to see what we're fighting for."

"We're fighting—"

"For all the little people who can't fight for themselves. Yeah, I've heard your speeches." He sniffed and turned to me. "This is different. It isn't some abstract idea of bringing agriculture back to Vespi 3-14 or putting more money in the pockets of nomadic asteroid towns. This is what VesCorp is doing to people, Jack. This is what *Diantha* is doing. And you need to see it so you can never doubt how evil she is again."

With a sigh, I gritted my teeth and stepped forward.

A person floated in the water, bound by straps at her wrists. At least, part of her was a person.

Patches of jagged scales covered her bare body, her legs fused into one limb from the knees down with a split fin at the end. Gashes on the sides of her neck suggested gills, but she still thrashed and gasped for air, struggling against her bonds.

It hurt, somewhere deep in the hole vacated by my soul. I felt her pain, echoing down through the generations. One of my ancestors, somewhere in the distant past, went through this horror, only to be discarded when they failed to live up to the ideal set forth by some devious corporation.

How many? Over the hundreds of years since the torture began, how many people had lived through it? Or died from it? Did they hide the survivors away in some dark warehouse, performing more experiments, or did they just execute them if they weren't perfect and try harder next time?

"I feel nine here," Theon said. His head jerked to the door. "We've got company—"

Too late. A scream cut off Theon's warning. Parthen.

By the time we reached the door, five soldiers lined the wall, weapons drawn. Merulo stood atop his cage between them and Parthen, roaring and beating his chest as he towered over them.

Intimidating as he may have been, they could have—and arguably should have—taken him down in an instant, but they didn't. Kind of a running theme lately, enemies not taking us down as easily as they could, and I'd about tired of it.

"What?" I challenged, stepping out from behind a blinking machine. "You gonna shoot us? Arrest us? Go ahead and try, but we're not going down without a fight." I hoped they hadn't seen the camera; I'd hidden it by the other tank, but it was still transmitting live to Cara, wherever she was.

No one made a move, and I considered calling for a preemptive strike. Slashing and biting, linoleum turning to floods of lava, maybe even a few flaming breaths to singe those caps right off their heads. And with a mind-reader telling us their moves before they made them, we might have stood a chance.

But one soldier gave me pause. The way she stood, the way she held her hand on her hip.

Lily. No wings, not that I could see, but definitely Lily.

She glanced my way and smiled before uttering two words that ruined everything. "I'm sorry."

CHAPTER TWELVE

It all happened so fast.

A ring of flames sprang up from the floor, surrounding us and the soldiers. One of them transformed into a snarling wolf, tearing open the seams of his uniform as he lunged for Merulo. Theon pushed me to the ground as a knife flew past my head, and a dozen more soldiers appeared above me.

I scrambled to my feet and punched one in the face, only to have him dissipate at my touch and throw me and my inertia into the path of another hurtling blade.

Ripped right through my forearm with a rage that burned through my body, the heat and pressure growing until I could contain it no longer.

Fire rushed from my lungs in a roaring tongue of orange and yellow that burned through more illusionary soldiers. Someone caught fire. Couldn't tell who through all the smoke and chaos, but it made me sick. These weren't faceless ships; they were people.

For a moment, the floor felt unstable beneath my feet. A hand grabbed my wrist as the wolf and Merulo flung each other to the ground; Parthen emerged from behind the tank that had been shielding her and came to stand in the center of the fray.

She knelt, putting her palms to the white tiles. The floor rippled, more of a liquid than a solid, and gave way. Didn't break, didn't collapse, just stopped being under us.

We plummeted into another lab, and with the floor fast approaching, I braced for a hard landing. But we didn't hit.

Lab after dark lab passed by in a blur lit only by the soft glow of tanks. How many people were they torturing in this place?

We finally came to a stop, and a far gentler one than I'd expected, given the rate of our fall, when Theon picked up Parthen and held her in his arms, breaking her contact with the floor.

Only then, looking at the hole above and the pool of water at our feet, did I realize Parthen must have transformed the floors to let us pass. Probably made the air into something thicker to soften the fall, too.

Parthen wriggled free from Theon's grasp, breathing hard and fast. "We have to keep going. They're coming. They'll catch us."

He grabbed her by the wrists. "We're on the first level! You let us through this floor and we fall eight miles to the planet's surface."

I wiped the blood from my arm, wincing at the wide gash. "How do you know? I couldn't count that fast."

He shrugged, putting an arm around a shaking Parthen and kissing the top of her head. "I stopped hearing soldiers' thoughts under us. Figured we were at the bottom."

Merulo groaned, hauling himself to his feet. Hairs singed, paws bloody, but otherwise apparently unharmed. Probably wasn't his blood anyway.

"Not Lily's," he assured me, following my gaze. "Never Lily's."

A cooling relief washed through my boiling veins, and I had to smile despite our situation.

I looked up, expecting to see the soldiers rappelling through the gaping holes of exposed beams and broken tile. Lily flying down, maybe. Some indication that they were after us, that our lives were in danger.

Nothing.

"Why didn't they shoot us?" Parthen wondered aloud.

"Why did the pirates flee?" I countered. "Why did the ship on Rouze give chase instead of blasting us to subatomic particles? Why does no one ever *actually* hurt us?"

I waited, hoping someone had an explanation for our continued survival against all odds, a reason why stronger and more capable enemies had suddenly started conspiring with the universe to keep us alive.

"Something is going on," I answered for them, "and we don't know the half of it. Hell, we don't know a quarter of it."

The quiet whoosh of an automatic door somewhere in the lab confirmed it, and I found the cause of my earlier unease.

This was Diantha's plan. Always had been. Altered to suit our individual abilities, but hers in every way that mattered. She had to have remembered it, would have been able to set a trap far in advance.

I took a deep breath, my fire my only weapon, and prepared for an attack. Merulo crouched beside me, fangs bared, with Theon and Parthen behind us.

Footsteps echoed in the shadows. Small, cautious.

The quiet tapping of giant insect legs on linoleum? The talons of a raptor? My mind ran wild with possibilities. What kind of supersoldier would emerge from the darkness, and with what kind of powers?

I saw her silhouette first, cast by the light of an empty tank, but I recognized her in an instant.

The girl.

Diantha's daughter. Maybe my daughter, too.

I put my hand out to stop Merulo and walked forward to meet her, searching behind her for any movement. Something could have followed her, or she could have led it to us on purpose. Couldn't trust anyone, no matter how her round little face and frizzy hair tugged at my heart.

"Are you okay?" she asked in concern, peering around me to wave at the others. "Hello, people."

They returned the wave awkwardly.

"You're bleeding," she cried out, noticing my arm.

"Ran into a flying knife."

"One of Billie's." She tore a strip from the hem of her flowing pink skirt and handed it to me, the pistons of the metallic exoskeleton on her arm firing to give her joints a smooth, natural motion. "You can use this as a bandage, but we have to get you out of here before they come for you."

She disappeared behind the equipment. I looked back at the others and helplessly followed, tying the material around my arm as I went. What else could we do? Bust through the door into a Castle filled with an army of what I had to assume were all genetically modified soldiers?

She led us to a back wall glittering with lighted buttons on a series of panels, and ran her hand across them with grace and precision. She had to stand on her toes to reach a couple switches, but the girl knew what she was doing. Her confidence reminded me of her mother.

A hidden door slid open in the wall, revealing a chamber that seemed to reject all ambient light from outside. Could have been a foot deep, could have gone on for a mile. The girl ducked inside and beckoned for us to follow, shrinking against the wall as Merulo wedged himself in the tight quarters.

"He won't hurt you," I told her.

She reached out and patted him on the leg. "I know. He just looks scary because he's trapped inside his anger."

I couldn't have said it better. Kid had a way with words.

"You know?" Parthen asked. "How do you know?"

She shrugged. "My mother used to keep surveillance on you, and she'd let me watch with her sometimes. Now she's too busy with the war. But I'm still watching. We got the video of the lab."

We?

The door closed behind us, leaving us in the dark, with walls brushing our shoulders and the low ceiling inches from my head, with only the daughter of VesCorp's evil general to guide us. It occurred to me that she could have been a cog in her mother's machine, and that my crew may have been following me faithfully to their demise, but that line of thinking wouldn't change the outcome.

First Diantha, then Lily...

If I couldn't believe in the good intentions of the little girl humming her way through the claustrophobic tunnel of doom, what could I believe in?

Humming. I knew that tune.

"That's our song," Parthen cried out.

"Yup," the girl confirmed, the sound of her footsteps changing. I think she was skipping. "My mom taught me to sing it. She says it's the music of our family, but she doesn't sing anymore."

"Not for a couple weeks now," I said. It felt like so much longer since we'd been on the stage, since our only concerns were getting to the next show.

"A couple months," she corrected, and curled her fingers around my hand. "It'll all make sense soon."

"It better," I muttered.

A tiny red dot cut through the black. The girl released my hand and sprinted to it. We waited, hushed breaths echoing in our ears, as she pressed her forefinger to the light.

Finally, a section of the floor slid away, a window to the world far below. No forcefield or glass in sight to prevent falls. Which, I realized, was the point.

Last time they let their failed experiments live, they learned to repair themselves and rose up against their oppressors. No one would make that mistake twice, and they wouldn't want to do anything with the bodies—cremation or export for disposal—that would draw attention to their clandestine operations. Since there were no civilizations directly beneath the floating city, no one would notice the occasional falling body.

Theon scoffed at my thoughts. "They don't throw people off the city to kill them, Jack."

"Yes, they do." In the light emanating from the hatch, I saw the girl staring at her feet, disappointment casting a shadow over her face. "Except she doesn't call them people. When they don't turn out right, they're freaks."

My heart ached for her. No one that young should have to see a parent descend so violently from the pedestal we put them on.

"Your mom was good once," I told her, not sure if I was lying. "She lived on a moon that never saw the stars because they all lived inside of her. You could see 'em sometimes, in her eyes and in her smile, and they were so bright, so beautiful, that otherwise level-headed guys would travel the universe against all logic just for a hope of seeing them one more time."

I caught Merulo looking at me with pity. He pretended not to, hastily rearranging his expression to hide it, but I knew that look. Not the first time I'd seen it while talking about Diantha, either.

"I'm over it," I told him, this time certain I was lying. I nodded toward the hatch. "This is supposed to be our escape route?" I asked the girl. "Because we can't fly, and you don't look like you'd make a very good landing pad."

She laughed—she had her mother's laugh—and leaned over the hole, her complete lack of fear sending shocks of panic to my chest. "Here it comes."

We heard the engines a second later.

The *Rubeno Mardo* heaved into view below us, her open dome coming to rest mere yards from the plate supporting the Castle. Cara waved from the captain's seat, the sleeves of her flannel jacket rolled up to show off both cyborg arms.

I looked at the girl in disbelief, wanting to give her a grand speech about hope, about how family meant more than people who shared blood, but the sound of distant footsteps echoing down the corridor rushed me to the end.

"Thank you," I said. "Are you coming?"

"They won't hurt me," she assured me. "I'm a princess. Kind of."

I patted her on the shoulder and joined my crew as we gathered around the hatch in an unspoken debate over who would go first. I won; whether I liked it or not, the captain had to risk his own life before he could consider letting his crew do the same.

Looked easy enough. Just had to drop into the bridge, try not to break my legs upon landing, and hope I didn't miss and go skidding down her rounded hull.

Long way to fall. A guy could spend a long time dying that way, alone with all his regrets and mistakes as the ground slowly threw itself at his face.

Give me a laser to the brain any day.

"You holding steady?" I called down.

Cara gave me a thumbs-up.

I crouched, gripping the smooth edge of the hatch until my fingertips turned white, and swung a leg into the opening. My body gave a sudden jerk downward when my second leg left the ground, and it took all my strength to hold onto the slick floor. Almost like the secret hole they used to throw people to their death wasn't designed for this purpose.

"It all looks good," Parthen said, peering around me. She looked over her shoulder in response to some sound I couldn't hear, but tried to hide the urgency in her voice. "You're fine. Just let go."

Easier said than done. I didn't dare look down. Couldn't look. What if the ship wasn't there anymore?

The girl appeared before my face. "Are you afraid of falling?"

"Afraid of landing," I corrected. "Falling is just like flying, until it isn't."

"Did you name the *Rubeno Mardo* after me?" she asked, switching subjects abruptly.

I didn't bother asking how she knew the name of my ship, or why she thought I'd name anything after her. She had to know who I was to her. "No. Dad named it after my mom."

"Oh."

"Why? What's your name?"

She looked down at me with a proud smile. "Ruby Marta."

"Well, Ruby Marta, I think you might have been named after my ship."

For a second there, I'd almost forgotten I was dangling from a floating city. Probably her intention all along.

I gave her a wink, took the deepest breath my lungs would allow, and I let go.

CHAPTER THIRTEEN

Never knew a guy who spent his life flying through space could miss the ground so much, but it felt damn good knowing there was nothing but solid planet for miles under my feet.

We sat outside the *Rubeno*, the sun casting a shadow in the shape of a floating city over a field of rippling grasses topped with tiny, white flowers that stretched on into eternity. The ocean's gentle roar behind us competed with the singing birds to provide the most tranquil sound.

If the perfect landscape existed, it probably looked a lot like this. Minus the odd femur jutting out from between the greenery as nature tried and failed to conceal the secret graveyard of our people.

I couldn't think of them as anything else. May not have known them, may not have been related, but the same injustice ran through us, and that made them our people. Our family.

"So how are we supposed to stop this?" I asked Cara, leaning back against the warm, sun-baked hull of the ship. Last thing I wanted was to talk strategy, ruin the last moment of peace we might ever have, but the unanswered questions swimming around in my head had already ruined it. "I'm guessing you know more than we do right now."

Like why Lily betrayed us.

"Where have you been?" Theon asked her. Struck me as odd that he had to ask, but maybe Parthen—sitting close at his side and flirting with the notion of holding his hand—distracted him from his ability.

"They recruited us," Cara said. "Me and Lily."

"Recruited you for what?" Parthen asked.

Cara shrugged. "They needed skilled workers to upgrade security. We figured it would help you if we were your inside men. And then I met Ruby. I didn't know who she was, just a bored girl wandering the Castle, but we've been working together to save her mother."

Merulo tore his attention from the sounds of a small creature rustling the nearby grass. "Save her from what?"

"Herself."

"Hang on a second," I said. "They thought Lily was a skilled worker?"

"No," Cara said, grinning at me for noticing that anomaly. "They've been trying to find descendants of the original freaks, examining millions of blood samples from VesCorp moons and asteroids for the genetic markers. They wanted to study us so they could make their own freaks with a trigger, like our song."

"How did they get so many blood samples?" Parthen asked.

"The mosquitoes," I said, finally understanding the strange scene back home on Stoval.

"The hypodermic micro-drones," Cara corrected, growing more animated as she revealed more information. I'd expected her to be more robotic, more of a machine in line with the way our powers had been amplified since the end of the song played. If anything, she seemed more human than ever. Outgoing and smiling, not so withdrawn. Almost looked like a normal kid, if you ignored the sheen of her skin. Probably the most normal out of all of us.

"...and Diantha never wanted to hurt you," she was saying,

though I thought I detected a hint of dishonesty in her voice, "but she knew you couldn't stay away if you thought she was in danger, so she had her allies try to damage your ship to keep you grounded. But she isn't playing around anymore."

I covered my face with my hands and laid my head against the ship. What kind of convoluted mess had I gotten myself tangled up in?

"So what now?" I muttered, sitting up. Triangular Vespi ships drifted through the clouds. Looking for us?

"Free the experiments," Cara said. "Then we release the video and show the universe what's going on in there. They'll know we're coming if we release it first; they'll move the freaks somewhere else. And then we can start the carnival up again." She smiled dreamily. "I was thinking we could fix up the carousel, put up some twinkle lights… maybe I can have a seat on the bridge?"

She was too damn earnest. Pure. "Yeah," I said. "We stop this, you can have the captain's seat."

"'This,'" Theon snapped. "What is this 'this' we're supposed to risk our lives to stop?"

Cara's response chilled my blood. "Diantha always wanted the moons to rise up, but they don't have the numbers or weapons to fight. She still wants that, but now she's trying to turn everyone on the moons into superpowered freaks so they have a chance. She wants everyone in the 'verse to be freaks like us."

Diantha's dreams of self-governed moons once epitomized hope and equality, but time had twisted her vision into an unrecognizable beast. Where had it gone wrong? Was there one moment that turned her, or just a slow descent into immorality? Would my insistence on her staying have made any difference?

The ships grew larger in the sky, deviating from their surveillance route and closing the distance between us with every pass. We craned our necks to watch, on alert for any sign of aggression.

"So do you know how to get the freaks out of their tanks safely?" I asked Cara.

"I can show you," she said with a confident nod.

"And you have a plan for getting back in there?"

"A plan our enemy didn't come up with?" Theon added. I didn't think he meant it as a dig at me, at my utter lapse in logic that led to our needless near-capture, but he should have. He couldn't say anything to me that I hadn't already said to myself.

Cara suppressed a smile at my expense. "Of course. It isn't far off from your original plan of using our powers to our advantage, but it won't be nearly as easy as you thought. For one thing…"

What would we have done without that nervous bundle of wires? I shook my head, hating myself for ever doubting her having a place on the ship. Maybe she had never felt at home there, and maybe we could have done more to change that, but I got the impression she'd never felt at home anywhere. From what little she had said of her family, they didn't strike me as the warm and huggy type. Not that we did, but at least we could offer a supportive environment and an outlet for her expertise in exchange for all this insider information.

A cloud of dust shot up a few yards away, and then another.

Laserfire.

One of the ships hovered on the horizon, facing us.

"Stay low," I commanded, and crawled to the *Rubeno*'s gangplank. My hand reached the rough wooden floor of the carnival as red streaks began raining down like fiery hailstones. One ripped through the sleeve of my shirt, missing my arm by millimeters.

Someone else wasn't so lucky.

The scream cut through the air. Not a scream of pain, but of horror. Of seeing the aftermath of a laser meeting human flesh.

Merulo and Theon paused behind me; I ushered them in as I turned around. "Get in, start her up."

I stuck my head outside. Dust and bits of grass in the air, stirred by the thousands of sporadic blasts, clouded my vision, but I could just see Parthen huddled in the shadow of the *Rubeno*'s tail fin, cradling Cara in her lap and sobbing over her lifeless body.

Nausea swept through me, soon replaced by an overwhelming sense of doom. One of our own, gone?

"Is she—"

Parthen nodded.

I ducked—for all the good that would do—as lasers struck the ground and pinged into the ship, and went to her side and held Cara's head in my hands. "Go inside."

The warmth had already begun to leave her body, and her half-closed eyes lacked any spark of life. No pulse, no breath, but no blood, either. Just entry and exit wounds in the sides of her head. Cauterized by the lasers, I supposed, not that I had ever seen someone shot by one.

I'd never seen anyone shot by anything. Not anyone I knew, not anyone I'd welcomed into my little piece of the sky and accepted as part of my family. Those people weren't allowed to get shot.

Parthen was still beside me.

"Go inside!"

Theon came out and dragged her into the ship. I lingered, staring at a face that had only just found reason to smile but never would again.

"This wasn't your fight," I whispered. "I'm sorry."

As I went to pick her up, the ship above switched from a scattered array to more targeted attacks. One struck Cara's chest, doing unspeakable damage. The next would be in mine.

I left her body in the field scattered with little white flowers and bones, and returned to my ship with lasers in pursuit.

"We can't leave her there!"

For a second as I closed the gangplank behind me, I thought the voice, so emotional and desperate, belonged to Pneuman, but it didn't. Theon, the most pragmatic and unsentimental man I had ever known, pleaded with tears in his eyes for me to protect what he once would have called an empty shell of a former person.

"She deserves better."

I wanted nothing more than to do right by such an amazing individual who had put her life in my hands, who had stepped on my ship with the trust that I would keep her safe, but I couldn't. I couldn't get myself killed trying to rescue someone beyond rescuing.

"It's our people's graveyard," I said by way of apology. "What better place is there for her?"

I pushed past him, stalking through the empty carnival and up to the bridge.

Merulo sat beside me. Don't know why; I'd sold off our weapons for fuel on the way to Stoval and we had no way to fight back.

I raised the *Rubeno* to match the warship's height, making a point not to look down at... at anything.

"Are you okay—"

"No."

"Okay, then."

I turned to face the other ship. Lasers tore through our hull.

We could have run. Probably should have. But they'd come after us and then we'd always be running, while the universe fell into a bottomless pit of chaos.

"This is a do or die moment," I said to Merulo and into the comm. "Maybe do *and* die. Anyone object to my doing something incredibly ill-advised?"

"Not as long as it's also incredibly reckless," Theon said, holding Parthen's hand—not a glove in sight—as they came up and sat with us.

Two empty chairs—Lily's and Pneuman's. Should have been three, but, as she had just reminded me, I never did get around to finding one for Cara.

"Then let's go." I cracked my knuckles over the throttle, then pushed it as far forward as it would go before taking cover below the instruments panels with my crew. The armored ship never expected full-contact battle from a ship half its size, and I prayed that would give us enough of an advantage.

Sparkling shards of glass rained down on the bridge, their last attempt to scare us off.

I tried to estimate time until impact, taking into account the distance between our ships and the *Rubeno Mardo*'s top speed in the atmosphere, but it happened before I'd begun the calculations.

If I didn't know better, I'd have sworn we hit the side of a mountain.

The inertia threw us into the wall in a crushing mass of limbs and bodies, stinging bits of glass flinging themselves at any flesh that dared to be exposed. Metal crunched and compressed, alarms screamed and the engines cut out. But the lasers stopped.

The *Rubeno*'s artificial gravity increased, sucking us toward the floor to compensate for our sudden downward trajectory. We were in freefall.

I pulled myself to my feet, using my chair and the instrument panels to support my increased weight, and overrode the engine cutoff. She struggled, injured in the crash, but finally roared back to life. Only then, confident in my ship's ability to get us out, did I look out the shattered window to see the ground spiraling above us.

We were upside down, a term that, while meaningless in space, meant everything and then some planetside.

With that in mind, I chose not to pull out of the dive. If the other ship, seen tumbling out of control in my peripheral vision, saw us recovering and managed to get a shot off, if we sustained any more damage, the *Rubeno* might have gone into emergency mode, turning off any unnecessary systems, artificial gravity included. Then it wouldn't matter if we had time to pull up or not, because there'd be no one left on the bridge to do it.

Waiting, watching the planet hurtle toward us amid the terrified screams of the people I loved, physically hurt me. I found I didn't have the time nor the energy to contemplate my regrets and mistakes, as it took every ounce of strength to keep my hand from staging a mutiny and pulling back on the yoke.

"Jack—"

"We're good," I told Merulo. He must have hated it, being pressed to the floor and unable to help. Had we landed differently, with anyone else within arm's reach of the controls, I knew they all would be right where I was, doing the same thing.

The other ship struck the ground. At least, I thought it did. Could only see the flash out of the corner of my eye, and I had to make the decision in less than a second. Was that an explosion as they crashed? Or laserfire as they recovered?

I pulled out of the dive with inches to spare, the jagged edge of our dome bending the tallest blades of grass.

As I righted the *Rubeno*, the gravity released its grip and I breathed a fiery, unlabored breath for the first time in what felt like hours but couldn't have been more than a minute.

"Everyone all right?"

"More or less," Theon groaned as they stood.

"Bleeding," Merulo reported.

The word triggered screeching pains from my own tiny lacerations on my arms and face—not to mention my earlier stab wound—that had been muffled by the adrenaline.

Beaten, battered, and bleeding, just like our ship. But we were all right, more or less, as we left the wreckage behind and flew off in search of a safe harbor where we could lick our wounds.

CHAPTER FOURTEEN

I made my living with words. The show and the carnival drew people in, the freaks thrilled and terrified them, but my part, the narration that flowed from the deepest parts of my soul, made them believe that the universe was endless, that it still contained wonder.

The words came without effort, always the right ones at the right time, taking on a life of their own and bending minds to see the world from a different perspective than any they would have found on their own.

I should have been good at giving a eulogy, at making the grieving people before me believe in some purpose to it all, in something beyond this life where Cara could find the peace this world never gave her.

Yet I stood on the stage with my family, and my words failed me.

What was there to say, when any word of comfort would be a lie? Even to suggest we channel our anger and devastation into taking down VesCorp felt like a weak attempt to find meaning in a meaningless tragedy, and implied that we couldn't do it without her death to spur us on.

"The people of Hodge," I said finally, paraphrasing the faint memory of a passage I'd once read in a book, "Cara's people, they don't have funerals. When your farms feed the solar system, there isn't time or resources to waste on ceremony, land to waste on burials, or energy to waste on tears. Instead, they let the bodies nourish the land and, after the next harvest, the family finally mourns with a feast of food fed by the deceased."

Merulo scowled. "They weren't her people. We were."

"I know." I stepped off the stage and swung open the door to the cargo bay, revealing a carnival lit by twinkle lights strung down the midway and around the carousel's pegasus. "That's why we're taking their traditions and doing it our way."

Most of the booths had fallen over in the crash, and the rides sat at odd angles with holes torn in their sides, but we were never going to have another carnival anyway. Might as well use it to honor our fallen sister.

I'd spread the last remnants of carnival food on a big table—the freeze-dried ice cream and the candies with so little nutritional value that they never went stale—as a feast, and though we had no photographs of her, I took her image from the *Rubeno*'s security feed and used a projector taken from the spiral slide's interior to display it larger than life among the stars on the ceiling.

"She didn't deserve what she got," I said, leaning against the wall as a rallying speech forced its way onto my tongue. "No one deserves that except the people who did it to her, and they got theirs today. There's more of 'em out there who won't hesitate to do it to us or anyone else who tries to stop them. I can't make you—"

"We're fighting," Parthen interrupted, gazing at the overturned booth where she used to sell elephant ears, at her fish in their little bowls—thankfully equipped with their own gravitational fields to keep them upright during battles. "We don't have anything else left, so we're fighting."

I looked to Merulo and Theon, who echoed her sentiments.

"Then we fight," I said, raising my voice until it reverberated from every part of the *Rubeno*'s dented walls. "We fight with every iota of our strength, and we don't give up until we're dead. Maybe not even then. It'll be ugly, and we'll probably have to kill." I met Merulo's reproachful eyes and added, "But we aren't going to lose ourselves in the ugliness. If Cara's short time with us taught us anything, it's that there's always room for beauty in the darkness, and that even the most broken clock can be fixed with a gentle hand and a—"

The faint sound of laughter drifted from an indistinct direction, and five people flickered into existence on the midway, standing side by side in their black uniforms with the red trim. Lily stood on one end, hat pulled low over her face. The others might have been the same we'd dealt with earlier; I didn't care either way, and stepped forward to confront them.

Merulo and Theon marched beside me but Parthen got to the soldiers first with a well-aimed throw of a metal ice cream scoop. The one she hit dissipated, only to return a few seconds later with a wicked grin on his face.

"You think we're that naïve?" he asked with a laugh.

The woman in the center, the shortest of them all but possessing an unmistakable aura that indicated she was their leader, nodded to the thin brunette person at her side. "This here's Maerian," she said. "They conjure up images in their mind, throw 'em out into the real world. They're our little genderqueer illusionist."

I tensed as she stepped closer to me, and grabbed a metal pole that had once held up a canopy.

"Won't be needing that," she said, reaching out to poke me in the chest. She flickered, like an image on a malfunctioning screen, only becoming solid when she broke contact. "Can't hurt each other. Not like last time." She patted the array of throwing knives strapped to her legs. "Fun as that was, we're just here to talk."

Merulo dropped to the ground, sniffing loudly. "They could be nearby."

"I don't hear anyone," Theon said. He beckoned Parthen to his side anyway.

"Mae's good," the blonde leader boasted. "They can cast their apparitions across galaxies, if they want. No way of knowing where we are, whether they're transcribing our words and speech in real time or just putting on a puppet show while the real Billie and Friends sneak up behind you."

I didn't give her the satisfaction of seeing me look over my shoulder, though I did check the reflection in the spiral slide's mirrored panels. Nothing.

"But you know all about puppet shows, don't you Jackie? Been the star of one for a decade now—"

"Get off my ship."

She pretended to consider it. "You know what, I think we'll stay. You know Lily, of course, but have you met the boys?" With a flourish of her hands, Billie motioned to a hulking bear of a man. "Dekker, shapeshifter extraordinaire. Heals remarkably fast, too. You can barely see the marks your little furball left."

Merulo gave a low growl.

"And this," she purred, running a hand down the arm of a tall, chubby man with fire in his eyes, "is my Saul. He's the reason you might want to hear me out."

The man extended a hand that glowed from within before it erupted into flames that danced on his fingertips. Big deal; I could set his whole body on fire if I wanted to.

"Saul can alter the temperature of the air, change up its chemical composition and all that good stuff," Billie said with a smile. "I'd hate to see what would happen if Saul ever got into your fuel stores, here in your safe little cavern behind the waterfall on the southern side of the tiny little island that no one could ever find, way out in the ocean exactly fifty-point-nine miles from the coast."

Merulo took off to check the perimeter. Didn't blame him, but I didn't think they were that foolhardy, either.

I looked to Lily, hiding behind her lowered brim. She wouldn't make eye contact.

"What are you doing with these people, Lily? This isn't you." Even if Cara had said she was playing double agent, I couldn't tell for sure.

"She's doing right by her kind," Billie answered for her.

Something about that woman irritated me. "Do you ever let your people talk for themselves?"

"I could ask you the same thing." She pointed at Parthen and Theon behind me. "And what the hell is this? You gotta hold the girl and comfort her when the big scary soldiers come in? She can't fight, or what? Let me tell you this, girl, you're stronger than any man in this ship—"

"What do you want?" I snapped.

"Me? I don't want a thing."

"Then get out—"

"Diantha, on the other hand, would like to talk with you."

***

VesCorp didn't take kindly to Vespi 3-14's last rebellion, and delighted in depriving the already dry moon of water. Crops withered to crumbling brown stalks; grasses disappeared almost entirely. Only a hardy, thorned plant in Diantha's garden seemed to withstand the drought, but she warned against eating its toxic berries.

Yet somehow, the people stayed hopeful. Maybe growing up the way I did had ruined that part of me, but I couldn't imagine loving a place so much that I'd stay there and die with the hope that something would change.

Nothing would change unless *we* changed. Stopped trying to take down the government without a real plan. Diantha's idea to seed the clouds was a good place to start, but it had ended up ruining everything.

I awoke in an empty bed to the sound of Diantha crying as she put on her good blue dress. Her hair stuck out in all directions, but beads and clips in it suggested an elaborate style had been attempted.

I came up behind her and put my chin on her shoulder. I'd never seen her cry. "What's wrong?"

Her answer came as a grave whisper. "My propane is gone. They used it to attack the mines." She waved out the open window to the dying world. "I did this. It should have seeded the clouds, brought rain. Not destruction."

Before I could even begin to argue, she had pulled away from me and wiped her eyes.

"But I'm going to fix it," she said with a resolute air, her voice only slightly constricted by tears.

"How?" I asked, knowing in the pit of my stomach that I wouldn't like it.

She stepped in front of a mirror to torture her hair into submission. "Did I tell you that Garon is looking for a wife? And his advisors say marrying a moon woman would be good for his image."

I crossed my arms, trying to appear angry to hide my growing devastation. She didn't have to say it, but I let her.

"So I'm going to offer myself in exchange for water and food for my people. It's the least I can do."

My world dropped out from under me.

I hadn't been on Vespi 3-14 much longer than a month, but I wanted to spend the rest of my life there. With her. I could clearly see my future before me—marriage and children and a home—but the illusion began to crumble.

And the worst part was that I couldn't be mad at her because I would have done the same thing. How could I hate someone for being noble and self-sacrificing? It only made me love her more.

"It won't be forever," she told me. "Just long enough for me to be accepted as their queen, then you can come and infiltrate the Castle with the others."

"Others," I muttered numbly.

"I want you to go out and find the other freaks. Bring them to Vespi. I've been in contact with some people up there, and I think I know a way to take them down."

She began detailing a plan to destroy the Castle from the inside, and speaking with only a slight quaver of emotion. How long had she had to get used to this idea? Why hadn't she let me in on it earlier?

"And of course I'll be helping, but this is really just Plan B. Hopefully I can kill Garon at the coronation."

"You're really doing this."

She looked me in the eye and gave a solemn nod. "I really am."

"And what if something goes wrong?" I asked, my voice rising. "What if someone realizes that you're working against them and—"

But she had thought of that, too, and calmly handed me a small box. A wireless receiver.

"I'll sing to you," she said. "You can set your ship's clocks to my time and I'll sing to you, same time every night. If I don't, you'll know something is wrong and you can come and rescue me." She put her arms around my neck and smiled, doing a good job of hiding her emotion.

Wish I could say the same for myself.

"I love you," she lied.

CHAPTER FIFTEEN

Water poured from above in thunderous sheets, forming a thick and sparkling curtain at the mouth of the sprawling cavern. The sky outside, visible through a thin slit on the side between rock and water, showed no evidence of enemy ships, but I wasn't taking any chances.

I nodded to Merulo. "Should have more than enough fuel to circle for a few hours and still have plenty to get back to the mainland later."

"Think it'll take that long?"

I shrugged. "I don't think it'll take more than a minute. She makes some plea for a truce, or whatever she's going to say, I tell her no thank you, and we go back to fighting. And hopefully this is a trap and we can take out some of her army." Even as I said it, I knew I couldn't kill again. The image of me setting that person in the lab on fire would haunt me forever.

Theon raised an eyebrow, most likely reading the doubt in my mind, and I preempted his question.

"And no, I don't think talking to her will change my mind. She's torturing and killing people. No amount of pretty face will change that." I stared at my boots for a moment, trying to believe my own words, then looked my crew in the eye. "Diantha's taken three of us. Cara with her lasers, Lily with god knows what sort of propaganda, and Pneuman may not be gone but he ain't here, either. I'm not losing another person to her, and I'm not gonna let anyone else lose anyone. So circle for a while, watch for danger, and I'll signal for you when she's gone."

With varying degrees of faith, they boarded the ship that scraped the roof of the dripping cavern. I stopped Parthen as she fell into line behind the others.

"I want you to stay."

"Because I suck at piloting?"

I smiled. "There is that, but no. I want someone else here in case it isn't a hologram."

The *Rubeno*'s door closed and her engines started up, her turbines stirring the dank, musty air. Tight squeeze, backing her out, but Merulo managed, even with his inelegant paws, and she parted the water around her hull before disappearing from view.

I peered through the gap, making sure they got off okay. The *Rubeno* had flown all right—more or less—after the impact, but her crushed front end contained some of her more integral equipment and I couldn't shake the feeling that she was worse off than we realized.

Parthen and I made one last circuit of the cavern's main chamber, using lights to illuminate the darkest corners and the black masses of bats contained within. Sprawling tunnels and passageways shot off into deeper sections of what had to be an expansive system of caves, but explorations the previous night had revealed only subterranean rivers and dead ends. No obvious way in, but something to keep an eye on.

"I know I'm I staying behind by default." Parthen's soft voice cut through the constant, irritating drip of stalactites.

"What are you talking about?"

She shrugged, burying her hands in her pockets. "You need Merulo to fly the *Rubeno*, and Theon's mindreading is useless against holograms or illusions or whatever you call what Maerian creates, and that leaves me."

I stooped to pick up a handful of pebbles from the cave floor. "I wanted you here because we're fighting an army of freaks. We're outnumbered, and if the worst happens, I want to have someone by my side who stands a chance against that." I pulled her hand to me and filled it with the pebbles. "You turn these into lava and throw it at a group of people, I bet you hit more than Merulo could claw in the same amount of time."

A small smile crept onto her face as she considered this. "Or I could turn the floor to water, let them fall in, and turn it back to stone with them inside."

I can honestly say I'd never been afraid of dying that way until just then. Never even knew it was an option.

"You okay with doing that, if it comes down to it?"

"No. But I will."

Good enough for me.

A faint figure in the center of the cavern caught my eye, fading in and out of existence like a specter. I recalled the first time I witnessed Diantha's ability to blend in with her environment, and couldn't be sure if this was an image projected from someone's mind or a real chameleon revealing herself.

I only knew it was Diantha, not the fancied-up queen but that barefoot goddess with the messy hair who had stolen my heart from my chest back on Vespi 3-14.

No, she hadn't stolen my heart at all. That implied petty crime, something done on the spur of the moment because the opportunity presented itself. She'd conned me, convinced me that I'd been waiting all my life to hand my heart over to her. I couldn't afford to forget that. No matter how she tried to look like the girl I'd fallen for, she wasn't. Maybe never had been.

I waited for her to fully materialize before standing in front of her. She beamed a smile filled with warmth and lies, and I tossed a pebble at her. Went right through her flickering white dress and pinged off the ground on the other side.

"No, I'm not really here."

"Just checking."

She looked so innocent, so sweet. On purpose, no doubt, but I struggled to understand how this face could have been the same one on the news, ordering an escalation of war. Had this face ever seen the misery she kept in the laboratories?

"I'm not gonna ask if you ever loved me," I told her.

"I did. I still do."

"No, you don't, but I'm not sure which is worse—being played from the start, or being betrayed. And I don't care why you kept it going this long. Did you like looking up at the stars and knowing there was a lovesick fool up there waiting for a sign that you were never going to send, or did you just want a contingency plan? If your people turned against you, that fool in the stars would swoop down and save you without a second thought?" I shook my head in disgust. At myself or at her, I didn't know. "Either way, it worked, and it really doesn't matter to me why you did it. I only care what you think you want from me now."

In an instant, her sunny façade crumbled, and she covered her face to hide her ugly, heaving sobs. "They *have* turned against me, Jack," she managed to say through the tears. Sounded real enough. "Just like I always wanted."

I looked to Parthen, who stood at the mouth of the cave, for confirmation that this didn't make any sense. She just shook her head, bewildered.

"All right," I said, crossing my arms. "You've got one minute to explain what that means and what you want. Then I don't want to see you again."

Betrayal lined her face, and she sat down with exhaustion on some invisible surface Maerian didn't bother projecting. "I'm supposed to die." Her every word trembled, saplings in a hurricane. "That was the part of Plan B I never told you about, that I've spent my life knowing I have to be killed for this war to end."

My chest tightened, and a lump pressed at my throat. Damn it. I still felt something for her. And what if she was telling the truth this time?

I sat on the floor beside her, wishing I could take her hand, take away her fear. "What are you talking about?"

"The universe needs a common enemy. Someone utterly awful to rally against. Me." The last word came out more as a squeak than anything else, and she wiped furiously at her eyes with no effect on the rivers pouring down her red cheeks. "I did love you, and I still do, but I've been trying to make you hate me so you'll be able to kill me. Be the hero, end the reign of Vespi and VesCorp, bring the 'verse together in the celebration of my downfall."

I don't know what I expected her to say, but that wasn't it.

I just stared at her. Whether true or not, how do you even begin to respond to something like that?

"The only thing I *want* from you," Diantha said, brushing her hair from her face and narrowing her eyes into a bitter glare, "is for you to let someone else be the hero. My army is stronger than I thought they would be, and I'm afraid they may kill you."

"Jack," Parthen called out. "We've got company."

I left Diantha, instantly regretting ever agreeing to this meeting, and sprinted to the waterfall.

Three ships circled like vultures, high above the defenseless *Rubeno Mardo*.

"Call 'em back," I told Parthen. "They'll pick us up and we'll go on as planned."

Diantha appeared at my side, her hands clasped as she pleaded for me to reconsider. "You'll die."

Parthen hesitated with the comm halfway to her mouth, glancing at Diantha beside me. "Are you sure? What if she's—"

"The Diantha I knew wouldn't let a single person suffer, even for the good of billions."

A chill swept through the cavern, an ancient wind from the depths of the planet. Maybe I shouldn't have said that in front of her. Maybe I could have feigned agreement to gain an advantage. At the moment, I didn't care. The bridge had to be burned sooner or later, and I *was* a firebreather.

"The Diantha you knew never existed."

I swear I felt her breath on my neck.

"I don't *want* you to die," she informed me, dropping the star-crossed lover mask in favor of the ruthless general. "But you will. You all will, starting with your crew and your precious little owl floozy."

I spun around and looked her square in the eye. "I'm not afraid of you."

"You will—"

"Yeah, I will be. I'll rue the day I ever laid eyes on you, the moment I did whatever I did to piss you off, and every word I said to encourage you to liberate anyone from VesCorp's grasp. Guess what? I already do. I hate myself for being so naïve to think our time together was the best time of my life."

Our laser glares fought for dominance, our heaving breaths the only sound breaking the stillness of the cave.

"I do believe you had good intentions once," I told her, "but the woman I loved is dead, and I am going to avenge her death and destroy VesCorp in her memory. I don't think you're redeemable and I won't waste my time trying to convince you to change, but if there is any shred of decency left in you that you think is worth saving—if you think you deserve to rot in prison instead of burning in a hell of your own making—then you need to start acting like it."

I pointed to her vultures.

"Call them off."

She turned to an unseen person. "Do it."

Not even for a second did I believe she was calling them off.

***

She fell.

Didn't struggle, didn't fight, just fell from the sky like a shot bird and splashed into the ocean.

My ship. My crew. My *everything*, sinking into oblivion.

I launched myself through the waterfall, scrambling down to the shore and flinging off my vest and shirt in anticipation of diving into the ocean after them.

Forget that I couldn't swim, forget the sharks, forget the war raging in the sky overhead. I had to go after them.

A hand grabbed my shoulder, jerking me back as my toes touched the first lapping waves. Parthen.

"Don't." She ran in front of me, putting out her hands to stop me. "Just don't!" she shouted through tears. "This is a suicide mission; let me help you."

Shaking, she removed her shoes and socks and took a tentative step onto the ocean. The water hardened into stone under her foot, a sturdy column extending to the sand below.

She walked with caution, as if expecting her powers to fail with each step and send her plummeting to a watery grave, but picked up speed as she headed in the direction of the splash. I followed, taking care to place my weight in the center of her small footprints. The thin, almost wispy stone pillars stretched into the darkness below, but I had no indication of how strong they were.

Every footprint, every second, brought us closer, yet every second it took us to reach them was a second longer they were struggling to stay alive. Did they have an air pocket in the sinking ship? Did her doors open to give them an escape route?

A mirrored fin stuck up on the horizon. The *Rubeno*'s. Another bit of hull sat a few hundred yards from it. She had shattered on impact, or maybe in mid-air.

Suddenly, I didn't want to know, didn't want to see the wreckage of my life. What if they were dead? What then?

At least we could survive this way, walking the miles to shore to find a town where we could buy a ship and… and what? We had nothing without them. We *were* nothing.

Parthen took off running as we neared the crash site, her feet pounding the water and sending jagged stone sprays into the air.

Why she wanted to get there so fast was beyond me. It had been too long. They couldn't have survived…

She looked back at me, her face red and wet, before leaping into the water.

I ran to the edge of her footprints. Though the oceans of Vespi sparkled with an unpolluted clarity, most of the *Rubeno Mardo* had already sunk past the sun's reach, leaving only a few torn segments near the surface.

A gaping wound in her hull exposed my quarters. I'd never sleep there again. Never do anything in that ship again.

The receiver was in there somewhere. I don't know why, but the thought of losing that memento of a lie hurt more than losing the ship.

Parthen should have come up by now. Could she turn the water to breathable air?

What if she couldn't? What if I was the last one?

"You just signed your death warrant!" I called out into the air, not knowing if Diantha could hear me and not caring either way. The hatred burned too hot; I had to let it out.

"Your perfect universe isn't going to solve anything. People will just oppress and kill others for the abilities they were born with instead of the moon they were born on. Instead of looking down on people for their religion or the way they choose to live, it'll be the way they use their powers. This won't eliminate the need for war. It will only eliminate the need for weapons."

My eyes stung and watered. Damn salty air.

"We don't need new ways to kill each other." I wanted to yell, to scream this so loudly that she would hear it wherever she was, but my lungs refused and it came out as more of a whimper. "We don't need to kill, and I don't want to. But I will do whatever it takes to protect them from you."

The small size of the footprints prevented me from collapsing in an overly dramatic outpouring of frustration and devastation, and I had to keep my balance while the tears from the salty sea air shook my body.

The water stirred before me.

Bubbles. Then a sweeping hand just beneath the surface turned a large swath of water into a wooden platform that bobbed in the waves.

I leapt to it and helped pull someone out of the water. Theon. Soaked to the bone and gasping for a breath he couldn't catch, but alive.

Merulo came next, clawing at the platform with desperation as I pulled and Parthen pushed. We almost fell in a few times, but eventually hauled him up in a dripping mass of fur. Never thought I'd be so happy to see anyone in my life.

Parthen pulled herself up and threw her arms around Theon's neck as a glittering rainbow of betta fish swam away behind her. "I almost lost you."

He hesitated, a look of deep loss in his eyes, before kissing the top of her head. "We all almost lost each other." He stared at her, maybe reading her mind, maybe coming to the realization they'd been drifting toward for a while. With a shaking hand, he lifted her chin and kissed her. She made no attempt to pull away.

"What happens next?" Merulo asked, averting his eyes.

Despite the misery surrounding us, I had to suppress a laugh at his appearance. Reminded me of a dog after a bath, with his sopping mats of tangled hair.

I leaned back on my elbows, staring up at the sky to keep watch for enemy ships. Not like we could do much if they came. "We find a way. Back to the mainland, into the Castle, free our people."

"And then?"

"If we survive that, we expose the truth about VesCorp. Up to the people whether or not they believe us and demand change, but we do what we can."

I made it sound so easy. Just find a working ship in the middle of the ocean and go save the world.

"That's not what he meant," Theon said. "What happens after? Where do we go, what do we do?"

After? Who could possibly think about that?

People with hope, I supposed. Better people than me. I hadn't had a single serious thought of the future since Diantha's last speech. Just wasn't a future to think about anymore. Not for me, anyway.

A bird flew by overhead. Too high to tell the color or species, but it might have been one of the ones we brought here, for all I knew.

It probably had never considered life outside that little cage. Not in any serious way. Didn't want to risk hoping when every disappointment hurt more than the last. What did the bird do after? Did it find a way, or wander aimlessly through a purposeless life waiting for a predator to come along?

"After," I said with a sigh, "we go back to before. We never thought the *Rubeno* and the carnival would come our way. Thought we'd have to live lonely, miserable lives existing without reason. It's gonna be like that again, maybe for a long time. Then one day, we'll find the smoldering wreckage of our father's ship, shine it up real nice and put in a new engine, and we'll head out into space to find our after."

CHAPTER SIXTEEN

I only closed my eyes for a second, and woke under a sea of stars. I guess I felt safe, sleeping on a beach out in the middle of nowhere. Safe—or maybe just exhausted—enough to let myself sleep, if only for a little while.

The others had succumbed as well, and I allowed myself a moment to watch them before the stress of the real world broke through my peaceful, half-awake fog.

Parthen and Theon in each other's arms, Merulo curled up with a paw across his snout. My crew, safe for now despite all the universe threw at us.

My earlier vow to end Diantha stuck in my head. Could I really kill her, if it came down to it?

People had died from my actions before. Even if I didn't blame myself for Cara and the pilot of the little ship on Rouze, I could think of two ships that crashed recently as a direct and purposeful result of my actions. Enemies, and I didn't know them, so that somehow made it feel... less awful that they died. I didn't think I could kill someone I knew.

But did I really know Diantha anymore? Had I ever?

A dark shape appeared in the sky, blocking out a patch of stars. My stomach gave an involuntary lurch, but no ships, to my knowledge, had wings that could flap with such absolute grace.

It moved in silence, soft feathers dampening the sound as it headed out to sea, but lingered as if waiting for me to follow.

I did. Call me illogical, call me gullible—I've called myself far worse—but I couldn't live with a distrustful mindset. I needed to trust that Lily meant us no harm, needed to know that living in close quarters with a person for years gave me some insight into their true self. If I let myself believe she really had abandoned us in favor of the enemy, that would be the death of my ever trusting anyone again, and I couldn't live in that kind of loneliness.

And so I followed her out to the wooden platform, relying on the light of the stars and a handful of Vespi's moons—maybe one of them was Vespi 3-14—to illuminate the trail of footprints that would be there long after any of us.

She stood on the border of two glimmering skies, one real but unattainable and one a watery illusion within arm's reach, her wings draped around her shoulders. She had shed the uniform of a soldier in favor of what first appeared to be an outfit made of fur, though a closer look revealed a layer of tawny feathers covering her body and ruffling in the breeze.

She turned away when I stepped onto the platform, hiding her face in a way that gave me pause. Lily, shy and vulnerable?

"How do I know you're real?" I asked softly. When she didn't answer, I reached out to touch her wing. Solid. Warm. "Are you still mad at me?"

"I was never mad at you."

"Right. You left the only home and family you ever knew to watch over a woman you never met, who you admitted needed no protection, because you loved me so much."

She turned to me. Two enormous eyes peered out from a feathered face as flat as a dinner plate. Her nose and lips formed a

165

sharp, hooked beak, though her cheeks and chin still showed the curves of human anatomy.

I must have recoiled—out of surprise, not fear or repulsion—and she shook her head in disgust. Her wide eyes remained locked in a forward facing position, but she looked like she wanted to roll them.

"I only left," she muttered, the two parts of her beak clicking together at the sounds that required lips to produce, "because it hurt to stay. My face was starting to change. I didn't want you to see me like this."

That wasn't the real reason. She hated that I still held a candle for Diantha.

But I played along. "See you like what?"

She motioned to her face and body. "I'm an owl—"

"Will you stop saying that?" I snapped. "You're not an owl, Lily! You're a woman. You might have wings and talons and a beak, but you're a woman. A strong, smart, beautiful woman. You're an angel."

For half a second, her armor slipped, and she almost let herself believe that. Then she crossed her arms, a wicked scowl narrowing her eyes to almost human proportions. "I'm trying to tell you there'll be a new ship here for you by morning, and how do you thank me? With some sappy speech—"

"You're giving us a ship?"

She shrugged, her wings flapping out involuntarily. "I can't promise anything fancy, but it'll get you to the city and it can't be traced back to me, so…"

"Why?"

"Because they said they could fix me, but they stuck me with needles and put me in a tank." She tried to stay calm, to speak as if giving words to the trauma didn't make it hurt all the more, but her voice started to crack. "They changed me so I have control over when the wings grow in, but it doesn't fix the face. It's always like this; always an owl. Their process didn't work for me, and they were going to clip my wings and throw me out of the city."

Tears welled in her eyes and spilled over, soaking into the tiny feathers lining her face.

"Because they only let me live so I could give them information on you and your ship, but I can't let them hurt you anymore."

Not having a clue what to say, I reached for her hand. She pulled away, curling her talons to her chest.

"So you're coming back with us?"

The image of Lily and I sleeping side by side on the starlit beach flashed to my mind and left me lightheaded and breathless. Last time I felt like that... No, I'd never felt like that before. Not even with Diantha.

And then Lily had to go and ruin it.

"No."

"What?"

"I'm not coming with you. I can't. Diantha would figure out where I went, undo what I've done—what Cara and Ruby did—to help you at the Castle."

Left unsaid were the words "and I still don't trust your judgment when it comes to Diantha," but her face said it all.

Couldn't blame her. I'd wavered over Diantha's trustworthiness too much, and even though I was fully committed to ending her reign no matter the cost, I probably wouldn't have believed me, either.

"We'll need you on board. The ship will need a pilot."

"Oh, please. Did you see the dive you recovered from?"

I raised an eyebrow. "Did *you*?"

"Cara hacked Diantha's system. I've been keeping an eye on you. Point is, you don't need a pilot."

"We need you."

She stared at me, waiting for me to change the pronoun and admit that it was me who needed her. I didn't think it needed to be said, the way I was looking at her. I thought she knew, but I guess I was wrong.

"The ship will be here by morning," she said, nudging my arm with her wing. "Don't get yourself killed, okay?"

I smiled. "I'll try."

"See you at the Castle."

Lily backed away, stretching our eye contact for as long as possible. When her heel reached the edge of the platform, she gave a small wave and disappeared into the sky with a hushed flutter.

She knew.

***

Lily said she couldn't promise anything fancy, and boy didn't she.

The ship arrived in the middle of the night in a thunderous sputtering of propellers hitting the water. Tiniest, most pitiful vessel I'd ever set eyes on, and the first rays of daylight did it no favors. I was surprised it even had autopilot.

Hell, I was surprised it had seats.

I rapped my knuckles against its hull, careful not to hit too hard lest the moth-eaten rust give way. It actually felt sturdier than it looked, though how well it would fly was anyone's guess.

"I never thought I'd think of the *Rubeno Mardo* as a large and luxurious ship," Parthen muttered. She followed my circuitous examination of the little jalopy and did her best to turn the rust back to aluminum.

"Will we all fit?" Merulo asked.

I leaned into one of the open windows. The interior of the *Mia Nubo*—as the peeling paint scrawled across its side called it—consisted of four seats, two by two, and a rudimentary dashboard. No quarters, low ceiling... Not what I'd call a ship, by any standards. More like an ancient airplane meant to ferry people short distances across a planet.

"Yeah," I said, climbing into the front seat. "We'll fit, barely. Real question is whether it'll lift us."

Loose sheets of paper filled every spare inch of the ship. Shoved between the seats, piled in the paltry cargo space in the back, all covered in a scrawling script.

I couldn't remember the last time I'd seen handwriting other than my own. And on analog paper, to boot. Guess my habit rubbed off on Cara, because the little ship's rusted seams almost buckled under the pressure of all the notes and books stuffed inside its narrow space.

"Diagrams of the Castle," Theon reported, flipping through a sheaf of pages on the co-pilot seat, "instructions for shutting down the tanks, profiles of the soldiers and their powers... Hmm. Apparently teleportation is exhausting; after one or two trips, you need time to recharge."

"And communicating with animals only works on mammals for this person," Parthen added, leaning in beside him to leaf through another pile. "Where'd Lily get all of this? And why paper?"

"Cara," I said with a smile. "Paper can't be hacked, can't be remotely altered. She's got our back. Always."

A light and airy sensation filled my body, lifting the oppressive darkness in my chest and loosening the knots in my gut. Hope, I think they used to call it, back when people had something to hope for.

We wedged ourselves into the ship, securing the flimsy safety belts, and I fired her up.

Not a smooth takeoff, with the Mia's props struggling and sputtering like an asthmatic cat hacking up a hairball and the whole ship teetering from side to side. Pretty sure we almost went down a few times, and though no one uttered a word of doubt or warning, once we stabilized there came an audible release of our collectively held breath.

Almost peaceful, flying through the wisps of clouds with what remained of my crew, though as we gained altitude and visibility increased, the sight of the city hanging in the distance gave me an uneasy feeling. No time to waste admiring the view.

"What's the plan?" I asked Theon.

Papers shuffled behind me. "According to Cara, the only way in without permission—other than storming the gates, which she says we 'don't and will never have the numbers for'—is from underneath."

"Same way we left it?"

"Different hatch, other side of the plate, but yeah." He flipped through pages, swearing under his breath.

"There are so many labs," Parthen said. "Dozens of them, each with so many tanks. We might not have the manpower to save them all, let alone the time."

Merulo and I exchanged a glance. Could we leave people behind? Could we live with ourselves after, even if we prevented anyone else from experiencing that misery and torture again?

A sadness came into his eyes, and he pleaded with me. "Not saving *is* killing."

I sighed, knowing I would have made the choice eventually. Best to plan for it in advance rather than scrambling during the siege. "You heard him," I called into the back. "We're saving 'em all, so find the time."

As we left the open ocean behind and flew over land dotted with tiny towns, ships began to pollute our empty sky, the sporadic swarms growing thicker as we got closer to the city. I held the unfamiliar controls with a tight but awkward grip, hoping the peculiar little *Mia* wouldn't draw too much attention.

"So we enter through a hatch under the Castle..." I prompted.

"And there's a lab—a bigger, backup lab, from the looks of it—twenty floors up," Theon said. "They shouldn't be expecting us, so there'll be people there. Scientists and soldiers. A few floors above that is some sort of control room. We have to go there and deactivate the tanks, which we'll probably have to do simultaneously while we deal with the soldiers..."

His groan, though muffled behind his hands, adequately summed up the frustration and anxiety we all felt.

How dare we think a handful of sideshow freaks could possibly accomplish something of this magnitude? Breaking into the center of universal government and dismantling the status quo from the inside… Where did we get the nerve to dream this big?

"We'll figure it out," Parthen said to Theon. "If some of us stay and neutralize any threats, then someone can go up to the control room and—" She cut herself off. "Jack."

I saw it, too. A pair of military ships set apart from the swarms over populated areas. Patrols.

I dropped the *Mia* a few hundred feet and slowed down, trying to take on the appearance of casual vacationers traveling between cities. Definitely not an army of anarchists en route to the Castle. Nope, not us.

The ships followed, pulling close on either side of us. They were only midsized vessels, about the length of the *Rubeno*, but they dwarfed us. If they wanted to take us down, nothing we did could have stopped them.

"They're just checking us out," I said, peering into their cockpits. One person in each. If they'd been looking for us specifically, they'd have had more people to man the many cannons jutting from their sides.

One of the pilots must have recognized us. I saw his hand move toward his trigger, and a missile blazed from his ship.

I tried to execute a sharp turn but found that the *Mia Nubo* was about as maneuverable as a boulder. In a panicked rush, I pressed an unlabeled button on her dash, hoping for something useful. A cloaking device, or maybe an ejector seat.

The *Mia Nubo* gave a horrific shudder that threatened to tear her apart, and then something screamed away from us. I caught a flash of movement out the side window, and the other ship's hull broke apart in a rain of fire and shrapnel.

Oh, yeah.

We had *weapons*.

I left the defense to Merulo, who mashed buttons with a vicious grin while I tried in vain to dodge their attacks.

The world exploded with noise. Blasts from either side, thumps of metal on metal, crumpling paper as our bodies shifted and pressed against Cara's notes. The sounds of battle fought for dominance and merged into an almost silent cacophony of white noise.

I dropped further from the sky, skimming the long grasses and ducking under treetops. With Theon reading their minds and calling out their intentions, we evaded the military ships long enough for Merulo to do sufficient damage.

They peeled off in opposite directions. Wouldn't be the last we saw of them or their siblings-in-arms, but Merulo's grin gave me hope.

"You knock out their communications?"

He nodded.

"Good. So one of us goes to the control room…"

***

When viewed from below, the plates suspending the Castle and the city of Vespi exuded a sense of grandeur surpassing that of any other angle. The gleaming towers and electric skyscrapers that touched the clouds paled in comparison to the two-and-a-half-mile wide shadow hanging overhead, obscuring the sky as far as you could see in every direction and offering only a ring-shaped slice of sunlight between the plates.

Standing on the streets of Vespi, people could forget they were floating above the ground on a flimsy sheet of metal, but down below… I couldn't possibly forget, even for a second, that the shadow looming above me weighed millions of tons and could fall at the slightest fault of its artificial gravity.

If any security ships lurked in the darkness, they failed to make their presence known, and we hovered in near-silence save for the intermittent sputtering from the *Mia Nubo*'s engines. Couldn't even tell how close we were to the plate until the *Mia*'s roof made contact.

"This is it," I said as I lowered her a few feet, gritting my teeth to quell the nervous aching in my jaw. I swung my door open and peered up at the plate, squinting to see the faint edge of the hatch.

"Are we under it?" Merulo asked.

"Right under." I tapped a hand on the plane's yoke, having little confidence in the *Mia*'s autopilot. "Keep her steady, Merulo."

With that, I grabbed the frame of the blown-out window for support and pulled myself out of the ship, careful not to look down as I stood on the edge of the doorway. I cautiously put one foot on her wing, then the other. My every movement set the *Mia* off-balance, the wing pitching up and down and threatening to throw me, but she stayed steady enough that I could stand straight and reach the hatch.

I ran through the plan for the thousandth time. All of us through the hatch, take out anyone who needed taking out, then Theon and I up to the control room while Parthen and Merulo handled the rescuing of the freaks.

Sounded easy enough, but each step contained countless variables that we could never prepare for, and I couldn't help but noticed Cara had neglected to include anything about an escape in her notes.

In that moment, standing on the precarious wing of a ship hovering between a floating city and certain death a long way down, I had the audacity to think about after. Would the universe be thrust further into chaos in the wake of the revelations about VesCorp, or have a chance to settle down? Would I have a ship of my own, maybe another carnival or even a legitimate career? My future was blurry, the specific bits and pieces undefined. But I was pretty sure it had Lily in it, and that made it a future I wanted to see.

I put a hand to the hatch. Designed as an exit only, but I could fix that.

"Get ready to move," I warned them, and felt the *Mia* shake under my feet as they shifted to the front to follow me.

Putting my face to the cold metal, I conjured up a burning breath and exhaled. The fire leapt to the plate, turning it a glowing white that radiated a searing heat. Sweat pricked my forehead, but I fared better than the plate.

Liquid metal fell in huge, blinding drops, slowly tearing a hole in the underside of the Castle.

I breathed more life into the heat, my power finally proving itself useful for more than mere pyrotechnics, and, once the hole was large enough, I stopped to let it cool.

"I could have done that for you," Parthen said from below.

"Yeah, but then I couldn't show off like this," I said with a grin as I put my hands through the gaping hole in the plate. Still hot, but not scorchingly so, and I pulled myself up into a passageway cloaked in a blanket of night.

Theon came up behind me, then Parthen. When Merulo didn't appear, I peered through the hole to see him crouched on the *Mia*'s teetering wing, furred arms clutching the doorframe. Would the ship right itself if he altered its center of balance too much, or flip over?

"Give me your hand," I called down, wincing at the way my voice echoed down the corridor. Theon should have alerted us to anyone in earshot, but even the sound of my pants rubbing on the floor sent a surge of panic to my heart.

Merulo slowly stood and his paw gripped mine, his claws digging into my skin. He slapped his other paw onto the floor beside me and lifted his feet from the ship. It pitched violently but remained in the sky, waiting for our return.

Merulo pulled himself up and we felt our way along the passage, counting steps as Cara's notes instructed. My hand soon struck an invisible ladder. No room for elevators in the tight quarters, I guess.

I craned my neck upward. How high did the darkness go?

If I were designing the Castle, I'd have put the secret labs higher than the first forty floors. But then, so would most people. If any visiting delegates thought VesCorp was hiding something, they'd assume it would be hidden at the top. Who would look so close to the ground floor? Those were probably just supply closets.

Brilliant, really, and my limbs were thankful we didn't have to scale hundreds of floors.

We climbed into the endless black, a tiny point of light near the lab door on each level acting as the only indication of passing distance. How did they ever get the freaks down to the hatch? Theories flitted to mind, each more disturbing than the last, and I decided I didn't want to know.

The twentieth light came into view, and I stepped off the ladder and onto a sturdy floor. We all stared at it, the red light above the lock, knowing we had to do it but no one making the first move.

"How many?" I whispered to Theon. My shaky voice took me by surprise.

"At least a dozen scientists," he whispered back. "Soldiers outside, but not in the room."

"What about the…" What was I supposed to call them? Freaks? Experiments? "What about our people?"

"I can't hear their thoughts; they don't think inside those awful things."

"Can't you feel them?" Parthen asked. When he didn't respond, she pressed, "Pneuman helped you feel their pain last time. You cried."

"Yeah. I feel them. Of course I feel them," Theon said, though uncertainty colored his voice. "I just can't distinguish them too well. They're all crying out with the same agony. Could be one, could be a thousand. Can we get this over with?"

By the dim red glow over the lock, Parthen positioned her hand over the set of fingerprints found in one of Cara's books. She pressed down, and the ink lifted from the paper, adhering to her fingertips as a new layer of skin.

Parthen held her trembling hand up to the biometric scanner. What if it didn't work? Would it set off alarms? More terrifying, what if it *did* work?

The three of us put our hands on hers, and together we activated the lock.

The light turned green. The door slid open.

CHAPTER SEVENTEEN

Blinded by the sudden white lights of the laboratory, it took us a good second to react, to launch into action and set the plan into motion. It would prove to be the last second of peace we'd get for a long time, the last second during which most of us could truthfully say we had never purposely killed another human being, and a second I wish I'd had the wherewithal to savor.

Alarms screamed the instant we stepped into the lab. Whether they came on automatically or someone set them off, I neither knew nor cared. It only mattered that people in fluttering white coats were coming for us, and while their weapons were limited to surgical instruments and hurtled pieces of machinery, their armed counterparts wouldn't be far behind.

I let a breath of crackling flames into the air, more a scare tactic than an actual attack. I might have been made to be a weapon, but I didn't have to comply.

Merulo lashed out with less reluctance, responding to Theon's directions and staining the pristine floors with ugly red streaks. I don't think the scientists got in a single blow.

Parthen, Merulo, and I kept in a tight group while Theon broke off, kissing Parthen goodbye before heading up to the control room.

The scientists weren't genetically engineered. Wouldn't be hard to overpower them, but that wasn't the way we did things.

My flames kept them at bay while Parthen sent ripples of water through the tiled floor. Like we did last time, the scientists dropped to the level below. Had to hurt, but wouldn't kill them.

Then it was over, just like that, and the sounds of the gurgling tanks softened the oppressive silence.

A few bodies lay at our feet. I averted my eyes from the one with a burnt face.

Something pinged somewhere, and the gurgling stopped. The lights dimmed, running on backup power.

We wasted no time going to the freaks.

With the tanks shut down—*thank you, Theon*—their stasis had been interrupted, and the stronger ones began to thrash and struggle. The mermaid we'd seen before freed herself, launching out of the water with her powerful tail.

Parthen attended to her, making sure she could breathe air, and we started pulling the rest out.

Slow work. From my perch atop one of the tanks, hauling out a woman who kept turning invisible, I counted twenty-five other tanks. They must have moved more in from the other labs after our first visit. I desperately hoped this was all of them.

Some had obvious abilities. Body that turned to metal, extra arms, black feathered wings... I could only guess at the rest of them, and few were in any state to talk.

A door opened. A tidal wave of soldiers poured in. A good number fell right away, some through the floor, others at Merulo's hands. Lasers and bullets pinged off invisible barriers.

At first I thought it was Parthen, then I saw one of the freaks with his hands raised. So exhausted that he could hardly stand, but he was fighting back. Another let loose a burst of electricity, and the mermaid dragged herself across the floor and struck with poisoned spikes that seemed to stun the soldiers.

Turning my back to the barking demands from the approaching army, I went back to the last tank and helped a gasping man with leonine features haul himself out.

Seconds passed like excruciating hours. If they were still shouting, still demanding we step away from the tanks or they'd shoot, I couldn't hear them over the sound of my own heartbeat surging in my ears.

I spun to face the army with my extended family. Fewer soldiers than I'd expected, to be honest. Only about a dozen, guns raised but firing ineffectually at our invisible shields.

Theon's voice came through the comm clipped at my waist. "Jack, we got a problem up here."

What could have been wrong? The tanks were off, the freaks safely out. The fear of imminent death stepped aside to make room for the fear that we wouldn't get out of here, that our lives and the lives of our ancestors were all just a waste of destiny.

"Coming as soon as I can."

In my panic, I fired with a burning breath that crackled furiously, and everything devolved into chaos.

Some soldiers took flight, wings of varying styles erupting from their uniforms. Others took to the offense, hurling balls of electricity and striking with galvanized fists that hit the shields like cannonballs. We could only last so long, and had no way to flee.

Fire blinded me, the breaks between breaths too short to see anything more than flashes of movement. A man made of stone, a woman with the body of a snake, Merulo swinging his claws like windmills.

"Scorpion!" a voice—maybe the mermaid?—shouted.

Faking right, I swatted away a barbed tail as it lunged for me, and blasted its owner with fire. I started to get a little lightheaded.

"Bird!" Merulo called out.

I looked up, but too late. The force of the divebombing eagle person knocked me to the hard floor. The air left my lungs and I lay there gasping as a feeling of death closed in.

And here I thought Lily had said something about helping us, but I must have been mistaken.

Lily. Figured my last thoughts would be of her.

The cold floor grew warm beneath me. Hot.

Molten.

"Parthen," Merulo growled breathlessly, and pulled me to his island of tile in a growing ocean of magma that was lit from within as if by the fires of creation.

Though the soldiers fought with every ounce of strength and abilities they had, throwing out bolts of lightning and spitting poison, the magma still consumed them, pulling them in and dropping them through the holes it ate in the floor. With the others out of our way, the bird people weren't much trouble for Merulo. I saw the self-hatred in his eyes with every slash.

Parthen stood at the edge of the chasm, beaten and bloody but alive, feeble freaks in line behind her. Some looked on the brink of death. The unconscious four-armed man Merulo picked up may have gone over that brink. But we got our people out, and maybe some would make it.

Parthen put her arm around a woman whose legs alternated between solid and semisolid, supporting her as they followed me to the elevator. "We did it."

The disbelieving laughter in her tired voice proved to be infectious.

We did it. A bunch of sideshow freaks, knocking down the first domino in a row that would lead to the end of VesCorp.

Diantha couldn't torture anyone else, the Castle and the city would soon lose power, and people would realize something was wrong. Then when the video went out, they would learn the truth. It would only take one person shining a light into the right dark corner of VesCorp's closet to discover all the winged and extra-limbed skeletons hidden away in there.

Because of something we did.

The euphoria carried into the elevator, and though hordes of soldiers may have been waiting for us on the four hundredth floor, I couldn't stop grinning. I hugged my crew, hugged all the freaks.

After the longest ride of my life, the elevator lurched to a stop, and though we prepared for an attack, the doors opened onto a bedroom draped in gold and silks and devoid of any military presence.

I squinted at the heavy brocade walls for any disturbance in the pattern. Much as I wanted—needed—to believe Lily would pull up to the balcony with a ship and carry us all to safety like we'd planned, this was Diantha's room, where she had delivered her addresses. What better place to lie in camouflaged wait for us?

I pulled sheets from the bed and curtains from the doorway and wrapped them around the freaks for warmth and decency, wondering if there were any more pulling themselves out of tanks in other labs, only to be met by the soldiers that would soon make their way to this floor.

I went to the balcony, startling into flight a bird that had been sitting on the railing. The setting sun glinted against the orbiting fleets and glowed on the mirrored buildings, competing for brilliance with the artificial lights within. No ships—enemy or ally—came for us, and I wondered why Cara sent us here.

As I went inside, I noticed a potted plant sitting by the doorway. Same toxic kind she used to keep in her garden. I'd bet my life she used that plant to poison her husband; only question was whether she knew what she'd be using it for when she brought it from home.

Vespi 3-14. The moon where it all started, where our people had once taken refuge and repaired their broken bodies.

In the hidden mountain prison.

Cold, sickening dread washed through my veins. "There's another lab. We need to get a ship, go to Vespi 3-14…"

Before anyone could respond, a smirking illusion appeared at my side. Billie, with the knives.

"You're actually not gonna want to go down there," she informed us. "You have better things to do here."

Like going up to help Theon.

Merulo snarled.

"Don't engage her," I said. "She's just trying to scare us, but she's too scared to even show up in person. She's seen the carnage downstairs, seen what we're capable of."

"Yeah, I've seen you struggle to save a few people. But can you save a million?" Her cocky attitude slipped, and vulnerability took her voice in a vice grip. "I hope you can. I don't want this to happen."

I almost believed her, but could do nothing until I knew what she was talking about. "Don't want what to happen?"

"Jack," Theon said over the comms. "Really need you up here. Something went wrong; all the backups aren't coming on fast enough."

"They don't have to die," Billie said. "You can save them, and she can fix them. Make 'em like us."

"Who!" I snapped.

"All of them," she said, a tear sliding down her cheek. "You can save them. Look out the window, and make the choice, because the rest of the universe is next."

Billie disappeared, and I went to the window, half-expecting to see flames engulfing the city below.

For a moment, all seemed normal. Peaceful, even. People going about their lives among towering buildings, coming and going in massive ships, surrounded by fleets of flying armories. But still peaceful.

Then the lights went out. One by one at first, then in sections starting from the inner ring and spreading outward as the power went down.

The artificial gravity systems failed next.

And then the city began to drop from the sky.
Because of something we did.

CHAPTER EIGHTEEN

Its wires snipped, the shining jewel of Vespi dropped from its place in the sky with alarming, heartbreaking speed. My soul died a little bit with every foot it plummeted. At least we were too far away to hear their cries of terror.

But there would be time to hate myself later. "How do we stop this? And 'we can't' isn't an answer."

Everyone stared, crowding the tiny balcony to watch the warships scramble. They didn't have anywhere near the time or capacity to save them all.

"Come on!" I snapped, the anger in my voice directed solely at myself. "I don't know the math, but I figure we've got a few minutes before their fall ends in a really fast stop. What can we do about it?"

Parthen pulled herself away from the balcony, covering her face in horror. "Okay, so the *Rubeno* had backup power, and she was just a little ship. A big corporation like this… it would be illogical not to have redundancies."

Something crashed to the floor in the bedroom. Merulo, thrashing and clearing off shelves with sweeping arms. "It did! Theon shut them down like the plan said!"

The urge to destroy, to throw and smash and stomp, ran hot in my veins, too, but I couldn't. No time.

"Then we find a backup generator, get it up and running again."

A vase shattered against the wall. "It won't work!" Merulo roared. "We overrode it! That's what Cara told us to do!"

He was right, of course, but it didn't sound like our meticulous Cara, overlooking a result as disastrous as this. Smart to disable the backups, prevent the Castle from recovering too quickly, but she never would have sent us in knowing what would happen and not having a contingency plan. Something must have changed since she died, making this part of her strategy obsolete and sending the city plummeting. Or she knew it would happen and thought she'd be here to fix it.

"They ain't dead yet. We just have to figure out how to keep it that way."

"We aren't falling," the mermaid pointed out, still gasping for air but looking less distressed.

"She's right," Parthen said finally. "*We* aren't falling. The Castle's gravity has its own power source. If we can find it and hijack it—"

"Protect them," I said to Parthen, Merulo at my side as we launched out the door and down an empty hall lit by dim, emergency lighting. "Everyone is probably at the front gates, guarding against enemies they don't know are already in." I didn't bother lowering my voice. Our racing steps and Merulo's bloody footprints would lead people to us anyway.

We found an old stairway, long since abandoned in favor of the elevators and hidden away behind an architectural feature in the wall, and we began our ascent.

My chest and legs cried out in pain as I ran faster and harder than ever before, counting each step, each second. Counting down to an unknown time. What if they had already hit the ground? How long did it take to fall from the sky?

Theon met us on the way down. "It's falling—"

"We know. Go help Par with the freaks."

Merulo kept pace with me, bounding up flight after flight on all-fours with considerably less labored breathing.

"This isn't your fault," he told me.

"I say it was?"

"Your face did."

I chose not to respond, and time both crawled and flew by. We arrived at the top of the Castle after an eternity that passed in an instant.

With no time for stealth, Merulo broke through the locked door, setting off more alarms, and we found ourselves in a dark little office. Twilight shone in through skylights high above, but shadows cloaked the room.

A wall of glowing screens and holographic displays silhouetted a woman hunched over a control panel.

She flung her arms over her head. "Please don't kill me!"

"Not gonna kill you," I muttered, sliding her chair out of the way as I took her place.

I hadn't the faintest idea what any of the information flashing across the screens meant, but one hologram drew my eye.

It was a simple display, made of crude three-dimensional models, but it wasn't hard to figure out that the floating disc represented the Castle and the rapidly descending plate below it was the city. Nearer to the ground than I liked to see.

"You know what all this means?" I asked the woman, nodding to the controls.

She removed her glasses to wipe her eyes. "There's nothing I can do. It's receiving some power from us, but it's only enough for me to keep it upright."

"What good does that do?" Merulo asked.

"Stops it from flipping." Her already small voice grew meeker, fearing our response. "Keeps people from flinging off and makes it easier to find the bodies."

I slammed my fist on the controls, then grabbed her chair and dragged her back. "We have power. You're gonna send it all to them. We fall, they don't."

She refused, shaking. "There's people here."

Not Diantha or Ruby, though, not anyone important, or she'd have said so. "The good ones are getting saved. Which side are you on?"

Merulo shot me a warning glance. What was I doing? Threatening a terrified girl, choosing to sacrifice one group over another? I never thought I'd have to make decisions like that. Definitely never thought they'd be so easy to make.

"I can make you like the others," she pleaded. "Able to control your gifts. I can fix you—"

"We ain't broken."

Someone laughed behind us. "Yes, we are." Lily. "I got a ship waiting downstairs," she said to Merulo. "Can you go load everyone up? I'll deal with the knucklehead here."

"Yeah." He motioned for the woman to follow him down the stairs.

"No," I called out. "I need her."

Lily disagreed with a silent nod to Merulo, who exited with the woman in tow. Why they saw fit to save someone working with *them* was beyond me, but I went back to the controls, determined to find a way even if I had to push every button and pull every lever on the damn blinking panel.

"It's too late, Jack," Lily whispered.

"Did they hit ground yet?"

"No, but—"

"Then it isn't too late."

"But we don't have time." She pointed at the screen. "There isn't time to stop them slowly enough. Stop them too fast, and it's just as deadly as hitting the ground."

She was right. I knew she was, but I couldn't believe it. Couldn't let myself believe my actions had led to the deaths of so many people.

"Sometimes we can't save everyone, no matter how hard we try."

I turned to her, squinting. Since when did Lilimeg Ascops believe in giving up? "How do I know you're real?"

With an exasperated sigh, she hooked an arm around my neck, pulled me close, and pressed her open beak to my lips. The sharpness of the edges startled me. I had no doubt about the damage she could inflict with that thing, but she made no attempt on my life, wrapping her wings around me in an embrace.

Never felt safer in my life. Never really understood the meaning of the word until that moment.

She held me—we held each other—feeling safe and afraid as the city of Vespi and all its beautiful, unique people succumbed to a death none of them deserved.

***

I could fly a ship. Anyone could fire up the engines and pull back on the throttle without crashing into the planet below.

But Lily could *fly* a ship, like no one I'd ever seen. The ship, be it the *Rubeno* or the new cargo ship she'd "commandeered" from some lovesick sap, came alive in her hands. It ceased to be an amalgamation of metal parts and cooling systems, thrusters and engines, and became a living being with a heart and soul. It danced among the stars, following her lead with a graceful daintiness alien to the other hulking masses of metal lumbering through space.

She owned that cockpit, yet her confidence didn't extend to herself in the way it usually did. She twisted uncomfortably in her seat, shying away from my gaze and picking at the feathers along her jawline.

"You look like an owl," I said, the first words either of us had spoken since the city fell. "What's wrong with that?"

She squirmed in her seat, as if trying to physically avoid my question as it moved through the air, and dedicated the entirety of her attention to outmaneuvering a microscopic piece of space debris.

I flicked on autopilot and used my foot to swivel her chair toward me. "There're worse birds you could look like. Vulture, toucan, them little guys that peck bugs and crap out of other animals' ears."

After a long pause, she lowered her head and said, "I don't want to look like any bird. I'm supposed to be the pretty one."

I knew better than to tell her she still was the pretty one, to compliment her beautiful eyes and long legs and confess that seeing her curves covered only by those soft feathers made my cheeks warm and my heart beat in double time.

"And what happens if you aren't pretty anymore?" I asked instead.

"Then I'm not anything."

I took her hand, letting my fingers trail along the lines of her palm. How did she not see it? How did she look in the cracked mirror every morning and only see the surface?

"You're the pilot. The smart one. The funny, outgoing, amazing one who makes us wonder why you keep us around because you could do all of our jobs so much better than we can. You're the Lily. And you're still the pretty one, even if you do look like an owl."

For a long moment, she said nothing, watching our hands and absorbing my words. Then she pulled away and went back to flying, shaking her head with a laugh. And that was the end of it.

Once out of Vespi's immediate orbit, the black cloud of warships thinned until it almost resembled the regular traffic of pre-war space. No one bothered patrolling the moons; they had allies, sure, but the allies took their weaponry to the front lines, leaving defenseless the people they fought to defend.

Sound enough strategy, since most moons and asteroids had little in the way of artillery or resources, making them undesirable targets for anything more than camping out to survey the real targets planetside. And probably why Diantha had gone unnoticed when she moved her operations to Vespi 3-14.

No way to tell what awaited us, but I had my crew and a ship, and we'd find a way.

"You asked me why I never tried to pull any of my tricks on you," Lily said suddenly. "I knew Diantha had played you the first time you told me about her. Someone like her, so dedicated to her cause and so hateful toward VesCorp, would never allow herself to be a part of it. You said it was a long con, and that she was the kindest and most pure-hearted person you'd ever known, but she supported the forced migration of the Lenians her first week as queen of VesCorp. It didn't match the person you knew, and I thought you would figure it out, but you never did."

I waited as she opened and closed her mouth without making any sound, her mind engaged in a civil war over whether to say the words screaming to be said.

"I couldn't stand seeing her break you the way I've broken so many men, but you loved her and I couldn't take that away. And that's why I never tried anything with you."

Not the words I wanted to hear, but then she didn't have to say them. I knew. We both knew.

She smiled at me, a barely discernible upturn of her cheek feathers and crinkling around her eyes, and a microscopic moment of happiness found its way into the cockpit before chaos came crashing down once again.

Shouts of distant horror echoed from the depths of the *Dorno Argenta*, our new ship, so similar in design to the *Rubeno* that I ran from the domed bridge to the cargo hold without giving thought to my direction or destination. I stopped at the top of the stairs, taken aback by the emptiness.

Well over a hundred people crowded the hold, most of them refugees from Diantha's experiments in varying stages of transformation. Some were freaks by birth, the genes passed down from the first generation, while others had undergone treatment to turn them. Lily had liberated most from the other labs—the ones I'd suspected Diantha had on other levels of the Castle—though some were soldiers from Diantha's army whom she'd coaxed over to our side.

All in all, easily the largest crowd we'd had on board in years, but still empty. Quiet. No rides taking up space, no music or lights or wafting warm aromas of food. Just masses of scared people, breathing as one in the echoic chamber amid the smell of rusted metal.

I scanned the crowd but saw no reason for the shouting, which had subsided by the time I arrived. Then my gaze landed on Merulo, cornering someone against the wall.

I stormed down the stairs. "Hey! What's going on?"

Parthen spoke for the group. "He attacked her."

"Who?" I asked, but then I saw her. The woman from the Castle's control room, cowering in front of Merulo. Her arm was bleeding.

I tried to convince myself that he wouldn't attack without reason, but at one time I'd have said he'd never attack, period.

"Wanna tell me what the hell's going on here, Merulo?"

"She's one of them." Rage stole the humanity in his voice, leaving it a rasping, feral husk. "Diantha's army."

The woman clutched her arm, pressing her back into the wall and trying to shrink into nothingness. Her eyes pleaded with me from behind crooked glasses. "I'm not," she insisted. "I worked in the labs a little, but I'm not... I'm not one of them." She glanced up at Merulo, then back at me. "Are you *sure* you aren't broken?"

I stepped between them, Theon and Parthen standing with a few others to hold him back if necessary, and confronted Merulo.

"We're about to land. Is this really the time to start something?"

He leaned close, his snorting breath hot on my face. "She changed. Became a beast when no one was looking."

"Anyone else see it?"

He snapped at me, his teeth missing my flesh by millimeters. "You don't trust me."

Damn right I didn't, at least in that moment, but nothing good would come from admitting it. Maybe some of us were broken after all.

"Look at her arm," he challenged.

Having never seen him in such a rage, I hesitated to turn my back. Did any trace of the man I knew remain in him?

"Look!" he hissed.

I knelt beside the woman and peeled her fingers away from the wound. Though covered in fresh blood, her forearm showed no signs of recent trauma. Only a faint scar ran through the blood, but even that seemed to fade the more I stared.

"Are you hurt?"

She just smiled, a malicious glint in her eye, and her arm began to contort beneath my touch. Muscles contracted, her limbs twisting. I didn't know whether to back away or try to help, transfixed by the process, and Theon had to pull me away when her muzzle sprouted fur.

"'Dekker, part of Diantha's personal security team,'" Merulo said through bared fangs, reciting something from Cara's notes. "'Shapeshifter, rapid healer.'"

The wolf stood on his hind legs and leapt for Merulo's throat, only to be thrown back against the wall and hit by simultaneous blasts of electricity and fire. I think the fire was mine. Didn't have time to think about it, but a lingering warmth coated my lips.

All available launched into action, pinning Dekker to the wall with every ounce of strength. I didn't doubt his ability to take the form of something larger and stronger, but for the moment it gave me time to think out loud.

"She's been Dekker all along." I looked to Merulo. "You saw her change, and you scratched her to prove she would heal?"

He hunched, panting calmly but ready to spring, watching Dekker snap at the newest members of our family. The lust for violence ran rampant on his face, the same I saw every time he fired at an enemy ship, except much stronger. Had he really seen the woman change, or did he concoct that story when she started to heal too quickly?

"But why would a spy reveal himself like that, Merulo?"

He stopped panting, stopped moving entirely, then turned his head to me with wide and frightened eyes that gave me my answer.

My world fell apart just when I thought the rebuilding process had finally begun.

He knew it was wrong, but could he control himself? Or would I find someone I cared about torn to pieces one day?

Like I needed more problems.

"Jack?"

Theon and the others strained to hold Dekker as he snapped and snarled.

They expected me to decide what to do with him, but how was I supposed to do that? Carnival problems tended to be limited to lack of money and excess of vomit—not every day I had enemy spies on board.

We had no choice except to kill him. Couldn't let him pass on the name of our new ship, or anything else that would aid in their finding and destroying us. Hell, with any luck, Diantha wouldn't know we were coming yet.

I looked at Theon, sending him thoughts of isolating Dekker in the cargo hold and opening the doors to the outside. "Spacing" him, they called it, or "airlocking." Awful way to go, with only a few reported instances, mostly during war or by pirates.

But what else could we do? We didn't have the means to keep him captive, nor the guarantee a more humane method would work. No way to know how fast he could regenerate.

Theon nodded, and I started ushering people upstairs, keeping some with the more offensive abilities close to the door in case anything went wrong.

Merulo caught on, and grabbed me by the shoulders, his claws piercing my skin.

"We don't have to," he said between snorts.

I couldn't tell if it was a plea for mercy or a threat, but it didn't matter either way. "We can't let him go," I said, throwing his massive paws off me. "He'll come back with an army and kill us all. And he can't stay here."

He backed off, looking alternately at his paws and the holes in my shirt, and the wild left his eyes as tears rolled down his furry cheeks. He didn't speak, but words had yet to be invented that could adequately articulate how badly he needed to not be a killer.

For a life dedicated to peace, to protecting and improving the lives of people and planets he hardly knew, his was stained with more blood than most. Be they enemy combatants or the leaders who polluted his home world, Merulo had killed more than I could count, and thoroughly enjoyed every one. We should all hope to find something that brings us as much utter joy as pulling the trigger of our cannons and blowing a pirate ship to shrapnel brought Merulo.

Living with that duality had to take its toll on his sanity. Couldn't blame him for needing to save someone, even someone who tried to kill us. Maybe he had smelled the wolf on her, or subconsciously noticed the way she seemed to recognize us. Either way, it was done and over.

I stood by what I'd said. Showing any mercy to that man would come back to hurt us, would turn the tides of the war toward Diantha, and I couldn't let her win.

But what good is winning if you lose what really matters? And maybe, if there was such a thing as karmic debt, sparing one life might be the start of making up for all those lives lost when the city fell.

I suspected I'd regret it, but I put my arm around Merulo and ordered the imprisonment of my first prisoner of war.

***

The rolling hills of lavender that once gave color and vibrancy to endless stretches of Vespi 3-14's countryside lay brown and dying like the towns it surrounded.

Maybe I only remembered it as the withered-but-hardy paradise where the sun never set and the skies clouded but never rained.

Maybe the perpetual sunshine had always burned as the years without precipitation desiccated the grass and the people.

I used to waste so much time dreaming of the day my ship would have the pleasure of entering this atmosphere again, of the life I would make with the woman I thought I loved. I'd have a little farm, she'd develop technology to make the farm sustainable, and we'd tell our children fantastic tales of how we fought VesCorp and gained sovereignty for all the moons and asteroids.

Now I couldn't imagine calling a single place "home." The only home I'd ever have was floating through the stars in an old cargo ship.

"Are you okay?"

I tore my gaze from the approaching landscape to see Lily eyeing me with concern.

"I'll let you know when I figure it out."

She pointed out the windscreen to where the dulled remnants of pink columns laid strewn across the ground, the last forgotten monument to the once great moon without a name. "So is that the famous marble city?"

"I guess it used to be."

Distant blue peaks jutted into the sky. The *Argenta*'s radar, a holographic display far superior to the old pinging screen on the *Rubeno*, showed a flock of ships circling the mountain range like buzzards. With no other ships marring the wide expanse of thin clouds, it was a safe bet they were guarding the second lab.

"I thought we'd set down in some of these ruins," Lily said. "Give us time to regroup, assess our new crew members, get a plan together."

And by "ruins," she meant villages. Villages filled with some of the nicest and most welcoming people the vastness of space had to offer. Villages that had never looked pretty but were somehow so much more than just ugly piles of rocks, now reduced to rubble.

A few neighborhoods seemed to have been spared the worst of the bombings, but I saw no signs of life.

"I should go down to the hold," I said, getting to my feet with a groan. "Say something. Been nearly an hour since my last incredibly inspiring speech, after all."

She laughed and saluted me. "Yes, go and address your army, General Jetstark."

I paused. "I'm not a general."

"You've got an army," she argued, "and you're leading the charge to end a war. If that doesn't make you a general, I don't know what—"

"Freakshow barker," I told her. "Nothing more or less than a guy who collects the misunderstood, says a few fancy words now and then, and, on extremely rare occasions, saves the universe."

I returned her salute and headed down to the cargo hold, giving an uneasy glance to Dekker on my way. Despite Parthen's repeated assurances that she and the other alchemists, as they were calling themselves, had encased him in the strongest material they could produce, the thought of him breaking free and the havoc he could wreak pierced my heart with constant nightmares. We should have spaced him.

He sneered through the small breathing hole. I didn't know if he could see or hear through the thick diamond shell, but I made a point to sneer right back as I passed.

Standing on the landing high above the floor of the cargo hold, I took in the soul-filling sight of people finding their purpose, discovering that others like them existed. They had regained most of their strength by this time, shedding the induced exhaustion of the tanks' sedatives, and cautious smiles graced some lips.

Probably the first time any of them had smiled in a long time. In my experience, freaks didn't have much reason to smile. Shunned, mocked, outcast by societies that didn't accept us. Even before we learned that we could fly or breathe fire, we were always the weird ones. The ones who used attraction for their own gains, who lived in seclusion because they knew nothing else, who dared to dream of seeing the stars up close.

Whether they were born this way or created, they all knew the feeling of rejection, of wanting from the depths of their souls to rise up and prove everyone wrong. I didn't need to rally them. Life had been rallying them for this mission long before I appeared on their radar.

"I want to thank you all," I said instead, my words taking on an imposing life of their own as they pinged off the walls. "There are other ways to make something of yourselves, less dangerous paths to find purpose. Any one of you could drop out, decide this isn't worth risking your life over, and our numbers would still be strong. But you didn't. Each and every one of you chose to stick with me."

The ship gave a shuddering lurch as we slowed to a halt and set down. Vespi 3-14 waited outside, in all her corrupted glory. One more sneak attack, one more rescue. According to Lily, Cara had sent the video files to Ruby for safekeeping. Assuming she was with her mother, we'd get them back and let VesCorp crumble.

The power of bad PR knew no bounds.

"No one would blame you for wanting out, least of all me. God knows this isn't the destination I ever thought my path would lead, and I would do anything to keep from having to do this. But I have to, and I would even if I was the only person in this ship. But one man can't defeat an army, and I'd get myself killed."

A hundred beaming faces looked up at me, some more human than others but each an invaluable asset not just to my cause but to the universe. It needed people like us. The strange and the wonderful.

"An army can beat an army, but we aren't an army. We're a family. An army will get you out of battle alive when all seems hopeless, but a family means nothing is ever hopeless. So thank you for joining the family."

CHAPTER NINETEEN

Nearly one in the morning, and the sun burned through the wispy clouds to pull the sweat from my skin. The planet Vespi hung in the sky, from this distance a peaceful blue and green marble faintly visible beyond the atmosphere, though news reports told of chaos erupting on its surface.

They called it an attack, warned ally planets to heighten security and screen every traveler to root out potential terrorists. Some planets cut off travel entirely, and brought their armies back to guard their home soil. There was only a passing mention of all the innocent people who lost their lives when the city fell. Maybe they'd get their names on a monument when the war ended. It'd have to be a pretty damn big monument.

"Maybe something carved in the face of the mountains," Theon said, joining me atop the *Argenta*. He sat beside me, wincing as his hands touched the searing metal of her hull, and leaned back against the bridge's dome. He was wearing Pneuman's souvenir freakshow shirt. "You found a pattern yet?"

I nodded, watching the ships crisscross the sky through the crevice in the rock formation that shielded us from their view. They circled the mountain at different altitudes and in different directions, but there was a moment, a brief second, when none of them could possibly see the entrance.

At least, we thought it was an entrance. Little alcove in the rock, covered by boulders and brush. A soldier had disappeared behind it a while back and never came out the other side. Barring any sort of portal technology, it looked like the way in to me.

"And you really think we can get through unseen?" he asked. "All of us in that short a time?"

"Just one of us. Lenore." I didn't even pretend to understand the physics of how xe did it, but Lenore, who identified as nonbinary and used xe/xyr pronouns, could bend the light around objects, make them more or less invisible. "We just have to get *xyr* there unseen. And then…" I let my sentence trail off. We had no inkling of what waited for us inside that mountain laboratory or how to destroy it. I only knew we had to try, had to hope we could end the experiments and bring the corruption to light. And if Diantha was in there… I didn't let myself think on that for too long.

"She is there," Theon confirmed. "Dekker must've been trained to resist mind-reading or something, but I've been able to get a little out of him. She's in there, with Ruby Marta, and she's planning something big."

Great. I let my head fall back against the dome.

"We'll figure it out," Theon said, though I had my doubts as to whether he believed it. "At least we have some intel. It's good you let Dekker live."

"Is it? Because I can't shake the feeling that this is all part of his plan. That he wanted to be kept prisoner so he could take us down from the inside. You get any sense of impending doom in his heart, Pneuman?"

Theon shook his head, picking at his fingernails. He looked as if he wanted to say something else, but didn't.

I dropped my volume to a near whisper, as if giving too loud a voice to the fear gnawing at the back of my skull would give it power. "What about the rest of them?"

He looked up. "What do you mean?"

He knew exactly what I meant. Just wanted to make me say it, make me hear the absurdity of my suggesting it.

"Are they all on our side? Have you heard any thoughts of betrayal?"

"No."

"Pneuman felt any—"

"These people believe in you," Theon snapped, standing up. "They'll give their lives for this cause."

With that, he disappeared into the ship, leaving me to devise infinite contingency plans for the siege. At least our family's vast and varied arsenal of skills gave me a lot to work with.

***

We walked as one, a mass of people seven wide and just as many deep, marching toward the mountain behind a cloak of bent light. Lenore, an anxious young person with dark skin that shimmered with an internal luminescence, led the steady and cautious charge, ducking behind every available tree or boulder on the half mile stretch of scorched grassland.

At my sides walked Jarry, who could turn himself to metal, and Arabel, a bird woman with an innate sense of direction. Further ahead were Esther, the autistic girl who saw into the past, Tavius with the extra arms... I hoped I'd memorized them all correctly, and I had to wonder if someone at the labs chose the abilities for them, or if it was random genetic chance that determined which powers arose in which person.

I could see them all perfectly. No matter how many times Lenore demonstrated xyr ability, no matter how strongly I believed in xyr, some part of me doubted that we were actually invisible from a certain point of view. And what about heat scanners? Radar? Maybe the circling sentries had no reason to turn their devices downward, being too concerned with the prospect of aerial attacks to bother with a few villagers.

Our plan wasn't perfect, but it was all we had at this point.

The craggy slate face rose into the sky, a sun-speckled empress looming over her domain. A deep crack in her base led into a shadowy passage with no apparent security measures. Whether this was an oversight in our favor or a luxury they could afford by having thousands of armed soldiers waiting just inside, we had no way of knowing.

Lenore crouched behind a boulder, looking back with uncertainty. I waited, feeling the weight of all their staring eyes, and watched for the gap in the pattern.

It came and went twice before I summoned the courage to give the signal and set off into the chaotic unknown.

Xe ran, feet skipping across the dead land like a gazelle evading the certain death of a lion's jaw, the rest of us scrambling in a desperate attempt to stay within range of xyr cloaking.

My toe hit the exposed root of a withered oak, and though I didn't hit the ground, the stumble made me fall behind as the sharp black wing of a sentry ship came around the mountain's peak.

Jarry stopped to pull me along, while the rest of them found shelter at the cavern's mouth. They could handle it fine without me, but my death would alert the army to our presence and ruin any chance at a surprise attack. And I didn't particularly feel like dying at the moment.

"Grippina!" I screamed, praying I had the right name.

The sky seemed to vibrate as our bodies dragged and bumped across the rough ground, only coming to rest when a rocky overhang blocked out the sun and the ships. The hand wrapped around my arm turned from an iron gray to its natural deep sepia as Jarry broke his connection to the magnetic field Grippina emitted.

We stood, pressing against the cool rock as the dozens of us tried to conceal ourselves in an area too small to fit all of us, and we waited.

No lasers, no soldiers. No sign that they were aware of our presence.

I raised my hand to signal to Merulo and the others in our hidden ship, who had stayed behind to keep the revolution alive in the event something went horribly wrong.

I looked to Lily and nodded toward the entrance, wishing we could afford to be stealthy but knowing we likely wouldn't get a second chance.

We fell into a practiced formation. Those with the ability for long-range attacks led the charge down the darkening passage, with the hope that we could take out any enemy combatants before they reached us, and those with more defensive powers stayed in the rear to protect the more vulnerable among us.

The passage grew narrower, boring deeper into the earth until the sunlight disappeared behind a twist in the tunnel. Quiet as we tried to be, the sound of a hundred simultaneous footsteps had to travel.

We came to a door. Metal, with a biometric scanner glowing beside it.

As I whispered for Parthen to come forward with her new fingerprints, the door clicked open on its own.

I pushed it ajar, and a dull glow filled the corridor as I peered into a laboratory.

Gone were the days of pristine white surfaces, shining metal, and the pretense that the operation was anything but a glorified torture chamber.

Centuries-old technology replaced the grand machines and panels of flashing lights. People languished in shallow tubs, hooked up to archaic monitors that ran on leaking batteries. Might as well have had the poor people floating in rusty barrels and been zapping them with short-circuiting wires.

Only a few people—scientists or soldiers or both, I couldn't tell—wandered the facility, dressed more like dirty cargo haulers than medical professionals and only occasionally looking up from their clipboards.

No one so much as glanced in our direction, and we paused, holding our collective breath. Maybe recon was a possibility after all.

Diantha swept into the room and stood on a rocky platform high above the lab, framed by ancient stalactites fifty feet long, and though I couldn't see her well from this distance, I recognized her in an instant.

Even without her gaudy, bejeweled gowns, even walking around in the uniform of a general with her hands behind her back and her hair smoothed into a bun, she somehow looked the same to me. Still that brave, funny girl trying to save her people.

She called out to someone, and two of her minions entered from an unseen chamber, dragging a screaming child to one of the empty tanks.

***

We must have been a sight, a seemingly unending river of bodies pouring out of the doorway in a glory of flames and wings, and though they wasted no time striking back, I dared to believe we had the upper hand this time. If they couldn't spare the manpower to guard the damn door, what chance did they have against us?

The world devolved into a blur of movement, noise, and pain. Flailing limbs and bursts of sparks, shouted commands and cries of agony, claws ripping and ice burning my flesh.

Dodging projectiles and dealing blows of our own, we moved toward the site where the bundles of wires converged in a mass of machinery cobbled together from a dozen different sources. The power core, the old one our ancestors stole. Take that down, and we'd finally put an end to the experiments.

Leading the charge gave me some peace of mind, as I knew with relative certainty that anyone in front was one of them and not one of us whose face I had yet to commit to memory, but it also gave me the brunt of the attacks. After a few seconds in the spacious torture cavern, I ceased feeling the individual blows as a single, blinding agony enveloped me. I never knew hair could sense pain before.

A body fell from above, landing limply at my feet. Not Lily. Some guy who looked like a bat. I stepped over him as his leathery wings caught fire, and elbowed someone in the face. Pretty sure it wasn't my fire.

Shrieks cut through the air, the echoes obscuring their source.

I turned around and for the first time saw the death in our wake, the bodies a tangled, indistinguishable pile of them and us over which only a few battered souls continued to fight. While we tried to limit casualties, sometimes it was just unavoidable.

I'd be reliving this day for a lot of sleepless nights to come.

A path of molten footsteps drew my eye to Parthen and Lua, another woman with the ability to change the physical property of an object, fending off a fiery specter of a man. They furiously turned the air to water, the ground to ice, but his flames boiled it off into a choking steam that filled the cavern. He absorbed my flames with no ill effect.

Parthen stepped closer to him, the air between them in a constant flux of water and steam, letting Lua make her move for the power core.

The man of fire lunged to stop her, but was flung upward at the last second as Lily, setting aside her own safety, swooped down and carried him off like an unsuspecting field mouse.

All the chaos fell away as I watched, transfixed by the beautiful and tragic sight.

The angel turned phoenix, the flames spiraling high into the inky night of the cavern. She dropped him, and for a moment she hung in the air, the orange and yellow light of her blazing wings dancing across the walls' hidden facets.

And then she fell, tumbling through the air on limp wings.

Stepping on the dead and dying with no concern for the battles still raging around us, I ran to catch her, diving to let my body cushion the impact. The fate of the falling city flashed through my mind.

She hit with the force of a meteorite, knocking the breath from my lungs. A sudden, brief downpour from an unseen freak drenched us and extinguished her scorched feathers. Time and my heart stood still, searching for any sign of life and finding none.

After what felt like an eternity, she gasped back to life and I held her to me.

The lights dimmed and flickered before going out, plunging us into a starless midnight as the machines went down. Just like when we cut power on Vespi.

"We did it," Lily whispered, her voice a gentle wind in my ear. "It's over."

Over.

The very word sounded foreign to my ears. Could it really be over?

One of the most illustrious cities in the universe couldn't just fall from the sky without the public demanding an explanation. And with Ruby and the video evidence of what was going on inside the Castle, no way things could go back to the way they were.

Yeah, I could see this as a means to an end. Finally exposing the true purpose of VesCorp and how far the corruption in Vespi's government reached might give their allies reason to finally reject Vespi's control over them. The moons might not gain sovereignty yet, but maybe some basic human rights would trickle their way.

The overhead lights came back on, seemingly of their own accord. Dim, but enough to make out the outline of the dead and count the living standing among them. Only twelve of us had survived, and though I hardly knew the fallen, my heart ached for every brave soul who gave their life in a war that should have ended years ago. Even her soldiers deserved better. They never asked for this.

I let go of Lily and walked in an unfeeling trance around the cave, just looking at the bodies, committing to memory the faces of those we lost. I stared for a while, searching for something but not knowing what.

I looked up at the platform above, framed by the stalactites. Ruby Marta stood where her mother had been, the girl from the tank and several other children at her side. No sign of Diantha.

"She got away," I said, lowering my voice so Ruby wouldn't hear. "It isn't over until she's dead."

CHAPTER TWENTY

When I was a kid, I'd stare up at the night sky, imagining all the exciting and wondrous worlds orbiting each of the millions of stars, unable to sleep for the excitement of knowing that one day I'd get myself a spaceship and visit every one of them. My days would be filled with adventure. Dodging asteroids, trading with the locals, discovering new lands of fantastic creatures never seen by man…

My romanticized vision of space travel failed to take into account many of the day-to-day realities of wandering the infinite. I never considered where I'd get money for fuel, if the locals would try to kill me and take my ship, whether the new lands would have a breathable atmosphere. And I sure as hell never thought I'd find myself bleeding and bruised, digging sixty graves with my daughter and an extended family of freaks at my side.

We buried her soldiers alongside our people. None of them asked for this, and at their core we were all the same. No us, no them, just broken people deserving of a final act of respect.

I leaned on my shovel, wiping the sweaty hair from my face, and wondered if my ten-year-old self would have considered my life adventurous enough. It checked all the boxes—peril, discovery, battles—but somehow it didn't feel right. I never wanted it to be like this, people dying and killing because I wanted to play hero.

No one died in the *Argenta*, though she bore more than a few dents from her victorious fight with the warships. I could be thankful for that, but what right did I have to choose who stayed and who sacrificed themselves for the cause? Why did anyone trust me to make that kind of decision?

"At least they'll nourish the soil," Theon said, redirecting my unhealthy thoughts to a nearby field of limp, bent wheat.

Agriculture, or at least an attempt at it.

People were still trying to make this place habitable, not giving in to the forced migration that had to feel like an inevitability, and not loosening their grasp on what little remained of their heritage. The dying moon with no name meant more to its children than their own safety or well-being. The blood of their ancestors ran in its soil, their lost history written in its hidden night skies.

Ruby Marta sat with the other children on a rock at the edge of the ancient graveyard, her back to us, halfheartedly playing a nonsensical game with sticks and pebbles that reminded me of Arlekenon.

In a misguided attempt at preserving their innocence, I hadn't wanted them to see the bodies or help with the burials, but they knew what was going on. Knew that people died, that a massive war raged through the skies, that the experiments were done on unwilling participants forced to become supersoldiers. And Ruby had to know, though perhaps not on a conscious level, that her mother had a hand in it all.

She deserved to know there was more to her heritage than death and destruction.

I looked past the crowd of grave diggers to the crumbling stone village, wondering if the little house with the stars in the roof was still there.

"Hey, Ruby," I said softly. "I want to show you something."

She came to my side and took my hand, holding it tightly in her little fingers and leaning into me as we walked, almost as if for protection. She was so good at putting on a brave face that I forgot she was just a little kid in a terrifying world, and growing up around freaks and assassination attempts didn't make it any less frightening.

The house still stood, more or less in recognizable shape. One wall had crumbled and the roof now bore so many gaping holes that the eternal sun stole the majesty of the stars, but it had survived. The house where I fell in love and set my life on a trajectory I never wanted.

The act of stepping over the threshold, once an image I held close to my heart, now repulsed me. Lies, every word and every touch nothing but lies. Nothing would have made me happier than to turn around and never look back.

But after all this, if I was lucky enough to have an after, the life I never thought I'd lead would have a little girl in it, and I needed her to know where she came from.

"My lineage ain't something you're gonna boast about," I said, "but in your veins runs the blood of heroes. People who were tortured and discarded by those in power, and came out of it stronger and braver than ever before. They felt no resentment toward their oppressors, but still fought against them for the good of all people."

With a hushed awe, Ruby swiveled her head to examine every inch of the house while never leaving my side, as if afraid touching anything would reveal the truth behind the illusion. "They lost."

"They did. They lost over and over again, and some of them are still losing today." I lifted her onto a chair so she could see the handmade medals of her ancestors, their frame undisturbed on a crumbling wall. "But they lived to fight again, lived to keep trying to make a better life. Not just for themselves, but for everyone. For all the little moons and asteroids that don't stand a chance on their own."

She ran her fingers across the carved wood and stone, letting them dip into every curve and line.

"Your mother grew up in this house, and she was amazing." I took the medals out of the frame and pinned them to her dress one by one. They were hers now. "Beautiful, funny, absolutely brilliant. The woman she's become is a lie, an insult to everything she once stood for, but she was amazing once, like those who came before her." I looked at Ruby, her frizzy hair glinting in the dappled light. "And those who come after."

Her attention drifted to a model of the solar system sitting on the bedside table. The planets and moons were supposed to rotate— Diantha had used it to show me how rare an eclipse was on Vespi 3-14—but it remained still as Ruby pressed the buttons on its base.

"It's okay if Mom lied to you," she said, sitting on the bed and leaning over to look behind the model. "It doesn't matter if it's a lie. It gave you hope, and didn't you say that's all that matters sometimes?"

It did sound familiar, but I couldn't remember ever saying it to Ruby. I'd said it to *Cara*, the first night she flew with us.

I bent to pick up a frayed cord that ran along the wall; probably led to the rooftop solar array. "Sorry, kid. Looks like rats chewed through this. You won't get that thing working no matter what—"

But the model started with a whir, its radiating arms tipped with miniature globes slowly orbiting around a central light. Without being connected to any power source except Ruby.

She laughed, grinning as the tiny worlds sped up and years passed in seconds, and I tried to comprehend this new information.

Our abilities were genetic. Being the daughter of two freaks must have given Ruby a higher chance of inheriting it. Only natural she and Cara, having a similar control over electricity, would have become friends and shared wisdom amongst themselves. My line about lies and hope, for instance.

Yet *everything* about her reminded me of Cara. Her manner of speaking, of walking, her cybernetic arm, the way she looked at the world with that infinite wonder...

"Ruby."

She looked up, stopping the model just as the rogue asteroid's erratic orbit finally swept between Vespi 3-14 and the sun.

"You have a special power."

"I can talk to electricity," she said with a nod. "It used to be only when I heard our song."

"And you've been able to do it anytime you want since you sang the ending?" I asked, venturing a guess.

She nodded again, spinning the planets and moons around the sun. "I found the sheet music a few months ago, and Mom taught me to sing it for you every night. I wasn't allowed to sing the ending for you, because it would ruin your show. But I sang it for myself once. That's how I always knew where you were; I followed the signal inside my mind, and I found you."

"And then?" I asked, though the answer seemed obvious. Outrageous and unbelievable, but obvious.

She stroked the little green marble representing Vespi 3-14 with a fond touch. "Why is it green when the moon is dead and brown?"

"Must have been made by someone with hope for the future. What did you do after you found us, Ruby?"

"I built a robot to keep an eye on you."

Of course she did. I rubbed my face and resisted the urge to laugh at the absurdity of it all.

"So you were Cara."

"Cara was me," she corrected, drifting to look out the window at the dying garden.

I joined her, leaning my elbows on the cracking sill. "And why exactly did you think we needed protection?"

"Mom stopped being Mom, and I was scared she'd hurt you like she hurt the other people with powers."

"She was doing that way back then?"

"Not as much. Daddy didn't like it, but then he got sick—

poisoned—and he wasn't in charge anymore, so I built Cara and snuck her on a supply ship to Hodge. I tried to keep you safe from all the ships Mom sent after you, by messing with their communications and sending them reports of incoming meteor storms and stuff." She paused, tracing the mountain range in the dusty glass. "And I wanted to know you."

All those moments when ships and soldiers hadn't killed us, when they could have blown us out of the sky but instead retreated or hesitated to shoot, suddenly made sense. And Cara trying to talk Merulo out of murdering the blackmarketer on the asteroid... She was trying to take care of her family.

"But like Cara told you, it all went wrong when we came on board. I knew you would all change when I sang you the ending, but I needed you to come help us. I'm sorry."

A shadow of deep pain came over her face, sadness and guilt like nothing a person her age should even know about, let alone experience. This was about more than just the song.

"The city falling?" I asked gently.

She nodded and fell into me, soaking my shoulder with tears. "I knew it would fall. I was supposed to lower it down safely," she said between sobs. "But I had to be in the Castle to talk to its energy because the wireless got turned off with the rest of the power, and Mom took me away. And now they're all..."

I held her as tightly as I could, not knowing quite how to assure a child she wasn't a mass murderer. "It isn't your fault, kid. It's your mother's for ever putting you in that position. I don't blame you, and I don't think any of them would, either."

There was silence for a moment, then, "Are you really going to kill my mother?"

Who knew such a simple question, asked in the tiny voice of a scared child, could hurt so damn much? The answer was clear to me, but I didn't have an answer for *her*.

I pulled away from her and looked up helplessly, searching for guidance among the artificial stars. Maybe Diantha didn't have to die. Maybe we could take her prisoner, keep her locked away until some government arose that could give her a fair trial. Was I an awful person for assuming nothing short of parading around with her head on a pike would ever completely end the reign of VesCorp?

"She isn't all bad," Ruby said. "She was good, and then she changed. She can change again."

"I won't if I don't have to," I promised, "but she's tried to kill me before and if she tries again—"

As if in response, a roaring shadow flew overhead, briefly blocking out the sun and shaking the air with the vibrating roar of rocket engines. A warship, and a big one at that.

***

We ran hand-in-hand through the empty graveyard, stepping around abandoned shovels and half-dug graves as swirling dirt particles from the recently landed ship buffeted our faces.

"Stay behind me," I whispered, preparing for the worst as Ruby and I walked up the *Argenta*'s open gangplank, wincing at the sound of our footfalls on the clanking metal.

I anticipated a siege. Enemy soldiers swarming and weapons firing, people shouting and killing with ice and claws…

The silence took me by surprise.

"Where are they?" I asked Holly, the mermaid, who sat in a tub of water beside the rest of our people standing shell-shocked in the cargo bay.

"They came and went so fast." Her voice trembled, and she curled her fingers into tight fists to keep her hands from doing the same. "We thought they were holograms until they… But they didn't try to kill everyone. They just…"

Someone pointed up the stairs to the crew quarters. I left Ruby with them and went to check it out.

The sight of blood pooled on the floor around a supine figure made my stomach lurch.

Theon.

I rushed to join the crowd kneeling at his side, brushing aside bits of broken glass. No, not glass. Diamonds. Tiny shards of glittering diamonds, like the prison Parthen had made for Dekker had exploded.

And it had. Dekker was gone, a pile of diamonds and a throwing knife in his place.

I made eye contact with Parthen, who was sobbing and putting pressure on Theon's abdomen. Pneuman's favorite shirt was slashed and bloody.

"What happened?"

Lily answered for her. "Billie and friends. We ran to our ship when they landed, ready to attack, but they just popped in, like teleportation or something, and broke out the wolf..." Her voice cracked, and she gnawed at her knuckle for a second, stopping only when her beak pierced her skin. "He tried to stop them. Dekker gave him one swipe, they said something about letting us destroy ourselves, and they were gone."

I lifted Parthen's hand from the wound. Deep. "To their ship?"

Lily shrugged her singed wings helplessly. "They aren't showing up on heat scans. Merulo's in the cockpit, waiting to fire if they appear. He is *not* in a good way."

With a weak groan, Theon turned his head to me. "Can't hear anyone. Definitely trained against mind-reading."

"Pneuman?" I prompted. "Can you feel them?"

Theon squeezed his eyes shut. "Pneuman's gone," he said, either laughing or crying softly. "He's been gone for a long time."

No one said a word, and it seemed as though time itself had paused to comprehend this revelation.

"He'd been fading away for a while, but the *Rubeno* crashing was the last straw. He's still here, in a way. Part of me, but..." Theon covered his face with his hands, and his voice grew weaker. "I don't know what to tell you. Mom always said we were two halves of one soul, split in the womb. Maybe he fixed us, put us back the way we were supposed to be."

I looked to Parthen, waiting for her to do something and realizing with every passing second that she wasn't going to. Did we have anyone else who could save him?

"Parthen—"

"I can't," she interrupted, wiping a tear from her cheek and leaving a red streak in its place. "I can't change another person. What if I..." She choked out the next words in a whisper. "What if I turn him to sand?"

"You merged your body to Theon and Pneuman's every night. Your bodies became one, your organs and veins connected. You can do this."

"When I did that, I was only changing my own body, letting it accept theirs. I took all the risk, not them."

In a fit of desperation, I grabbed her by the shoulders and shouted at her. "He's dying, Parthen! I'm not impressed with him either at the moment for not telling us about Pneuman, but he's one of ours and we take care of our own because no one else will."

She wiped her eyes again and leaned over Theon. "I hate you right now," she said, kissing his forehead. "But I loved him, so I'm going to try."

I couldn't bear to watch as she put her hands to the wounds, and I went up to the cockpit.

Merulo sat hunched in the captain's seat, paws curled tightly around the triggers for the *Argenta's* entire arsenal and eyes locked on the ship parked beside us. Why not just fire?

"He won't let any of us near the controls," said a winged young man with his back pressed against the glass, watching while keeping as far away as possible.

I dismissed him with a nod to the stairs, and sat next to Merulo. "You're scaring people."

"Not the first time."

The glass of the dome was aglow with amorphous pockets of color—the optical lens that let us see ambient heat around us. It showed only residual heat coming from the Vespi ship beside us. No sign of life, but it stood to reason that if they had someone who could teleport, they probably had someone who could hide their heat signature.

"You don't want to kill," I said quietly, "but you've seen what happens when we let them live."

He glared at me from the corner of his eye, his lip curling to reveal his fangs. Purely a display; he didn't have it in him to hurt anyone. "Dekker didn't escape. They came to get him. Billie didn't want to hurt anyone."

I believed it. The blonde knife thrower had shown despair at the prospect of losing the city of Vespi, and if she wanted my crew dead, we'd have lost a lot more blood. But it didn't really matter anymore.

"You're right," I said, laying a hand on his shoulder.

"So when does the killing end?"

"When the war's over, I guess." I sighed. "Is there a reason you won't let somebody else take charge of the weapons? I don't want to do it, but I will—"

"They aren't in there," he interrupted. "Ship's a decoy, to make us waste our artillery."

"Well, would you look at that?" trilled a familiar voice. Billie, and a hologram judging by the way she flickered as she walked through the seats beside us. She was drenched in an eerie blue light. "A member of Jackie Boy's crew who thinks before he acts. That's a rarity on par with Lily not trying to seduce a random stranger."

I bristled at her comments but opted not to respond as I scanned the sky for incoming ships. Why would she come if not to act as a diversion?

"That's cute," Billie said, "the way you get all defensive over your bird. You actually think she loves you, don't you? Has she told you about all the guys in our ranks she's been with?" She cackled and called down the stairs, "Or would it take less time to list those you haven't—"

"If you had the means to kill us, we'd be dead. You're ghost soldiers, forever fighting a war you've already lost. And I'm not sure you even want to fight anymore, but you don't know anything else."

"I won't deny it. That's the great thing about you and I, you know, we've got the same power." She twirled a knife. "No, not this. You can't throw to save your life, and if I could breathe fire you wouldn't have your eyebrows. No, we've got this innate sense of the truth. We read people, situations. We speak the truth; can't do otherwise. Go on, try saying your bird loves you; bet you can't."

To be honest, I didn't hear most of what she said. That blue light that enveloped her bothered me. I'd never known a ship that didn't have something resembling sunlight.

Because they weren't in their ship. If they could teleport, if they could be transmitting her image from somewhere farther away...

I knew that color light. I'd discovered my true self in a similar unnatural blue glow, under the marble city that now lay in ruins miles away. Some part of the bunker could have survived the years of bombings. It was a stretch, sure, but they were Diantha's army; she could have told them about the caverns.

"So you've got a teleporter?" I asked. "Two trips in such a short time; I bet he's pretty tired."

I walked through Billie to sever her holographic connection to our ship and, in the seconds it took her to reappear, I went to the controls and punched in the approximate coordinates. When I reached for the trigger, Merulo grabbed my hand.

"The war isn't over," he said, and pushed it himself.

In a roaring flare that shook the ship, one of our missiles rocketed across the landscape. It disappeared in seconds, and Billie realized what we'd done a moment later, panic crossing her face.

Teleportation was exhausting; after one or two trips, you needed to recharge.

"Yeah, we might be the last gasp of a losing army," she said under her breath. "Or maybe we were just stalling until the reinforcements got there."

CHAPTER TWENTY-ONE

The ships came one by one at first, a variety of vessels from all corners of Diantha's empire. The frequency of their arrivals quickened, and the flock of armored birds soon dominated the sky as an impenetrable shadow.

Darkness came to Vespi 3-14, the stars above not stars at all but the glowing red lights of a thousand lasers, torpedoes, and missiles ready to lay waste to the few remaining dwellings that had the audacity to survive all the past raids.

With the fleet covering the sky clear to the horizon, we'd have been shot dead if we so much as moved the *Argenta* from beneath the massive stone arch we had taken refuge under. And forget about fighting our way out.

Ruby had sent out the video to every news outlet she could reach. We'd won, or we would soon enough. But us? I'd thought we'd get out alive.

"I'd hoped we'd have more time."

Lily leaned against me, just a reminder that we weren't alone, even if neither would admit we needed someone. "You're not giving up."

"I don't know. A ship full of freaks against the armies of a hundred planets paid for their loyalty?"

I stood at the front of the *Argenta*'s hull and stared out at the endless black sky. I could hear the clock ticking down, my mortality drawing closer with each shaking breath. At least I wouldn't live long enough to get past the denial stage.

"I thought this was our purpose," I told her, "to end these rebellions and get something like a standard of living in places like this. But then I guess that's what the first generation thought, too. There are more of us out there, waiting for their time. Maybe our purpose was to set up their dominoes."

Lily took me by the shoulder and turned me to face her. "I'm sorry," she said in a voice devoid of humor, her pupils eclipsing her yellow irises. "You thought that was a question; let me try again. You are *not* giving up. If I have to personally fly up there and—"

"And what? Flirt with all the pilots until they join our side? We don't have time for that."

As soon as the words left my mouth, I wanted to call them back.

"There's a way out of this," Lily said, crossing her arms, "but it starts with us working together, not tearing each other apart. And for the record, I know you think I seduced someone for this ship. I didn't. I traded for it. Figured we'd need something expensive sooner or later, so before I left the *Rubeno*, I took all the gold and jewels and fancy gadgets men have given me over the years."

I nodded silently, not sure if I should apologize or thank her.

She sounded so confident that we would survive. Confident in *me*.

A way out? How could she see a way out of this? With a wall of warships between us and any chance of escape, ready to destroy us on sight if we even tried to find Diantha and take her down, I couldn't begin to fathom a strategy for anything except protecting the citizens of Vespi 3-14. They didn't deserve to die just because we brought the front lines to their door.

The bunkers beneath the marble city extended for miles. Our missile destroyed part of it, but maybe some parts were still accessible and secure. And if what Diantha said way back when was true, there'd be a fleet of ships hidden somewhere down there.

"Think we could get them to the city?" I asked, a smile forcing its way onto my lips. "The people in the town, I mean. The eyes in the sky will be looking for our ship, but if we walk…"

Lily just looked at me, shaking her head almost imperceptibly.

"I'm not giving up," I assured her, my feet slipping on the slick metal as I ran for the bridge. "Not even close."

***

We didn't have to run. The ships paid us no mind as they drifted overhead, waiting for a signal that would never come.

No, we didn't *have* to run, but we did anyway, a mass migration of bodies moving as one across the plains painted with the blackness of space. Our feet slammed against the ground like countless drumbeats, our harried breaths providing a calming, metronomic rhythm.

Questions and concerns tried to intrude—Were the bunkers safe? Had Diantha escaped to her mountain refuge when the missile hit? If not, where was she?—but I couldn't let myself think of anything but getting the survivors to the city. Everything else would come later.

A spiraling flame whistled through the sky, striking the ground up ahead and exploding with a blinding light that, for a flash, illuminated the glistening ruins of the distant city. The sound followed a second later, the ear-splitting crack of the air being torn in two.

"They've figured out Diantha's army is dead!" Did I even have to shout? I couldn't see two inches in front of my face, let alone anyone else in our group. I thought I was leading, but the sound of frantic footsteps on hard-packed dirt surrounded me in all directions.

Another bolt of fire, closer this time.

Merulo's voice hit my ear in rapid, hushed bursts. "They're not going to stop. We won't all make it."

True, the town's citizens ranged from infants to the elderly, with many of them in less-than-peak physical shape. But running for their lives as lasers fell around them invigorated the human spirit with enough adrenaline to overcome old age and weakness for a few more minutes, and the strongest carried those who were unable.

***

Like their villages, the citizens were survivors, and everyone arrived unharmed at the ruins of the city. Parthen, one of a few who had gone ahead to scope it out, met us at the entrance to the tunnels, a trail of lights leading the way down the dark passage.

"Is it secure?" I shouted over the explosions.

She nodded. "I saw evidence of a cave-in from our missile, but no one got out alive."

Never thought the deaths of fellow human beings could fill me with such relief, and I allowed myself a moment to reflect on that as we ushered people in.

Had I changed in some way since the night the song played to the end? The old Jack Jetstark, the lovesick barker of a decrepit carnival, never would have led an army, gotten involved in a war, kissed a pretty owl...

But had that always been in me, waiting for the opportunity to show itself? Or had the music altered my DNA, giving me the ability not only to breathe fire at will but to become the fearless, adventurous captain I'd always dreamt of being?

And did it really matter?

"Theon is doing well," Parthen told me, pride beaming from her wide grin, and I realized I had been afraid to ask.

"Good. You did good."

"I don't think Pneuman is gone." She looked surprised by her own words.

"No?" I said after a moment.

"You know they always told me—both of them—that they shouldn't have split in the womb. That they knew, somehow, they were just two parts of a whole." She wiped at her eye with the hem of her sleeve. "I can't explain it, but I can see it now. They, he, whatever… There's happiness there now. They're complete."

I put my arm around Parthen and squeezed her shoulder. Only when the last person had entered the tunnel did she and I go in, shutting the heavy door behind us. A warm yellow glow permeated every nook in the carved rock walls, though upon closer inspection what I had assumed to be a string of bulbs was, in fact, a series of handprints.

"I turned the rock to luciferase," Parthen said. "It's the chemical that makes fireflies glow. Diantha's people might have had the electricity working, but I think our missile broke it."

"We'll have it fixed soon, with Ruby here." I suspected she had messed with the ships' radar again. How else could so many advanced vessels miss hitting a crowd of people at such a close distance?

The passage of time had neglected to reach its meddling fingers into the bunker, leaving everything just as I remembered it, right down to the shelves of canned goods. Memories floated on every dust mote stirred up by our steps. Some of those memories had yet to be ruined by the truth about Diantha.

"Where's Theon?" I asked Parthen as the others got settled in the caverns.

"Let me show you." Her face lit up, and she led me across a room scattered with rubble.

She had set Theon up in a corner, where he lay half-conscious on a cot. His abdomen showed no sign of damage, and he raised his head to give me a tired smile. She was right; there was something different about him, a whole new… aura. A peace that I don't think either brother had ever found separately.

"He's going to pull through," Parthen said. "He's in pain, but he isn't bleeding. And he isn't—they aren't?—as much of a jerk now that Pneuman is in there, too. I don't really know the grammar for this, or what happens next." A lovesick kind of conflict swirled in her eyes. "But we don't have to decide now, and there's something I wanted to show you."

We went around a corner, through more rubble and up a gradual incline into a large, open area. I could make out vague forms in the darkness, but it wasn't until my eyes adjusted that I realized what they were.

A fleet of one-man ships, dozens of them, hidden away years ago and waiting all this time for someone to need them. Not the prettiest things, tiny and inelegant like the *Mia Nubo*, but they looked spaceworthy and each undoubtedly had enough weapons and projectiles to equip a small army.

I breathed easier for a moment, the weight of looming death lifting from my shoulders. Wouldn't make much of a difference against the ships, but at least it was something. A chance.

We went back to the main room and told the others of the discovery.

"If we could work out a strategy," I muttered, leaning my back against the cool stone wall, "so we could coordinate our attacks on one ship at a time..."

"The people with natural defenses on the outside of the pack," Lily added.

I nodded. "We'd never take them all down, but if we could eliminate a few, we could carve out a path to Diantha. I can only assume she's back in her mountain."

"She is," Ruby confirmed from across the room, where she and a few kids from the town were poking around in a box of belongings left behind by a previous group of refugees. They found an ancient camera, and marveled like it was a priceless artifact.

"Or we could blast a hole in the fleet that would allow us to leave the moon," Parthen suggested. "We could come back with reinforcements."

"Who'd bother coming here to fight?" Merulo asked. "This is a nothing moon."

Theon stirred, wincing as he raised his head. "What are you

talking about?" he said with a pained grin. "Jack'll give a speech and convince the whole damn universe to come and help."

I raised an eyebrow and chuckled as the ground quaked. If only.

Although…

I went over to Ruby and picked up the old camera. "Can you connect to the wireless systems and transmit video from this?" I asked.

She nodded.

"Can you overlay my voice and picture with the footage from the labs? And send it to every screen you can, all across the 'verse?"

"I *think* so."

"Great."

I wasted no time, positioning myself and Ruby in the blue light she'd restored and making sure she could see as many freaks as possible. She started the transmission, and I spoke from my heart.

"Gentlefolk of the universe, I don't need to tell you there's a war going on. Some of you can see it out your windows, some of you are fighting in it, and a lucky few among you have only seen images on the news. On the surface, this is a revolution, the result of the perpetually trodden-upon banding together and saying 'no more.' Their homes have been destroyed by mining, and for what? For energy none of us get to use, because it all goes to the Castle."

I signaled to Ruby.

"The images you're seeing come from secret laboratories in the VesCorp Castle. Be thankful you can't hear the screams as people are tortured in an attempt to change their very DNA. This is the true purpose of all the mining, to power the machines that try to turn people into warriors and, all too often, create mutated freaks. This is why moons are dying, and it's been going on for generations."

Ruby turned her camera back on us, broadcasting our true selves to every screen in the universe. We were entertaining onstage for a few minutes, but the crowds had to know the show was fake. I could all but feel our audience cringing at the thought that we were anything but performers in elaborate costumes, that something as hideous and alien as us really existed.

"This is not a war between freaks and non-freaks. This isn't even a war between planets and moons. This is a war to save human decency, that increasingly elusive voice in our heads that tells us it isn't okay to let others suffer, that our lives are rendered meaningless if we don't do everything within our power to help another person."

The ground shook more than it ever had. Loose dirt fell from the ceiling.

"We've taken refuge under the surface of Vespi 3-14. A thousand warships are trying to kill us, not because we dared to fight but because we dared to win. And we did win, but we're—" I looked at Lily and smiled. "We're a small army, and we don't have the manpower for the final battle."

I stared into the lens. My reflection stared back, a broken man with desperation in his eyes.

"I have no right to ask for your help, and you have no obligation to provide it. But you will. I know in my heart that you will because this isn't some little skirmish on some distant moon. This is the fight for the future of all people across the entire universe. This is your fight. Your future. And it's in your hands."

CHAPTER TWENTY-TWO

The song played every night, just like she promised, and every day I watched her on the news being adored by the Vespi people. There was no problem with them accepting her, and the wedding happened so soon after that I hadn't even begun to look for the other freaks.

I went to the coronation, expecting her to use it as a platform to expose corruption inside VesCorp and call for the dethronement of Garon and a total overhaul of the government. Maybe even kill him right then and there.

She didn't. She married him instead.

In my heart, I believed it was part of some larger plan. She still sang every night, so she must not have needed rescuing.

The house—hell, the entire moon—was empty without her, and I decided all I could do was find the rest of us and prepare for her to call us to action. Not like I could afford a ship, but I'd heard reports of a wrecked cargo hauler out past the city. Thought I might see if anything could be salvaged.

I recognized her the moment I set eyes on her. My dad's ship, full of holes and with her snapped-off tail fin laying a hundred yards away on the new shoots of grass. She must have been caught in the siege all those months ago.

No sign of the old man inside. Probably hitched a ride offworld. Good. As much as I despised him sometimes, I liked knowing he was alive. I wasn't about to go looking for him, but for better or worse he'd helped shape the person I'd become.

I made my way into the ship, treading carefully along her walls that had become floors when she landed off-kilter, and reached the bridge without much difficulty. Beautiful ship, in her own awkward way. Dad said he named her for my mother. I never met her, not that I remember, but she must have been an amazing woman to have her name on such a resilient ship.

She actually started up, with a wheezing engine and short-circuiting display panels, and we got all the way to the next star over before we had to set down for repairs.

The metal shell of Jaz blocked out all the stars, so while I waited for the *Rubeno Mardo*'s new parts to be delivered, I went down to the cargo hold and painted some. You could hardly see the unsightly iron patches across the ceiling once they bore the inky blue-black of space, and every dot of yellow served to further camouflage the repairs.

I left the cargo door open to let in the cool night air, and Diantha sang to me as I sat on the scaffolding near the ceiling, the heat from my breath setting and drying the paint with every meditative brushstroke.

"What was that song?"

The voice echoed in the spacious hold, and it took me a few seconds to locate the source—a blonde woman standing on the gangplank with her arms crossed over a low-cut, sequined dress.

"It's called *The Libramo*," I said, recovering from the surprise.

She stepped inside the ship. "But what *was* it?" she asked quietly.

At the time, I didn't know how it had affected her, how wings had sprouted from her back as she walked past the ship on her way to work, so I just shrugged.

"Is this your ship?"

"I guess so."

She tilted her head up and peered at the ceiling half-filled with constellations, her heels clicking on the metal floor as she walked around. "I don't get it," she said at last. "Is it supposed to look like something?"

I stared at her; she was serious. "It's the sky."

"No," she said after a moment's thought, "the lights in the sky are installed in perfectly straight lines. Yours are all wonky and different sizes."

"It's the sky," I repeated. "The real one, outside."

Understanding dawned on her delicate features, replaced by awe as the stars she'd only heard about danced in her eyes. Her little universe unfolded unto the infinite the same way mine had when I first set foot on the *Rubeno Mardo*. If I could only bring that indescribable feeling to all the people who would never leave their own world...

She shook her head. "There's so many of them."

"And each one with its own planets and moons and people." With my paintbrush, I indicated a small star in a constellation Diantha had called the Selfless Dragon. "See that one? That's where I'm from. And here?" I pointed to a giant fireball of a sun, the eye of the Harpy, who ate the heart of every man until she found one worthy of her beauty. "That one's your sun."

She wiped her eyes with the back of her hand and searched the cargo bay for a change of subject. "So what do you do with this flying deathtrap? Haul stuff?"

I hadn't really thought that far ahead. If I was supposed to go out and find the other freaks, I'd need money for fuel. "Hauling was kind of my dad's thing," I said. "And it's awful on the back, but I don't know what else to do with the space." I looked down at her. "Why? You got any ideas?"

She smiled up at me. "You could always start a carnival."

***

We had no way of knowing if the message got through, or if anyone would come. I hoped my words hadn't fallen on uncaring ears. There had to be good people out there; the universe wouldn't have lasted this long without good people keeping it together.

The ground shook almost constantly, the brief stillness between attacks a welcome respite that never lasted. The ceiling crumbled more with every passing hour.

"This bunker wasn't designed for so many direct attacks," Lily said, brushing bits of debris from her hair. She looked toward the hangar but said nothing more on the subject.

"I know," I told her. "We're going."

In the other room, Ruby regaled freaks and common folk alike with the history of our people. The tales would live on, even if we didn't, but I intended to put off the deciding moment for as long as possible.

Prolonging the inevitable sounded just fine to me, but my desire to keep my family alive did absolutely nothing for all the other families in all the other towns out there.

"We've got forty ships." My voice thundered down the corridors, competing with the blasts. "I want our best people with me. Pilots, fighters, girls with magnetic hands... But I'm done deciding who lives and who dies. If you want to do this, claim your ship. There's no shame in staying behind."

A sea of people, exhausted and beaten beyond anything their bodies had ever felt, raised their hands. Far more than I had ships for, and a light, airy sensation filled my chest. Pride?

Even Theon, whose abdomen was still bandaged and who had to lean on the wall for support, offered himself for the cause.

"My girl patched me up," he said, countering my thoughts. "All I have to do is sit in a chair and push a couple buttons. I've been training for that my whole life."

"You lied to me; I'm not your girl," Parthen informed him, though she did flash him a smile as she stood beside him.

"It would be nice," Merulo advised, "having a psychic up there with us."

"You're going?" I tried not to sound too surprised, abandoning any doubt that he would be unable to kill for us. "Of course you're going. I can't go into battle without my first mate."

An electric energy filled the air, an audible, buzzing combination of excitement and terror. It ended here, with the answer to the question we'd been afraid to ask: did an army of farmers, discarded science experiments, and sideshow attractions stand any chance against the armies above?

I took off my vest and gave it to Ruby, letting it hang limply over her narrow shoulders. "I'm not gonna tell you to keep this safe for me," I said, crouching to her level. "You've got your mother's brilliant mind; you'd see right through that. And you already know there's a chance I'm not coming back."

I turned her to face the people staying behind, the restless crowd who had seen the universe and seen that it was filled with mystery and wonder and, on rare occasions when the stars aligned, the right conditions for miracles to happen.

"I want you to keep *them* safe for me. Keep their spirits up, tell them stories. If the bombings stop and we don't come back, bring them to the ship and be their captain. They're your people, too."

She smiled, a beaming grin that warmed my heart and gave me every reason to make it back alive.

***

The display glowed a soft green, its dials and gauges the only source of light in the hangar now that they'd closed the heavy doors behind us. Almost looked like they hung in the air of their own accord, tiny emerald stars with reflections that danced on the windshield as I moved my head.

I could just make out Lily's form in the ship beside me. She had her wings out, their sparse, burned feathers crowding the already cramped cockpit. Maybe it gave her a sense of security, hearing the light flutter as she moved and feeling the softness against her skin. I know I felt safer with them around me.

In the row of ships directly behind us sat Merulo, Parthen, and Theon, with the extended family and a few skilled citizens of Vespi 3-14 filling in the ranks further back. They all waited in the dark for my command, while I waited for… I don't know what. Someone else to take over, to tell me that I wasn't qualified to lead a carnival, let alone a war.

Of course no one did, and I had to face the fact that, whether I liked it or not, my entire life had been leading up to this moment.

Hours spent memorizing every aspect of other cultures meant I could rattle off an enemy ship's specs with only a silhouette to go by, running from pirates on our last drops of fuel gave me an unrivaled ability to devise evasive strategies on the spot, and there was nothing like keeping an intergalactic traveling carnival going to make a guy learn how to help people work together.

I had to do this, had to accept that maybe I was the only who could.

I raised my hand to signal, and the heavy doors before us slid open with an ominous scraping of stone on stone. The artificial night extended into infinity, broken only by the streaking lasers and fiery explosions across the landscape.

"We focus on the big one," I said into the radio, pointing to the vague outline of a ship. Enormous thing with a pointed nose and wings wider than it was long, taking up ten times the space of any ship surrounding it. "It's a Vespi dreadnought, fitted with enough artillery to blow a hole clear through this moon. We try anything while it's still flying, we die. It's probably the command vessel, the queen bee if you will, so knocking it out will make taking out the others a little easier."

"Weaknesses?" Merulo prompted.

"With those wide wings? Narrow doorways." If anyone laughed, they didn't have their comms on, and an eerie silence engulfed me. "Look," I said, rubbing my face with my hand. "It ain't gonna be easy. Might not even be possible, but we have to try. If it helps, think of it as revenge. These people took lives. Let's make them pay. If that doesn't do it for you, then remember that we're going out there to honor just as much as avenge. Picture that smiling face you're never going to see again, and do this for them."

A soft sniffle came over the radio. Parthen.

"We're doing this for Pneuman, and for everyone who has ever suffered or died because of these people. We knock as many as we can from the sky, pray to every god we can name that reinforcements come, and we try to clear a path to the mountain."

With that, forty ships fired up, a quiet hum amplified by the sheer number of engines until it became a roar louder than anything the warships could hope to produce.

We rolled out, lifting into the sky in formation, and any semblance of strategy fell to the wayside as a screaming laser forced us to scatter. I lost sight of the other ships, and found myself alone in the darkness with the endless enemy above.

I locked onto the dreadnought, its wide, triangular shape obscuring the lights of those hovering above it to create a swath of black in the artificially starred sky. Wouldn't even know it was there otherwise, with nothing on its underside to give away its position.

Blurs of light flashed in my periphery, either fireflies or our other ships zipping by. They disappeared before I could get a good look, and I could only hope they wouldn't cross between me and the target.

I fired and my ship, which I suspected was not originally designed to carry weapons of that magnitude, was rocked by the force of launching the projectile. The missile streaked through the sky, but exploded in mid-air with no apparent cause.

They shot back, a red-hot laser that came so fast I just had time to roll my ship out of its way. Or maybe not, I amended, seeing the glowing hole burned through my left wing.

More missiles went up all around, only to go off prematurely. A volley of lasers followed each one.

"They have a forcefield!" I shouted into the comm, dodging a piece of shrapnel from another ship. "We can't hurt them!"

We fell back, but streaks of red light filled the sky as the ships above began to lower toward the ground, creating a funnel pointing directly at the dreadnought.

Trapped.

I fired. We all fired. Theon and a few others reported running out of ammo, but the few ships we managed to hit didn't matter. We could take them all down, and the big one would still destroy us in a single blast.

My heart sank, and the constant sound of explosions around me faded as I stared out at the family. Couldn't tell who that was, falling to their death in a ship torn in half. It didn't matter anyway. It would be all of us soon enough.

No sound, no turbulence. Just silence. Stillness.

And then, over the comm, came our song. Slow at first, but rising to the familiar tempo of the tune I never thought I'd hear again, filling my deflated hope with something lighter than air.

At that moment, a ray of sunlight cut through the darkness, a solid beam of sparkling particles stretching straight on to the ground.

I looked up, and laughed in disbelief when I saw blue sky through the hole in the center of the dreadnought. Bright, beautiful blue, with spiraling wisps of white and a dozen tiny ships zipping by.

Another jagged hole tore through the warship, and the lasers ceased as every enemy ship rose up to defend themselves. The forcefield didn't extend to the top of the dreadnought.

As the fire of Ruby's voice burned within me, our army dove en masse out from beneath the swarm, moving as one entity. My stomach dropped as we flew straight up and over the enemy, into the gloriously blinding light of the perpetual sun.

The ships below us stretched for uncountable miles, an impenetrable sheet of iron and steel and cannons. And above, more ships. Circling, darting vessels in every shape and size, from personal transports to the most massive cargo haulers, glinting silver and gold as they returned fire.

Reinforcements. Hundreds of them, from every corner of the universe. I recognized some as the ships that fought with us on Rouze, and I must have been under mind control because I think I saw my dad in the bridge of a small, undoubtedly stolen, cargo hauler.

"Thank you," I said, tears welling in my eyes. "I thank you, and the people of the moons and asteroids thank you. Someday, stories will be told about what's about to go down. So let's make sure those stories have happy endings."

With that, the battle truly began. Rockets blared past my windshield, shrapnel of unknown origin striking my hull. Another pilot and I dropped a small warship with simultaneous hits to both its wings.

Radio chatter turned to chaos, each pilot shouting commands and coordinating strikes, warning others of incoming attacks and taking cover behind their more-armored compatriots. It was an inelegant mess of violence and desperation, with ships bleeding fuel and too many good people struggling to stay afloat, but such was the nature of war. Anyone who says otherwise is a fool.

I found a rare moment of stillness and locked eyes with Parthen as she came up beside me. She stared with deadened eyes, her face shaded with a sickly gray pallor. I guess war did that to people; I could only imagine what I looked like.

And then she fell from the sky. Whether something hit her or her damaged engine finally gave out, I couldn't tell.

I dove after her, so fast that I lifted from my seat, but couldn't catch up. The hulls of the ships below fast approached.

Another ship—Theon—appeared seemingly from nowhere, hooking her stalled propellers in his landing gears and sweeping her up away from danger.

I pulled out of my dive and leveled off, dodging a barrage of missiles as I watched the conjoined ships work in synchronized harmony. He lifted her immobile ship, while she supplied the ammunition he had long since depleted. Whether they realized it or not, their missiles struck their targets to the beat of Ruby's song.

They'd been through more than any couple deserved, and maybe things would never be the same between them, but Parthen and Theon would survive. Together, in one way or another, inseparable until the end of time.

The music shifted to its tribal phase, with Ruby clapping her hands like a drum in accompaniment to its low, rhythmic melody.

Something struck the back of my ship, sending me tumbling tail over nose. Ground and sky flashed outside my windows. I struggled to get my hand on the yoke, let alone regain control.

Roaring turbulence and the smell of propellants filled the cockpit, and my somersaulting heart pounded in my chest. Part of my tail section was gone, torn open as if with giant claws.

A violent nudge set me back on my previous trajectory. Merulo, I realized once I regained my bearings, using the brute force of his ship to right mine.

The enemy ship rose above us, a gleaming black arrow without so much as a scratch. Its broad tail fin indicated it hailed from McKinley 3, and should have had a vast arsenal. If it'd wanted to destroy me, I'd have been dead.

Lasers and missiles zipped by in all directions, but nothing from the warship. A graveyard of twisted metal lay below.

They'd run out of ammo. My display showed a similar situation.

The ship's engines roared, and it charged toward us at full speed, intending to knock us from the sky. I nodded to Merulo, hovering beside me, and, in a decision both ill-advised and reckless, we returned the charge.

Our ships clipped the ends of its wings, a violent hit that rocked us but hardly affected them.

I darted off to the side and circled around to face the unseen enemies behind the blacked-out windshield, drawing their attention as they gave chase.

For a moment, though I knew Merulo would come through, I let fear take over. My palms grew slick, my jaw ached from clenching my teeth. In my heart and in the pit of my stomach, I knew death was near.

I looked back through the hole in my fuselage. Even if they didn't catch me, how long could I stay airborne?

Without warning, the warship cartwheeled off its trajectory, hurtling into the path of one of its compatriots and dying in a fiery crash. The top of Merulo's ship showed severe damage, but we both came out of it alive.

As the song switched to its most beautiful portion, more reinforcements arrived in a shimmering ribbon from space. They'd have an easier fight, the sky now far less dense with warfare and the ground littered with steel and iron skeletons.

The mountains jutted up in the distance, surrounded by ships but with a clear path from here. Diantha would be in there, waiting in vain for our defeat or surrender so she could be rescued and resume her reign. But wasn't my responsibility here, protecting my people?

A one-man ship glided to a halt beside me, firing at the barrage around us and protecting me from attack. I made eye contact with its angelic pilot, and she waved me on, telling me to get there while I still could.

She may have looked at other men, but she saw only me.

The music swelled to its climactic end, and Lily blew me a kiss.

"She loves me," I said to myself as I peeled off and headed straight for the mountains.

CHAPTER TWENTY-THREE

Though her body blended with the craggy walls of the dim cavern and rendered her invisible, her footsteps rippled in the rivulets of fuel bleeding from my wounded plane.

She made no attempt to escape or attack. If any of her army had survived, they did not show themselves.

The ripples came to a halt mere feet before me. Once upon a time, the thought of being in her proximity would have given my soul goosebumps. Now I only wanted to get it over with and rejoin my family.

When she phased into view, it wasn't as the ruthless queen or the comely villager, but a Diantha I'd never seen. The real Diantha, I could only assume.

Dressed in a floor-length maroon jacket and with her hair corralled into a messy braid, she stood with her hands clasped in front of her, staring at her boots. Her body shook with tears barely repressed.

"Jack—"

She didn't deserve a chance to explain herself or to make peace with her gods. Didn't deserve a damn thing, after all she'd done, but I guess I'm a sentimental fool because I kept my mouth shut and let her talk.

She looked up at me, eyes wide with fear. Her lips moved without sound until she rediscovered her voice, little more than a tired whisper.

"I thought this was the way. I never thought it would end like this. With a war. I thought people would see the corruption, would see how evil we were." She wiped her eyes. "They looked the other way, because we paid them to. *He* paid them to. And you know, I didn't try to hide the fact that I killed him. The only one who cared was Ruby, but by then it was too late for me. I loved the power."

For the first time since I'd known her, I felt I truly knew her. A vulnerable and scared woman, caught up in an underhanded political world she had no place being.

I couldn't let it change my mind, yet the igniting breath caught in my throat.

Diantha took me by the hand, stroking my palm with her shaking finger. "It wasn't really my plan, you know, for you to kill me. I just said it because I thought you would fall for it and give up. But now I think you have to do it. If you don't, you'll never forgive yourself. And I won't stop. I'll rebuild, I'll start new wars and destroy lives and homes all over again. And I'll never forgive you for not stopping me when you had the chance."

All those nights I'd spent dreaming of the reunion with the girl I thought I loved, it never turned out this way, never occurred to me that she might beg for me to end her reign of terror.

"I'm not going to kill you."

Her brows furrowed together. "Don't you think I deserve it? Don't the people deserve to know I died a horrible death?"

"Yes," I said, believing it to my core.

"Then why—"

"Because our daughter thinks you're redeemable, and I'm inclined to trust her judgment."

I took her face in my hands, committing to memory the true visage of the most amazingly complex person I'd ever had the pleasure and misfortune to meet.

"Yeah, maybe you deserve it, and maybe the people who hate you have earned the right to dance on your grave. But Ruby deserves to believe that you're not the monster she saw you become."

The fumes from the fuel hung thick in the air.

"Here's what's going to happen," I told her. "You're going to turn invisible, I'm going to set this place on fire, and then I'm going to tell Ruby that you escaped and are heading to some distant moon to live an honest life under an assumed name. Whether or not you do, I don't care. But that's what I'm telling her."

Diantha gave me a sad smile, and then she was gone. Did I imagine the footsteps running to the mouth of the cave?

I sighed, a long exhalation from the hottest depths of my lungs, and that was all it took.

The air erupted with roaring blue flames, suffocating the oxygen in the cavern with oppressive heat. They didn't dance, didn't leap and cast fanciful shadows. They just consumed.

I turned and walked away. A burning smell came from my clothes. I stepped outside, and the piercing heat of Vespi 3-14 felt cool on my sweaty skin.

Only a few ships remained in the sky, and all of them ours. The wreckage of the other armies lay in crumpled heaps across the landscape, hundred-foot-tall memorials to the dead.

Could hardly see the sun through the clouds, made thick and dark from the battle's smoke and exhaust. Almost looked like rain.

It was over.

It was over, and we'd won.

Even as the words came to me, I rejected them. There was still too much to be done to call this winning. Not until all the wars ended, until the moons and asteroids had the same rights as the planets... It was coming, and hopefully soon, but not just yet.

A drop of sweat fell to the ground between my feet, quenching the cracked soil and turning it a deep, fertile brown.

Another drop. Not sweat at all.

I looked up at the heavy gray clouds, and a drop of rain hit my face.

They fell sporadically at first, big and wet and spattering the ground with spots of dark and light, then faster and more frequent until they came in curtains of visual static.

The rain slapped against its own puddles until it became the grateful cheers and applause of a dying moon without a name. All that propane in the air must have seeded the clouds. Just like she'd always wanted.

***

It poured late into the night, saturating the thirsty soil with the liquid life it so desperately needed. When the storm clouds finally gave their last, they fizzled into wisps of nothing to reveal the sky they had concealed.

Stars. Uncountable millions of tiny points of light, sparkling like gems on the black velvet of night.

The faintest crescent of sun peeked out from behind the enormous asteroid making its regular, if infrequent, pilgrimage to Vespi 3-14.

We lay on the damp ground, the entire extended family, inhaling the scent of rainy soil and gazing upon stars no living soul on that moon had ever seen. Wherever Diantha was, I hoped she could see them.

"Which one are you from?" Ruby whispered, as if she might frighten the stars away if she raised her voice.

I pointed to the eye of the dragon constellation. "That one there. Swampy little moon, where the air is so thick that you have to learn to swim just to survive."

She looked at me for a moment, brows furrowed in skepticism. "That isn't true."

"Maybe not, but it could be true somewhere. Look at them all.

You think a puny little species like us could ever visit all the planets orbiting all those stars? And what about the stars so far away that their light hasn't even reached us yet?"

"I want to go," Ruby said. "Explore them all. Is that what we do now?"

I looked around me. Dozens of eyes stared back, waiting for my answer. I realized then that this was it. This was our after, an unwritten future stretching before us into the infinite.

What happened to us now? A few of us looked normal enough to find work where we wouldn't be judged for scales or wings, where our abilities could prove invaluable. Parthen and Theon, for instance, though maybe we were all a little too damaged to ever fit into the real world.

Merulo's bright blue eyes shone through the night. The kindest, most loyal man I'd ever known, but he'd be lucky if anyone gave him the time of day, the way he looked. They'd probably hunt him down and kill him for being a monster, along with the others among us armed with fangs and claws and tails. I wondered if any of them wished we hadn't destroyed the labs.

Who was I kidding? Even with all the vastness of space before us, none of us had anywhere to go. A bunch of winged, furred, psychic freaks with violent tendencies, messed up relationships, and the insatiable urge to collect others like us. Maybe no one would ever accept us, but so what? We found the few people in all the universe who did, and sometimes that's all that matters.

"So?" Lily prompted, resting her feathered head on my shoulder. "What do we do now?"

I put an arm around each of my girls and sighed. The *Dorno Argenta* sat in silhouette against the starry sky.

"Well, we've got a couple dozen freaks and a big, empty cargo ship. We could start a carnival."

ABOUT THE AUTHOR

Jennifer Lee Rossman is a disabled and autistic freak, and proudly so. Her work has been featured in many anthologies and her debut novella, *Anachronism*, was published by Kristell Ink in 2018. She blogs at http://jenniferleerossman.blogspot.com/ and tweets @JenLRossman.

ACKNOWLEDGEMENTS

This book almost joined the Graveyard of Abandoned Chapter Ones haunting my hard drive. I had a great concept, *Heroes* meets *Firefly* with a magical song that gives people superpowers, but the actual plot fizzled out somewhere after the orphan girl with the mysterious past joined the space carnival. Then I heard a magical song of my own: "American Pie." So my first thanks have to go to Don McLean, who wrote the song that saved the book. From the music dying to the city of Vespi eight miles high and falling fast, your lyrics shaped Jack's universe, along with the Beatles and the Rolling Stones and all the other great musicians that shaped *my* universe.

My eternal gratitude to everyone at World Weaver Press, but especially Sarena Ulibarri, who took what I *thought* was a final draft and showed me how to fix all the problems I couldn't even see. Also, that cover art!

My mother gets a paragraph all to herself, for a lot of reasons but mostly because she told me to watch *Star Wars*. That movie made me a sci-fi geek, so all of this is kind of your fault.

Sabrinna, thank you for telling me to watch *Heroes*. And Terry and Matt, thanks for letting me watch it at your house when we didn't have a DVD player. (Also, hello to Conway the Very Good Boy.)

Thank you to my family and everyone who gave their input on the cover art, and for never getting tired of my "omg, you can't show this to anyone yet but please scream about it with me!!!" emails: Peanut, Daisy Duck and Donald Duck, Aunt Carol, Mo, Penny, Jacki, Gaven, Lizz, Claudie, Chasia, Jen, Galia, and Minerva.

To my doctors and healthcare people (because I love the looks on your faces when you see your names in my books): Dr. Dutkowsky, Dr. Chanana, Dr. Rammohan, Dr. Cummings, Mallory, Lori, Danielle, and Shawna.

To Liza and Kate, for figuring out my problems and helping me edit them.

To Nanette. Best teacher ever.

Hi, Jennifer from downstairs. You're awesome. (You may show this to your son as proof.)

Neil deGrasse Tyson, I don't know you but the thought of you reading my work and finding errors in my science is the most terrifying thing this nerd can think of, and it led me to change several plot points, do a heck of a lot of research, and try to learn how to calculate the terminal velocity of a falling city. Emphasis on *try*. I probably did it wrong, but welcome the chance to be corrected. (Also, my local bookstore took down one of your books to display one of mine, so I'm pretty sure we're rivals now.)

And finally, thank you. Yes, you. That weirdo who doesn't fit in, who doesn't look like everyone else, who looks up at the stars and wonders if there's a planet out there that will accept them. I wrote this book for people like you and me. We're freaks, and that's a beautiful thing even if it hurts, because we're the ones who are gonna change things.

Thank you for reading!
We hope you'll leave an honest review at Amazon, Goodreads, or wherever you discuss books online.

Leaving a review helps readers like you discover great new books, and shows support for the author who worked so hard to create this story.

Please sign up for our newsletter for news about upcoming titles, submission opportunities, special discounts, & more.

WorldWeaverPress.com/newsletter-signup

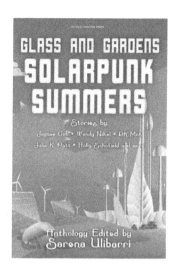

Glass and Gardens: Solarpunk Summers
Anthology
Edited by Sarena Ulibarri

Solarpunk is a type of optimistic science fiction that imagines a future founded on renewable energies. The seventeen stories in this volume are not dull utopias—they grapple with real issues such as the future and ethics of our food sources, the connection between technology and nature, and the interpersonal conflicts that arise no matter how peaceful the world is. In these pages you'll find a guerilla art installation in Milan, a murder mystery set in a weather manipulation facility, and a world where you are judged by the glow of your solar nanite implants. From an opal mine in Australia to the seed vault at Svalbard, from a wheat farm in Kansas to a crocodile ranch in Malaysia, these are stories of adaptation, ingenuity, and optimism for the future of our world and others. For readers who are tired of dystopias and apocalypses, these visions of a brighter future will be a breath of fresh air.

Featuring stories by **Jennifer Lee Rossman**, Jaymee Goh, D.K. Mok, Julia K. Patt, Holly Schofield, Wendy Nikel, and more.

Mrs. Claus: Not the Fairy Tale They Say
Anthology
Edited by Rhonda Parrish

When you think of Mrs. Claus, do you imagine a quiet North Pole homebody who finds complete fulfillment in baking cookies, petting reindeer and crafting toys alongside elves? How about a magic-wielding ice goddess, or a tough-as-nails Valkyrie? Or maybe an ancient fae of dubious intentions, or a well-meaning witch? Could Mrs. Claus be a cigar-smoking Latina, or a crash-landed alien? Within these pages Mrs. Claus is a hero, a villain, a mother, a spacefarer, a monster hunter, and more. The only thing she decidedly is not, is a sidekick.

It's Mrs. Claus' turn to shine and she is stepping out of Santa's shadow and into the spotlight in these fourteen spectacular stories that make her the star! Featuring original short stories by Laura VanArendonk Baugh, C.B. Calsing, DJ Tyrer, **Jennifer Lee Rossman**, Kristen Lee, Randi Perrin, Michael Leonberger, Andrew Wilson, Ross Van Dusen, MLD Curelas, Maren Matthias, Anne Luebke, Jeff Kuykendall, and Hayley Stone.

World Weaver Press

Publishing fantasy, paranormal, and science fiction.
We believe in great storytelling.

www.WorldWeaverPress.com

Damage noted:
10-29-20 83
P.170

CPSIA information can be obtained
at www.ICGtesting.com
Printed in the USA
LVHW041431051218
599370LV00020B/1123/P

9 781732 254633